SCORPIO RISING

BY MASTER STORYTELLER
MONIQUE DOMOVITCH

If you purchased this book without a cover, you should be aware that this book is stolen property. It was reported as "unsold and destroyed" to the publisher, and neither the publisher not the author has received payment for this stripped book.

SCORPIO RISING

Copyright © 2011 by Monique Domovitch.

This is a work of fiction. All of the characters, organizations, and events portrayed in this book are either a product of the author's imagination or are used fictitiously.

All rights reserved. No part of this book may be reproduced or transmitted in any form or by any means, electronic or mechanical, including photocopying, recording or by any information storage and retrieval system, without written permission from the author, except for the inclusion of brief quotations in a review.

Published by Lansen Paperback Publishing.

ISBN-13: 978-1463790738
ISBN-10: 1463790732

First Published August 2011

Dedication

*To Ed, who cooked,
so I could write.
You are the butter on my bread.*

CHAPTER 1

The days were getting shorter. The boy looked up in surprise at the sky that had suddenly grown dark. He pulled his worn sweater tight against the October chill, blew warm breath into his cupped hands and hurried on. The newspaper bag he carried strung across his shoulders was now almost empty. He no longer had to put it down for a moment at every street corner and massage his sore shoulder. He was almost home.

Alexander Ivanov lived at the end of the world. To the twelve year old, that was exactly what Brooklyn was, 'the end of the world.' Maybe because the one time he had been to the city—that was what he called Manhattan—it had taken forever on the subway.

Alex hated living in Brooklyn and never more so than when his mother talked about her youth in Leningrad with tears running down her face. She would revert to Russian, which he didn't understand, but the passion in her eyes spoke more volubly of the beauty of her old country than words could ever convey.

On his way back from school every day, weighed down by the load of newspapers, he passed the same dusty old stores, their signs barely legible from the peeling paint; the same ratty tenement buildings in which people suffocated in the summer and shivered in the winter; the same old women in their ritual wigs and shapeless dresses, vacant and blank expressions of hopelessness etched on their faces. Hopeless, that was how he sometimes felt, and then he would remember Manhattan and feel better. If there was one single thing Alex wished for, it was to live in Manhattan.

He walked through the streets of Brooklyn where pickles marinated in barrels, salamis swung from hooks and sausages dried in their cotton bags, oblivious to the sights and smells. One by one, he took the papers from his bag and with a quick experienced motion, he threw them. His aim was almost perfect.

Tomorrow was collection day. He would stop at each house along his route and wait while his client went to get their money. He would make change, and thank each one of them politely, even though most never bothered to leave him a tip. His work would take him more than twice as long as on normal delivery days. Still, he looked forward to it. Collection day was when he could go home, count out his profits, and decide how much of that money he could save. This week, if all went well, he might reach the fifty dollars mark in his bank account. *Fifty dollars!* It was a fortune.

He reached into his bag, pulled out the last newspaper and aimed it with unerring precision at the Kodesky's front porch. At that moment, the door swung open and old man Kodesky stepped out. The paper flew through the air like a projectile and landed with a thud in the startled man's well-padded stomach.

"Hey, you no good little piece of shit." He waved his fist and continued. "What the fuck do you think you're doing?" Alex did not hear a word. He was a million miles away, dreaming of the day he would escape the hell of living at the end of the world.

Even now, two years later, he could still remember every detail of his trip to Manhattan. After a long subway ride, he had emerged in the city, surrounded by skyscrapers so tall he could only see the top by looking up high and leaning back. People on the street rushed about in the lightly falling snow, pushing and jostling each other, their arms full of brightly wrapped packages. It was one week before Christmas and there was a dizzying feeling of joy in the air. Alex was almost drunk from the excitement. *This must be what Leningrad is like.* Deep in his dreams of unlimited delights, he walked home. Three blocks later, Alex climbed the stairs to the dingy one bedroom apartment where he and his mother lived. Before he was born, his mother had tried to make the apartment look warm and inviting. She had hung pretty paper on the walls and crisp curtains on the windows. The furniture was inexpensive but attractive and functional. Whatever nesting instinct had once inspired Marlena Ivanov's efforts had long disappeared. For the last twelve years she had done nothing more to improve her home. Indeed, she had not done even the most basic of repairs. With time, the wallpaper had become worn and faded. The curtains lost their freshness and the once attractive furniture became old and shabby. The sour stench of poverty clung to the apartment like old dirt.

Alex closed the door quietly behind him and dropped his canvas bag on the floor with deliberate neglect. He sniffed the air and wrinkled his nose. From the kitchen came the smell of boiled cabbage.

"Is *dat* you Alexander? Where were you? *Is* nearly six o'clock and dinner *is* been ready for hours," his mother's heavily accented voice called out from the bathroom. "I getting ready to go out. You will have to eat by yourself."

Through the thin door came the sound of the toilet flushing. A moment later Marlena appeared wearing a tight pink sweater set and a black satin skirt. Her dark hair was freshly coifed, the marks of the bobby pins still imprinted between each wave. Her mouth was painted crimson in the shape Joan Crawford had made popular a decade earlier. From ten feet away the smell of vodka on her breath overpowered.

"Will you be coming home by yourself?" asked the boy suspiciously.

"What you vant me to do?" She picked up her purse abruptly and threw in her lipstick. "You vant to eat. I not do this for me. A boy need food to grow big, strong. Someday you understand." A moment later, she was gone.

Marlena Ivanov was a bitter woman. She made no secret of the fact that raising a boy by herself was a heavy cross to carry; one she deeply resented. Alex sometimes thought his mother hated him almost as much as she did his father. He had never seen his father. He knew, only because his mother repeatedly told him, that Pavel Ivanov had been a gambler and a womanizer. Whatever wages the man had earned, he had just as quickly spent on those two vices. The day Alex was born was the day Pavel Ivanov decided that married life was not for him. He disappeared, leaving his seventeen year old wife to deal with the struggles of working and raising a son by herself.

After a dinner of cabbage soup, Alex turned off the lights and climbed under his blankets. In the dark, he could clearly see his mother's empty bed a few feet from his own. He turned his back to it and curled up in the fetal position.

Hours later, the muffled sound of laughter woke him up. The bedroom door swung open and the light turned on.

"Turn *dat* off. You wake up boy." His mother ordered in a shrill whisper. The light flicked off. "*Das* better. I like dark." She laughed. "Now come to Marlena." Clothes rustled. From his cot, in the corner of the room, Alex guessed every gesture, every movement. Old springs creaked. The sounds were loud, magnified by the stillness of the night.

Alex covered his ears. By trying hard, maybe

he could keep the noises from reaching him. It was too late. The guilty stirring in his loins had already begun. His mind swirled in a mix of emotions too strong for him to understand. Maybe if he thought of something else. *Yes, that's it. Think about something else. Someday, I'll drive in from the city in a brand new Cadillac. I'll show them all...*

The next morning, Marlena kissed the man good-bye and turned triumphantly to Alex. "See *dis?*" She pulled out a ten-dollar bill from between her breasts. "Dis can buy food for whole week."

Alex looked away, embarrassed and ashamed. She did this for him, he thought, returning to the picture he was drawing in the back of his spelling book.

* * * * *

By the time he became a teenager Alex Ivanov believed his dreams were just that, dreams. He still felt that raging desire to be rich, but except for the endless stream of buildings he drew, which everyone agreed were beautiful, he had no special talent. And other than the goal of saving up a lot of money, he had no real plan.

Alex kept delivering newspapers and watched his savings account grow. *At this rate, I'll never have enough money to move out of here.*

He decided to look for other opportunities. Soon, he found what he was looking for. He sold his paper route to a younger boy for two dollars, the amount of a normal month's profit, dipped into his bank account for another five dollars and invested in a second-hand bicycle with a large wicker delivery basket. The next day he began to work for Yonah Schimmel's Knishery.

From then on, every day after school he raced down to Schimmel's and loaded up his basket with bags of sweet smelling homemade knishes, jars of savory borscht and fine yogurts with a crust of cream on top and packaged in drinking glasses. With a speed never before seen from any of Schimmel's boys he raced through his deliveries until Yonah, himself, came up to him one day. "What are you trying to do, boy? Get yourself killed? Slow down," he told Alex. "No sense in going so fast. Slow but safe, that's the way to go."

Alex nodded politely, but just as soon as Yonah turned away, he jumped on his bike and sped off.

Alex was tall and well built for his age. The years of delivering newspapers had helped develop his once lanky frame into a strong, muscular body. His shirts, which were often a size too small, hugged him in a way that exaggerated the ripples on his chest. His hair was black and his eyes ice blue in a face that could only be described as sensual. The sight of the young and virile teenager, slightly flushed, and carrying Schimmel's parcels, did strange things to his female clients. Often, when Alex would ring a doorbell, the woman would appear even more flushed than the delivery boy. Alex would smile and greet each client politely by name. "Good afternoon Misses Zawisny." And he would walk away with a fresh knish, and more often than not, with a generous tip. Within one month, he had made enough money to cover the expense of the bicycle, plus what he would have normally saved with his paper route. Alex was beginning to feel like a rich man.

The way women reacted to him was a constant source of amusement to Alex. Since he had started shaving the year before, he knew the effect he had on the opposite sex. But he had no interest in any of them, except maybe in Miss Mateus, his homeroom teacher.

Rita Mateus was a big-busted brunette in her mid-thirties, with smoldering brown eyes that made Alex blush when she looked at him.

Sometimes he caught himself dreaming about what he would like to do to her, given the opportunity. Never in a million years did he believe the opportunity would come, and that when it did, it would prove to be his ticket out of Brooklyn.

For months, and to his great pleasure, every time he asked Miss Mateus a question, she would leave her desk, come up to him and as she bent over his books, she would rest her ample breasts on his forearm. One day, as he prepared to leave class after school, she asked him to stay. For the next hour, Miss Mateus went over his homework book, studying drawings one after another, while her breasts brushed against his back, his arms and even his cheek. "You're a talented boy. I love this drawing of—what is it?—the empire state building? What do you want to be? An architect?" The fourteen years old boy blushed and stammered, praying the whole while that she would not notice the huge erection in his pants. Miss Mateus, or Rita as she asked him to call her, noticed. Then she did the most shocking thing. She put her hand right on top of the swelling in his crotch. She looked at him with limpid eyes and said in a melting voice. "Why Alexander Ivanov, you're not a boy any more. You're a grown man."

The next day after school, Rita invited him to her apartment. Alex raced through his deliveries faster than he ever had and arrived at her doorstep in record time. She invited him in and poured him a glass of Chianti. "What sign are you, Alex?"

He looked at her, confused. "Sign?"

"What's your birthday?"

"November fifteenth," he replied still perplexed.

"November, hmm, that makes you a Scorpio." She leaned forward and traced a lazy finger along his upper lip. "Scorpio men are intensely passionate and ambitious. But beware a Scorpio's sting." She smiled, and his heart skipped a beat. "But, you won't sting me, will you, Alex?" Before he could think of an answer, she rose and picked up a deck of cards from the table. "Do you play cards Alex?" He shook his head. "Well you're going to learn."

That night, Alex learned two things, strip poker, and the grown up game of sex. After that, the routine never varied. Every day, after school, Alex would rush through his deliveries, spend a few hours with Rita, and then rush on home.

It was months before his mother noticed how late he was getting home in the evenings. When she asked him about it, Alex brushed it off easily. "I go to the library and do my homework."

Marlena chose to believe him. "I no cook for you when you late."

She's happy she doesn't have to worry about fixing my supper. Alex told himself and swallowed the lump that formed in his throat. Then he thought of Rita and his heart filled with joy. *I love Rita and she loves me. That's all that really matters.*

* * * * *

Every night, as soon as Alex walked in the door, Rita pulled out the cards. It was her favorite foreplay. In the beginning, Alex invariably found himself loosing and naked, but in time, he began to win occasionally. The promised vision of Miss Mateus pulling off her bra was enough enticement to make him yearn to win. He remembered the first time it had happened.

"You win Alex." Rita pulled off her bra and stood triumphantly before him. The loser thrilled to be vanquished. "You like my tits, Alex?"

"Oh! Yes!" he answered, not daring to move.

"Touch them."

"W-what?"

She came closer. "You heard me. Touch them."

Small beads of moisture broke out on his upper lip. He hazarded a hand out to the soft mounds of flesh and thought he would come right then and there."

"Kiss them."

He took a nipple in his mouth and felt it harden. Rita moaned. It was too much. His erection, which had been dangerously close to bursting, exploded in his shorts.

"Hey sweets, the idea is to keep a little for me." Rita motioned him toward her bed. "Lucky you're young. Let's see how long it takes to get you going again." She cupped his balls into her hands and took him in her mouth.

"Oh God, I love you," he cried out. He had never felt anything so delicious in his life. It was so good, it hurt. This time, he didn't come until Rita begged him to.

After sex, Rita liked to talk. Surprisingly she seemed to enjoy their conversations.

"I don't know why that surprises you Alex, you're a bright boy. With a mind like yours, you can do anything you choose."

I can do anything I choose. It was a staggering thought. Maybe he really could be an architect. It was a dream he'd never dared voice.

The next day Alex went to the one place in Brooklyn he loved. At Highland Park, he climbed the hill to the old reservoir from where he could look straight out to the skyscrapers of Manhattan. He sat on the cold, damp grass and thought about what Rita had said. He didn't want a job just for the sake of earning a living. What he wanted was a position with prestige. He wanted people to look up to him with admiration and respect. He wanted Rita to be proud of him.

His eyes wandered back to the skyscrapers across the distance. Skyscrapers like those he dreamed of building. From his position, they looked like monuments. *Monuments to the builder.* That was what he would be. He would build big important buildings, buildings like those skyscrapers.

Rita laughed when he told her. "Be serious Alex. Why don't you want to be a plumber or an electrician? An architect! That would take years of studying. I know I told you that you're smart, but not that smart. Besides, sweets, you don't really expect me to wait for you to grow up, do you?"

The words were like a knife in Alex's heart, but they only made him more determined. Rita meant everything to him. He would have to show her.

The relationship endured his entire senior year, until he was ready to go to college. One day, when he rushed over after his deliveries, he found Rita in bed with another man. For a few minutes, he hid behind the door and listened in horror as Rita said to this stranger, all the special secret things she had said to him. "That's it baby, don't stop. You're the best, baby. The very best." He heard Rita's familiar moans rise until she screamed. Tears welled in his eyes. He closed the door silently behind him and went home. All night he tossed and turned, amazed at how much pain he felt. Never again, he vowed. *No other woman is ever going to hurt me.*

The next day after school, Alex went back to Rita's as usual, and made love to her as though nothing had happened. Afterward he had a talk with her. "Rita, does anybody know about us?"

"Don't be ridiculous," she answered sharply as she straightened the seams of her stockings. She sat on the edge of the disheveled bed and watched him covertly.

"I guess you'd be in real trouble if anyone ever found out. Right?"

Rita adjusted the straps of her brassiere and paused in her dressing, long enough to light a Lucky Strike.

"You might lose your job," he continued.

She took a long drag on her cigarette and exhaled slowly.

"You might even be prosecuted for, what is it, something about a minor?"

She exhaled, blowing the smoke in his direction. "What do you want Alex?" she asked coldly.

He told her.

At his next report card, Alex Ivanov was at the top of his class. He was accepted at NYU with a full scholarship; he had seven hundred of Rita's dollars in his bank account; and the pain of finding her in bed with another man was just a distant memory.

* * * * *

CHAPTER 2

Half way around the world, Brigitte Dartois also liked drawing. But rather than buildings, her pictures were of her family—*Papa, Maman*, and herself under a bright sun. Sometimes she drew trees and flowers. Her subjects were the same as any other child's her age, but her pictures were different. They were strong, arresting.

"*Viens voir*, Colette," her father called her mother. He held up a bright drawing of a garden. "*Regarde*, don't tell me our daughter is not talented."

Colette Dartois looked, but to her, those colorful scribbles were no better than those of any other nine year old.

She shrugged. "You shouldn't compliment her too much. It will go to her head. Brigitte, put that away and go do your homework."

Often, Colette would look at her husband and her daughter with a vague discomfort. He paid so much attention to Brigitte, and so little to her. Every day when Louis Dartois burst through the door after work, it was Brigitte to whom he opened his arms after a perfunctory kiss to Colette. Gradually, Colette's love for her husband and daughter festered into resentment and jealousy.

Then, when Brigitte was thirteen years old her father died suddenly. Three months later, her mother married Lucien. "Consider yourself lucky. Not many men are willing to be a *papa* to an already grown girl like you. You better be nice to him." But the girl was filled with anger, feeling betrayed by her mother's indifference. One night, when Brigitte was alone in the house with her stepfather, she was awakened by a pair of rough hands moving over her body. "This will be our little secret," Lucien told her when she opened her eyes. "If you even think of telling anyone, I'll kill you," he said. Then he raped her.

Her mother worked the evening shift as a barmaid at a club down the street, and for the next three years, it became a nightly ritual for

Lucien to stop in for *une petite caresse*, as he called it. Every night he gave her the same warning. "You tell anyone and you're dead." Sometimes he went into gruesome details of what he would do to her if she ever told. Brigitte believed him. And she kept her mouth shut.

Once the top student in her class, her grades began to slide, until she was close to failing. She slept at her friends' whenever she could. At home, she was silent and withdrawn. Her mother barely noticed. "What's the matter with you?" she asked. "You keep it up and you'll be kicked out of school."

One night, while Lucien was in her bed and forcing himself on her, the bedroom door flew open. Her mother stood in the entrance, an expression of horror on her face. Lucien jumped up and fumbled with his trousers. "It's the girl's fault," he said, his voice coming in halting breaths. "How's a man supposed to resist. She's always coming on to me. As soon as you leave in the evening, she takes off her *camisole* and lets me see her body. Colette, you've got to stop her, she's trying to break us up."

"Get out!" Colette shouted and her voice was like ice. The girl sobbed in relief. At last, her ordeal was over. She would never have to see her stepfather again. "You're no daughter of mine. Get out you *putain*."

In shock, Brigitte realized her mother was speaking to her. She had lost! Lucien had won! She dressed as quickly as she could, threw a few of her things into a pillowcase and slipped silently down the hall to the closet where her mother kept her purse. *Sorry, but I'll need this more than you will.* She took all the cash she found. Then she left.

Two days later, a sales-help-wanted sign in a store window, caught her eye.

* * * * *

Marcel Latreille was a tall, colorless man, in his late forties. His road to success had been marrying the vapid Hélène Richoux, of the Richoux chain of fashion stores. For twenty-two boring years, he remained faithful to his dull wife, reminding himself regularly of the union's one important benefit. Thanks to his wife's shares in the company, he was in total control of the stores. Without her, he might still be selling ties in the men's wear department.

Marcel Latreille was bright and ambitious. Under his tutelage, the chain grew into one of the most successful in France. Over the years, the stock doubled and quadrupled, sometimes yearly, until it was worth nearly a hundred times what it was worth on his wedding day. It was an enviable record, one that should have made Marcel a very happy man. In reality, it only served to make him feel bitter. Although, as president and managing director of the stores he received a generous salary, he owned no company shares. These remained jealously in his wife's hands.

Although dull, Hélène Richoux was not stupid. As willing as she was to lend her husband control of the company, she never gave him the power that would provide the means for him to leave her side.

The day Brigitte walked into Richoux's main store on the rue du *Faubourg St. Honoré*, was a particularly distressing one for Marcel. That morning, over breakfast at the George V with his chum Aurèl, he noticed that the server did not smile at him the way she did at most of the other customers in the room. Even when he tried to flirt mildly, the woman simply ignored him. Later, on his way through the store to the office, he walked by a mirror and was jolted when he realized that the drab looking person he saw reflected was himself. *My lord, I have finally turned into a male version of Hélène.* It was a depressing thought.

Marcel Latreille was forty-seven years old, an age when a man should feel in the prime of his life. Instead of taking pleasure in his success, he felt bored and empty. If he didn't do something soon, his life would be over before he ever enjoyed it. *If only I wasn't stuck with Hélène.* At that moment, he walked by the personnel department and his eyes fell on the pretty young girl filling out an application form. Although she was tall, thin and curved in all the right places, what attracted him was the pain in her eyes and the desperation in her voice. When he reached his office, he called the woman in charge of personnel.

"Who is that girl, filling out the questionnaire?" he asked.

"There's nobody here at the moment *monsieur* Latreille."

"Yes of course there is. I just saw her. A young woman, red hair, about twenty, she was standing at the counter a minute ago."

"Oh! That one. I didn't keep her application. She's only sixteen and has no experience."

"What did you do with it?" He was surprised

to hear himself yelling. That was something he rarely did.

"I threw it in the garbage. Just a moment. I'll fish it out." She came back a moment later. "Here it is. Her name is Brigitte Dartois. There's no telephone number or address."

"Stop her before she leaves the store. I want to see her in my office now." He slammed down the phone.

Brigitte was nearing the main exit when a burly *guardien* stepped in front of her. "Sorry *mademoiselle*. You'll have to come with me."

"Why? I haven't done anything wrong." It flashed through her mind that her mother must have pressed robbery charges against her.

"Marcel Latreille wants to see you. He's in charge here."

Heart hammering and feeling faint with fear, Brigitte entered the large wood-paneled office.

"*Mademoiselle* Dartois is here to see you," the officer said.

"Show her in. Have a seat *mademoiselle*. Brigitte isn't it?"

"Yes, thank you." She sat and nervously smoothed down the folds of her skirt. She still could not understand why she was summoned here.

From his seat behind the desk, Marcel Latreille studied the girl with curiosity. With a knowledgeable eye, he noted that she was lovely in spite of her unflattering attire. *She has the face of an angel and a body made for pleasure. What a beauty she would be with the right clothes.* The thought intrigued him. "You're looking for a job," he said. "What kind of work would you like to do?'

"Anything sir. I have no experience, but I can learn fast."

"How would you like to work in the cosmetics department? With a face like yours, women will be begging to know your beauty secrets."

Brigitte nodded.

"Fine. You're hired." He pushed the intercom button. "Jeanne, could you come in here for a minute please? There's a young lady I want you to meet."

Jeanne walked in. With her upswept hair, expertly applied makeup and well-tailored suit, she looked every bit the sophisticated and capable corporate secretary. She glanced at Brigitte with curiosity and looked at her employer.

"Jeanne, meet Brigitte. She and I need your help. Here's the situation." Marcel quickly explained what he wanted and Jeanne jotted down a few notes. Once in a while, she glanced at him in surprise. "So, what do you think?" he asked finally.

Jeanne tapped one perfectly manicured fingernail against her notebook, and inspected Brigitte with a critical eye. "You're right. It's an exciting idea, but you're not giving me much time."

"Two days. No more. What I want is discreet elegance, nothing flashy. And I want her to get to work as soon as possible."

"I'll do my best." Jeanne smiled to Brigitte. "Ready to get to work?" The feelings of revulsion Jeanne felt were carefully suppressed. It was clear to her that Marcel Latreille had more on his mind than training a new employee.

"Yes Madame," replied Brigitte eagerly.

Jeanne had forty-eight hours to do a total makeover. What the girl needed first was a proper wardrobe. Jeanne took her to the young-designer section on the fourth floor and began rummaging through the sales racks under the expectant eyes of Brigitte.

"So which one do you like?" asked Jeanne. She pulled out two blouses and held them up for Brigitte to inspect.

The young girl was overwhelmed. "I don't know. They're both so beautiful."

Jeanne glanced down at the blouses. Both of them were silk. One had raglan sleeves and a Peter Pan collar. The other was a more tailored style, almost like a man's shirt. "You're right," she said. "You really need more than one. We'll take both." *Why not*, she thought. *If Marcel Latreille has designs on this child, he can bloody well pay for two silk blouses.*

"Oh, but I didn't mean..."

"I never imagined you did," she said. "Now let's not waste time. We have a lot to do." Next, Jeanne selected a classic brown wool skirt. With it, she chose a matching hound's-tooth jacket. "This is perfect."

Brigitte agreed enthusiastically.

"Now you need shoes and accessories." In the shoe department, Brigitte immediately spotted her favorite pair—simple pumps with a small heel. To her joy, Jeanne pointed to that very pair and asked the salesman to bring them in Brigitte's size. A few scarves and silk stockings later, the shopping spree was over.

"I've never in my life had such beautiful clothes," said Brigitte, so overwhelmed she thought she might burst. Visions of herself dressed in all her new finery danced through her mind. "Is *monsieur* Latreille so nice to everyone here?"

"He's being very nice to you," replied Jeanne, eyebrows raised and mouth pursed. "Very nice indeed." She hesitated for a moment, and then continued. "Brigitte, if you ever need to talk to someone, don't hesitate to come and see me."

Brigitte looked at her, puzzled. "What do you mean?"

"I only mean that you're very young and that if you ever need the expert advice of an old lady like me..."

"Oh, Jeanne, you are so beautiful. You are probably the most beautiful woman I've ever seen in my entire life." Brigitte's admiration was sincere.

Jeanne smiled. "Thank you. That's nice of you to say." She sighed deeply and patted Brigitte's hand. "But enough of this chit chat. We still have loads of work to do."

Next, Jeanne took Brigitte to see Olivier. The hairdresser, a tall skinny man with a thin black mustache, took one look at Brigitte, put the fingers of his right hand to his mouth a made a loud kissing noise. "Beautiful," he exclaimed. "And just look at all that hair. It will be a pleasure working on you ma *jolie.*"

"Olivier," said Jeanne. "*Monsieur* Latreille wants something classic and easy enough for Brigitte to maintain by herself."

"Trust me." Olivier was walking around Brigitte, touching her hair and rubbing the stands between his fingers. "So thick," he was talking to himself. "So shiny, and with a face like that, anything will look good on her."

"Olivier," repeated Jeanne in a warning tone.

"*Oui, oui, j'ai tout compris.* Come with me my lovely." He guided Brigitte to the sink and ordered an assistant over. "Louisette, give her a shampoo. Finish with a touch of cream rinse, then bring her over to my chair."

A few minutes later, Brigitte sat in Olivier's chair and watched as he ran his fingers through her hair. He picked up a pair of scissors and began to clip.

When Brigitte emerged from the salon, she looked like a new person. Instead of the gawky teenager of a few hours ago, was a beautiful and elegant young woman. Her new clothes were simple and well cut, emphasizing her long and slender silhouette. Her red hair was trimmed to shoulder length and tied off her face by a simple twisted silk scarf knotted at the base of her neck.

Jeanne stared at her in shock for a moment. Finally she recovered enough to speak. "*Mon Dieu*, who would have believed. *Monsieur* Marcel has a good eye. Every one of our customers will want to look just like you. Come. Our boss wants to see you."

* * * * *

"So how do you feel?" asked Marcel. The girl stood in front of him, shyly staring at her feet.

"Like Cinderella," she answered. Marcel burst into laughter. Jeanne felt her heart sink.

"Jeanne, you did a tremendous job. She is beautiful." Marcel looked at Brigitte again. It was difficult to believe this was the same girl who had stood trembling in his office only two days earlier. "Now, I think she's ready for some sales training."

He nodded his dismissal, and Jeanne and Brigitte turned to leave. Just as they walked out the door, Marcel called out after them. "Brigitte, do you have a place to stay?"

The girl blushed. "I haven't had a chance to start looking," she answered stammering. She had slept huddled inside a Metro station for the last few nights.

"Do you have money for an apartment?" Before she had a chance to answer, he continued. "Jeanne, see that she has an advance on her salary. As a matter of fact, why don't you take a few hours to help Brigitte find a place to stay?"

Brigitte could not believe her luck. If not for Marcel Latreille's generous help, God only knew what would have become of her. She smiled at her benefactor gratefully. "Thank you so much *monsieur* Latreille. If there is anything I can do for you... Anything," she said innocently. "How can I ever pay you back?"

"That's very sweet of you my dear," replied the man vaguely. His eyes ran over her body as she left his office. *A body made for pleasure*, he thought again.

* * * * *

Chapter 3

Although all he had done was cross a bridge, Alex felt like an immigrant arriving in New York for the first time. He walked steadily through the streets in disbelief at the immensity of the city around him. Manhattan! The city of his dreams. With evening coming on fast, he headed back toward the apartment house he had noted on East 45th. One-room apartments, cheap, the sign had said.

Nothing was cheap in Manhattan, not even the broom closet he rented as an apartment. It was far from perfect, but it would do. There was a bed and a small table tucked under a window that looked directly into a neighbor's bedroom. He opened the old refrigerator and the smell nearly knocked him out. He quickly closed it again. Not exactly the Plaza, he told himself, but at least I'm in Manhattan.

Once settled in his apartment, he armed himself with a list of what he needed and went shopping.

For the past three years, Alex had studied Rita's fashion magazines. The time had not been wasted. He now considered himself an expert at distinguishing those with money from those without, solely from the way they dressed. He had learned that the upper classes dressed quietly, in well-cut clothes that lasted years. On the other hand, flashy clothes immediately marked a person as being from a less affluent background.

Carefully, he examined and studied every garment he bought. Was the fabric of good quality and resistant? Did the cut seem classic enough to last a long time. He badgered the sales clerks with questions until he felt sure of his selection.

Loaded down with parcels, he walked back to his new home and gingerly put away his clothes. Then he went out again. A few blocks down the street, he found what he was looking for. He walked into the barbershop and described the cut he wanted. Later that night, when he saw himself in the mirror, he was looking at a different person. Now he was ready to start his new life.

Alex woke up the next morning, his body stiff and sore from the lumpy mattress, but his heart was filled with joy. Today was his first day of class. *My first step toward success.* His stomach growled voraciously and he went in search of food. Visions of scrambled eggs, bacon, sausages and ham filled his mind. The small, but now clean refrigerator in his apartment was bare so he grabbed his new wool jacket and headed for the university cafeteria.

He walked along the street, aware that among the students on campus he was anonymous, just another face in the crowd. Nobody knew about his background. Nobody knew about his mother. He would be judged for his talent and achievements alone.

The cafeteria was crowded with students. Alex found himself a table and concentrated on the food before him. As he ate, bits of conversations drifted over to him.

"...Calculus 101 with professor Morrow, then principles of design with Anderson, a cinch..."

"...Not looking forward to analytic geometry. That'll be a real bitch..."

He turned his attention to the next table. Even before seeing them, he could have described the boys perfectly. Tall, medium builds classic Ivy

League haircuts, intelligent eyes and dazzling white teeth in well-tanned faces; they were the very picture of young men living the American dream. *And that is exactly how I look now. Who would ever have believed I would be here some day. I got this far. I'll make it the rest of the way.*

* * * * *

NYU's architectural program was everything that Alex had expected it to be. For the first time in his life, he threw himself in his studies with enthusiasm and energy. Until then, school had been a necessary evil; one he had endured giving it the bare minimum of effort. Now, his mind was like a sponge in search of knowledge. The courses included drafting, building and construction, design, algebra and professional practice. At the end of each day, he could hardly wait until the next morning's classes. He worked harder than he ever had. His dreams were finally within reach. *Nothing will stand in my way now.*

The campus was full of pretty girls. The first time Alex noticed one that appealed to him, he quickly reminded himself of his goals. *I don't have time for such things. A girlfriend will only slow me down*. That night, as he settled down to a few hours of study, his mind kept wandering back to her. Much as he tried to concentrate on his books, the vision of the girl's blond hair falling loosely on her shoulders, of her trim figure in the crisp white blouse and pleated skirt, of her legs tapering down to slim ankles in rolled white socks, of her small feet in shinny penny loafers and of her smile when she looked back at him, interfered with his efforts. Try as he might he could not stop his mind from conjuring up images of the delights those prim clothes hid so well. It had been months since he had last seen Rita and Alex's sexual appetite was screaming to be fed.

The next morning, after a fitful night's sleep, he hurried over to the library, where he had last seen the girl. He hunted through the rows of bookshelves until he spotted the familiar blond head. She was standing on her toes in the Psychology section, her back to him, inspecting the titles of the books on the upper shelf. He unhurriedly walked over, searching for an excuse to talk to her.

The girl reached for a book, tugged at it and just as she managed to grasp the edge of it, it slipped out of her hands and crashed heavily down on one of her feet.

"Ouch!" The cry was heartfelt. She stood on

one foot, holding on to the shelf as tears welled up in her eyes.

"Let me help you," offered Alex, solicitously. He picked up the book and put one arm around her narrow waist. "Lean on me." He walked her slowly over to the study section and helped her into one of the chairs. Alex slipped off her shoe and massaged her foot gingerly.

"Ohhh! That feels better," she exclaimed.

"That book weighs a ton." He stopped massaging for a moment and looked down at the lump that was quickly forming. "That's a nasty welt. Maybe you should go to the infirmary."

"No, no. I'm feeling much better already. It was nice of you to stop and help."

"Nice!" exclaimed Alex in mock horror. "I'm not nice. I fully expect to be paid for this."

She looked up at him, surprised, and noticed the deep blue eyes and the easy smile. "What are you talking about?" she asked, suddenly suspicious.

Alex looked back at her innocently. "I never do anything for nothing. I did something for you, now you have to do something for me." He paused before adding. "Have lunch with me."

With his easy charm and deep blue eyes, he really was irresistible but still the girl hesitated. "I don't know. It's too early for lunch, besides I have work to do."

"I'll settle for coffee," he said, beaming.

"Are you always so pushy?" she asked playfully.

"Always." Alex chuckled. "And if you're about to accuse me of purposely making that book fall on your foot, I admit it. You're right. I took one look at you and said to myself, 'how am I going to get that girl to notice me?' Then I made the book fall, and the rest, as they say, is history."

She laughed. In spite of herself, she found that she liked this brash young man. "Okay. Coffee. But only a quick one. In the cafeteria in an hour?"

Alex nodded. "It's a date."

* * * * *

Over coffee, Alex learned a lot about Linda. She was nineteen years old, in her first year of college and was studying to be a child psychologist. But what Linda wanted most in life was to get married and have children. Alex was smitten. He could not take his eyes off her. Linda Hyde was beautiful and sexy. The thought of her beautiful body under his, drove him wild. He could not wait.

On their first date, he took her out for a burger. At the end of the meal, over ice cream, he told her about his dreams. He talked about the buildings he wanted to build and the money he wanted to make. "I guess I want what every guy wants." He paused for a moment and put his hand on hers. "I want to be successful, get married and have a family." It wasn't really a lie, he told himself. He did want to get married—someday.

Linda listened with rapt attention. "You know, you're the first boy I've ever met who doesn't mind talking about his plans."

"Should I stop?"

"Please don't. I like talking. Most boys just try to get me into bed. If I mention that I want to get to know them, they get impatient. I can't be attracted to a boy I don't know."

Alex nodded. He leaned forward and kissed her. Linda blushed but did not pull away. For the rest of the evening Alex told her all about himself, changing the details of his childhood until it sounded nothing like his life and altering his ambitions until she believed that settling down was foremost on his mind.

On the second date, Alex took her to The Starlight Club. *This is sure to break my budget, but what the heck. She's worth it.* On the dance floor he pressed his body close to hers during the romantic songs. With every dance, her body melted closer into his. With every kiss, her breathing became shallower. Alex pressed his hard body against hers and she pressed back. He could feel her resolve weaken. At the end of the evening, when Alex invited her back to his apartment, she accepted. And when Alex slowly undressed her and covered her body with his kisses, she believed she and Alex would spend the rest of their lives together.

Long after Alex had fallen asleep, Linda stayed awake remembering every delicious detail of their lovemaking. Their naked bodies, moving together as in slow motion, Alex's hardness tearing into her until her passion equaled his and she cried out for more. Then she had exploded into waves of sheer ecstasy. At last she knew what love was. She turned and gazed at the face of the man who had awakened such deep emotions. In his sleep Alex looked like a little boy. "I love you," she whispered, then curled up close to him and fell asleep.

* * * * *

Linda was sitting across from him in the coffee shop. "I was speaking to my parents last night and they mentioned that they would like to meet you."

Alex looked up from his espresso. "Why would they want to do that?"

Linda giggled. "Don't be silly. You know why. You're my boyfriend. They know that we're in love with each other and they want to meet the man I want to marry."

"What do you mean 'marry'?" Alex was shocked.

"But Alex, I'm not talking about getting married now. I'm talking about eventually, next spring, or next summer. Maybe we'll even wait until you graduate. You do love me don't you?"

Alex swallowed hard. Suddenly he wasn't so sure what he felt. "Love? Whoever said anything about love?" How could anybody be sure of being able to love only one person for the rest of their life? He wasn't ready for this. Linda was nice, but he didn't want to be saddled with marriage and babies. Visions of being stuck in a small apartment with a family to feed flashed through his mind. He saw his dreams of a brilliant future, vanishing. He was near panic. "Sorry sweetheart, I think we got our wires crossed. You're a great girl, but I'm just not ready for that." With that, he turned and walked out of the shop, leaving a tearful Linda behind.

* * * * *

Chapter 4

Richoux's cosmetics department occupied the entire first floor of the store. Displayed along soft pink counters were the world's most expensive beauty products and perfumes. It was a place designed to make a woman feel beautiful and feminine. It was brilliant marketing.

At Richoux's a customer could, in the privacy of a curtained booth *bien entendu*, re-powder a shiny nose, try a new rouge or lipstick, apply a touch of mascara or eye shadow and study the results in the rose-tinted mirrors that invariably made one look younger and more beautiful than nature allowed.

Brigitte followed Jeanne to the Mariane

Marceau counter. "Yvonne, I would like you to meet Brigitte. She is going to be working with you. I want you to teach her everything, consultations, professional makeup, everything," she repeated. She turned back to Brigitte. "Good luck. I'll be back at the end of the day to see how you did."

Yvonne was a self assured young woman, given to wearing bright colors and heavy, but expertly applied makeup. Where Jeanne left off in Brigitte's training, Yvonne took over with energy. In no time Brigitte's life was completely transformed. She loved her job as a sales girl in Richoux's cosmetics department; and to her surprise she excelled at it.

"You really have a knack with cosmetics," Yvonne told her one day. "I can't believe it. You've been here only a few weeks and you're already much better at makeup applications than many of the other sales girl." And indeed it was true. Brigitte's ability with the makeup brushes was astounding. She could, in minutes, transform a pale or sallow complexion into a young and healthy glow. With a few strokes of color, she could turn a plain woman into a vision of beauty.

Brigitte was ecstatic. *My life could not be better*, she thought. She had a regular income. She had a home, a small rented room a few blocks away from the store, and she had friends, one of whom was *monsieur* Latreille. She had begun to think of him as a father. As a matter of fact, the man bore a slight resemblance to the real father Brigitte had loved and lost.

Every morning on his way to work, Marcel stopped at the rooming house and had a cup of coffee with Brigitte. His behavior was friendly and always correct. He listened patiently to the young girl's chatter about her work in the cosmetics department and was full of helpful advice. The few minutes with Marcel every morning became precious to Brigitte. For the first time since her father, a man cared for her without seeming to have any ulterior motives. "If you need anything let me know," he told her repeatedly. "I want to make sure you have everything you need."

I can't believe how happy I am, she thought, and pinched herself to make sure she wasn't dreaming. She no longer dreaded the nights. She slept easily, without fear of Lucien's advances. She enjoyed food again, and ate with a hearty appetite. She began to put on weight and only looked more womanly and beautiful.

One morning, as she hurried down to the dining room to meet Marcel, the smells from the kitchen sent her stomach heaving. She ran back upstairs and made it to the toilet just in time.

Afterward, she sat down and calculated quickly. In horror, she realized it had been months since her last period. She could be as much as four months pregnant. She splashed water on her face and went down to face Marcel.

Marcel looked up eagerly as she walked in. "Are you all right?" he asked as he pulled her chair for her. "You don't look well."

"I'm not sure what's wrong with me. I think I might have a touch of the flu."

There was concern in his voice. "Take the day off. You look like you need it. I'll stop by tomorrow morning and see how you're doing."

"No, I don't feel that badly. I'd rather go to work."

"Well, if you're sure you feel up to it."

At Richoux's Brigitte quickly put on the white lab coat that was the cosmetic girls' uniform and hurried over to the Mariane Marceau department.

"Bonjour Brigitte. How are you today?" Yvonne greeted her. She picked up a bottle of spray window cleaner, squirted some on the pink counter and began to wipe. "Hey, what's wrong? You look terrible. Did you spent the night with your lover?" she asked teasingly.

Brigitte thought fast. "I didn't sleep all night. A girl friend of mine came over." She paused for a moment, wondering whether she should continue. "She's pregnant and she's not married."

"That's a drag. Won't her boyfriend marry her?"

"He left her and she has no money."

"Listen." Yvonne lowered her voice. "I have a friend who had an abortion. I'll try to find out where she went. It's not dangerous if it's done by a proper doctor. How far along is she?"

"I'm not sure—I mean—she doesn't know for sure. She hasn't had her period in over three months." Brigitte's eyes revealed nothing of the turmoil she was feeling.

Yvonne groaned. "Why did she wait so long? I wouldn't want to be in her position."

A woman approached the counter and Brigitte immediately flashed her Richoux-sales-girl smile. "Good morning madame. Can I help you with anything?"

* * * * *

CHAPTER 5

The euphoria of such a short time ago had turned into despair. Life had suddenly become a nightmare. It took all of Brigitte's energy to get through each day. Nights she lay sleepless, worrying. No matter how she looked at it, her situation was impossible. Yvonne had come back with the news that the abortionist who had taken care of her friend's problem had since been arrested. The information only made Brigitte feel more worried. What she wanted was not only dangerous but illegal.

A year ago, a girl from her school underwent an abortion. The operation, it turned out, had been performed in a dirty apartment by some quack that had no idea what he was doing. It had cost the girl her life. The whole *lycée* had buzzed about the tragedy for weeks. *Even if I could find a decent doctor to perform it, I don't have enough money.*

On the other hand, having the baby would mean giving up any chance of a happy life. She would be that child's prisoner just as surely as she had been Lucien's prisoner. *I can't have this child. I would rather die than have that man's baby.* The more she thought about it the more hopeless her situation seemed. There has to be a way out of this, she told the peeling ceiling above her bed. Marcel Latreille must never know about this. *He's a decent man. I'd lose the only real friend I have.*

The idea grew slowly. She would have to do it herself. It was the only solution. Brigitte looked at the clock next to her bed. Five thirty in the morning. It was time. Whatever happened, she was ready.

There was something almost ceremonial about the preparations. From the closet, she pulled out a wire hanger. She walked back to her bedside table, untwisted the hook end of the hanger and lit a match. The flame licked the end of the wire over and over until it burned her fingers. She repeated the procedure until there were no more matches.

She watched the water as it filled the tub. *Soon it will be red with blood.* The fear was gone.

Instead, was a feeling of peace. *What will be, will be.* She stepped into the scalding water, and with a bar of disinfectant soap she scrubbed herself until she was raw.

Crouched in the bath, her legs apart, she took the long wire and carefully inserted it inside herself until she felt resistance. *Oh mon Dieu! Give me the strength.* With a sudden hard thrust, she pushed the wire further. *Oh! Help me.* The pain came suddenly. She bit the inside of her mouth to keep from crying, and watched the blood trickling down her legs. She crawled back into her bed and sank into the pain, deeper and deeper, until there was nothing but blackness.

* * * * *

After his frightful experience with the lovely Linda, Alex concluded that although his sexual appetite needed tending, he would have to find a way to feed it without really getting involved. No girl was worth abandoning his dreams. Soon, he found that seduction came easily to him.

On a first date, he invited a girl to dinner. Over a meal, Alex would talk about his dreams and goals. He made her feel privileged to be sharing such intimate thoughts with him. He hinted about how special he found her and talked about wanting someone in his life. The second date was similar to the first, but ended with some deep kissing and heavy petting. On the third date, he took her dancing. During slow romantic music, he held her tight and let her feel the hardness of his body. It worked nearly every time. When he asked a girl back to his apartment, she said yes. There the girl would spend the most romantic and sensuous night of her life. In the morning she would leave convinced that she had found the man of her dreams. After that, she would never hear from Alexander Ivanov again.

Whenever he felt guilty, Alex quickly reminded himself of everything he wanted to accomplish. *I don't have time to fall in love. There's too much I need to accomplish.*

* * * * *

By mid term, Alex had a problem. Even though his scholarship covered tuition fees, he still had to come up with money for food and other living expenses. His patiently nurtured bank account was diminishing quickly. With winter coming, there were new boots and a warm coat to buy, and countless other expenses that he could not afford. Although he would have preferred to concentrate all of his spare time on studying, his financial situation would not allow it.

As fate would have it, a few days later Alex opened up a newspaper and found what seemed to be a possible solution. In the classified section was an ad for a second shift watchman, five hours a day, from 4 PM to 10 PM. He applied at Durring and Durring Construction Materials and was hired on the spot.

"It's not a hard job," the foreman told him. "You have to check the loads as they go out. Make sure nobody tries to sneak anything out. In between inspections, you do what you like."

Perfect, I can bring my books and study.

From then on, every night after classes, he took the subway all the way to the rusted crumbling dockside along the equally pathetic West Side Highway. There, among a myriad of eyesores, stood the huge and decrepit warehouse that was headquarters to Durring & Durring. A high wire fence with a heavy metal gate surrounded the building and lumberyard.

He was stationed by the entrance, in a hut not much smaller than his apartment. In one corner was a cot, in the other a wood-burning stove that provided heat during the winter months, in the center were a small table and two chairs. *All the comforts of home*, thought Alex.

* * * * *

"Hey kid." The yard supervisor closed the door heavily behind him and walked up to the table. "There's another big project going up near the airport." As he came near, Alex noticed the smell of alcohol on the man's breath.

"Really? What kind of a project is it?"

"How the hell would I know? All I know is, they get their supplies from us. I have the approval sheets for them to pick up the material. I don't care about anything else." He gave him the necessary papers and continued, "I got a fifteen minute break. Mind if I have some of that coffee? It's warmer in here than out there." He moved closer to the small wood stove in the corner as he spoke.

Alex shook his head. "I don't mind Barney, as long as you don't mind if I read."

"Read? What are you reading?" He was already standing over Alex's shoulder, trying to read his notes. "Basic principles of architecture. Well what do you know? Are you studying to be an architect?"

"That's right," he answered exasperated. The last thing he wanted was to waste time chatting aimlessly. He had hundreds of pages to read, tons of material to learn. He opened his book and buried his nose inside. Maybe the supervisor would get the hint.

"No kidding? Isn't that a coincidence? My son used to be an architect."

Alex nodded. "Really..." he mumbled, uninterested and kept reading.

"You don't believe me do you? Well, it's the truth. He used to work with James B. Southern." The name was one of the most respected in the profession. Barney saw the disbelief on Alex's face. "You think I'm making this up? I'll show you. I'll bring you some of the plans he drew. Then you'll believe me."

Alex noticed that Barney spoke of his son in the past tense.

The next evening, when Alex arrived for his shift, Barney was already waiting for him. "Take a look at these." The old man trembled with excitement as he unrolled the sheaves of paper. "I haven't taken these out in years."

Alex bent over the plans. Even at a glance, he knew they were good. His eyes traveled to the lower right corner. There, in block letters, was the stamp, 'Sidney R Taylor'. "These are good Barney. What is your son working on now?"

The old man looked down at his feet and shrugged. "He's dead!" Alex could read the misery on Barney's face making him look years older. He turned slowly and huddled out of the cabin. A few autumn leaves blew inside and the door slammed shut behind him.

Fall became winter and for weeks, Barney avoided Alex. Then, one day, the door to the shack flew open and Barney stormed in. "Hey, kid, it's cold out there. Mind if I come in to warm up?"

Alex pulled out the second chair for him. "Grab a seat."

Barney closed the door and hurried to the stove. He warmed himself for a few minutes and began to talk. "He was a good architect, you know." He spoke bitterly.

"I know."

Alex's response took Barney by surprise. "Yeh?" he continued testily. "More than that, he was damn good."

Alex nodded. "I saw his plans. They were great."

Barney moved closer and his eyes shone with fervor. "You do believe me, don't you? Don't make his mistake Alex. Damn liquor." He looked at Alex shamefully. "That's what did him in. And now he's gone."

There was nothing Alex could say. He hesitated for a moment. "Barney, I'd like to hear about your son. What was he like? What were his dreams?"

Barney's eyes lit up. "Really? You're interested in hearing about him?"

"Do you mind?"

Nothing could have made the old man happier. Having found an audience, Barney launched into his son's story with abandon. "Sure. I'll tell you about him. But if you want to be successful like him, I'll tell you how he did it. The first lesson is the easiest and the hardest. Are you listening to me boy?" He searched Alex's face, to make sure he was listening. "The first lesson is learning to dream big dreams. That's what Sidney did."

"What do you mean?" asked Alex, surprised.

"Listen to me boy! You go ahead and dream up the most incredible buildings, buildings that are impossible to build. Then make them possible. Sidney found a solution for every insurmountable problem. Architects who build easy buildings, are a dime a dozen." His eyes twinkled with excitement. "But my Sidney, he could dream! So tell me boy, can you dream?"

A few nights later when Barney looked at Alex's sketches, he burst out laughing. "Well, these sure aren't chicken shit. What is this? The tallest building in the world?"

"That's right," replied Alex, without a trace of a smile.

Barney was thoughtful for a moment. "Well, like Sidney always said, dreams are free, so you might as well go ahead and dream big."

* * * * *

CHAPTER 6

It was the noise that awakened her. Brigitte was lying on her bed, naked, when Marcel broke the door down. As he came closer, he saw the blood. "What the hell..." He turned and ran back outside. By then a small group had gathered in the doorway to see what all the commotion was about. "Get an ambulance," he ordered the first person he saw. The woman looked at him with an expression of mild annoyance. "I said, get an ambulance," he screamed. "Or do you want that girl to die?" The woman turned and ran. He walked back to the bed and covered Brigitte with a blanket. "Don't worry. Everything will be all right."

* * * * *

The hospital was a tall gray building. On the seventh floor, the surgical team rushed to try and save the girl's life. When the bleeding stopped, the chief surgeon inspected the damage. "Peritonitis from a ruptured posterior fornix," he said, his voice showing no sign of emotion. "She has a fever of 103°." He stopped and shook his head in frustration. "Why the hell do young girls risk their lives that way? Don't they know they can kill themselves?" Once again his voice became professional. "Give her 100% O2, Ringer's lactate 100c.c. per hour and put her in I.C.U. Make sure you report her to psychiatry."

* * * * *

Brigitte hovered between life and death. One minute she shivered violently from chills only to find herself sweating profusely a moment later. Everything was hazy. The walls, the sheets, even the intern who adjusted the intravenous and gave her medication, looked more like an apparition than like a living person. Brigitte lay in the bare room, not sure where she was, and not caring. There was no more life inside of her. That was all that mattered. Nightmares of her stepfather crawling into her bed would start her screaming.

A moment later, she laughed hysterically. She had no idea how close to the edge of sanity she was. When the nurse who came in to help her eat, tried to talk to her, Brigitte could not make out what she said.

※ ※ ※ ※ ※

She slept on and off, for three days. Then her fever abated. When she woke up, Marcel was sitting next to her. "You're going to be all right," he said. "You and your baby will be fine." The words and their meaning echoed through her mind. *You and your baby... baby... baby...* She had not succeeded. The child was still alive.

Brigitte looked away and began to cry.

※ ※ ※ ※ ※

The next day, Brigitte received the visit of Doctor Swanson. With his full blond beard and his long disheveled hair, Swanson looked more like an escapee from an insane asylum than like the reputed psychiatrist he was. He sat at the foot of Brigitte's bed with a stack of papers on his lap and stared at her intensely. *He looks like he's trying to get into my mind*, thought Brigitte. As though he had heard her thought, Swanson smiled and began to talk.

"You had us all scared there for awhile." His manner was calm and reassuring. He paused for moment before continuing. "Can you tell me why?"

Brigitte looked down at her hands folded neatly in her lap. The urge to speak was almost overwhelming. She felt a torrent of words pushing against the dam inside of her. *Tell him. Just tell him.* She held back with the knowledge that if the dam broke, there would be no controlling the pain that would come with it. She looked up at him. "The important thing," she said, her voice steady, "is that I won't do it again."

Swanson looked at her. Her eyes were clear and her jaw set. Instinctively he knew he would get nothing more out of her. "You're absolutely sure about that?"

"Absolutely." Her voice was sad but firm.

"What are your plans?"

"I've given the matter a lot of thought. I'll have the baby, and I'll give it up for adoption," she answered.

"That is probably the most sensible thing to do, but it still won't be easy." He peered at her more closely. This girl surprised him. After the physical ordeal she had just gone through, most others her age would be frightened and weepy. Instead Brigitte Dartois was firm and determined. *A strong girl*, he thought.

Brigitte looked at him and smiled. "Nothing is easy."

He nodded. "You're right, but when people find themselves in difficult situations, life can be easier when they know they are doing the right thing." He scribbled a few words on the top sheet of his pad and put his pen back in the breast pocket of his white lab coat. "I'll sign the release forms as soon as you're better." He tore off the bottom of the sheet and handed it to Brigitte. "Here's the name and telephone number of a good adoption agency. Give them a call as soon as you can." At the door he turned and looked at her again. "*Courage,*" he said and gave her the thumbs up sign. Then he walked out.

* * * * *

Brigitte waited for each of Marcel's visits with nervous anticipation. Surprisingly, and to her immense relief, he had not asked her a single question about her pregnancy. His only comment had been, 'you should have come to me.' He seemed to understand intuitively that the entire experience had been tragic for Brigitte, and the last thing he wanted to do was cause her any more pain.

In fact, after the initial shock, Marcel had come to the conclusion that he should not have been surprised. The girl was after all, sixteen and on her own. Still, Brigitte was a puzzle to him. From the little he knew of her, she had struck him as being reserved and sexually immature. He had no idea what to think.

He knocked at Brigitte's hospital door.

"Come in," Brigitte called out, and smiled as she saw him. "*Bonjour pa...* Marcel. I'm so happy to see you." She had almost called him *papa*."

"How are you?" He handed her the bunch of flowers and watched as she buried her face in the fragrant blooms.

"Lilacs, my favorite! Thank you Marcel. You spoil me."

"This is not spoiling you my dear. This is nothing."

"I have good news. I can go home tomorrow."

Her eyes clouded over. "I don't know what to do. The doctor says I can't go back to work right away."

Marcel saw the flash of pain and desperation in her eyes and he immediately felt protective. *If only Hélène was vulnerable like this girl*, he thought. *The only thing my wife wants is a slave to order around.* He patted her hand sympathetically. "I don't want you to worry about a thing. I'll help you whichever way I can. What are friends for?" he asked with a chuckle, amazed at how good her helplessness made him feel.

* * * * *

Chapter 7

Going to school all day then working the second shift was an exhausting schedule, one, which, Alex often worried, would break him, but there were indisputable advantages. Aside from his generous salary and the hours of often undisturbed studying he was able to do, there was the added bonus of always knowing the location of every latest real-estate development where the company's materials were used. On weekends, armed with his Durring & Durring work pass, Alex was able to visit the sites of every important construction project in the city, gathering and incalculable amount of knowledge in the process.

Every stage of construction held a magical fascination. Alex watched as gigantic cranes dug holes the size of football fields. He gawked as steel frames went up. He gazed in wonder, as giant metal skeletons became beautiful modern structures of strong, rich, gleaming marble and shimmering iridescent glass. It was at moments such as those that he knew beyond doubt that choice of career was the right one.

Still, Alex's double life—student by day and watchman by night—was difficult. It demanded unwavering discipline and countless sacrifices. Late at night, when he counted out stacks of plywood in the back of some truck, or when he fought to stay awake during class the next morning, Alex pushed himself on with the same thought. *Someday....*

Three years later Alex graduated at the top of his class. He was the only graduate without a family member or friend to watch him receive his diploma. As he stood on stage looking into the sea of smiling faces in the audience, he felt a million miles away from Brooklyn.

* * * * *

CHAPTER 8

The apartment was beautiful, more than any Brigitte had ever seen. The ceilings were high with intricately carved moldings. The rooms were large and well proportioned; and the windows were on the west side of the building, offering plenty of sunshine and a lovely view of the courtyard. There was a large master bedroom and a second, smaller room with a balcony. The living and dining rooms were generously proportioned, and the kitchen was equipped with modern appliances.

It was the kind of apartment Brigitte had seen, lavishly furnished in decorating magazines; the kind where wealthy people lived. *Not the kind of apartment I can afford*, she thought soberly.

Still weak from her ordeal, she clung to Marcel's arm for support as he showed her through the empty rooms. "Marcel I can't afford an apartment like this. I need is a small place. I don't have any furniture."

Marcel saw the worry in her eyes and quickly reassured her. "Brigitte, I don't want you to worry about a thing. Leave everything to me."

"But I could never repay…"

Marcel put his index to his lips. "Shhhh! I don't want to worry about having to repay anything. I only want to help. I am a rich man and I can afford this. Besides, you don't have only yourself to think about anymore. There is the baby."

At the mention of the word baby, Brigitte's heart sank, but she said nothing.

"Trust me, Brigitte. I'm only thinking of you. Besides, what other choice have you got?"

Brigitte's eyes swept over the apartment again. Every room was lovelier than the last. She imagined living in a place like this, where the floors were polished wood, where the kitchen was sunny and modern, where closets were so large one could walk right in. This could all be hers. Everything would be so much easier. All she had to do was say the word. If she did not accept

Marcel's kind offer, then what? *He's right*, she thought. *What choice do I really have?*

"Yes," she said. "Yes, I'll take it," and felt as if a giant weight had just been lifted from her shoulders. *God bless Marcel. He treats me as well as a real father would.*

Marcel threw himself into the role of benefactor with enthusiasm. He took charge of Brigitte's life with a concern and efficiency that was almost frightening. "Leave everything to me," he told Brigitte as soon as she said yes. He rushed off to work, leaving her in the bare apartment. Back at his office, he closed the heavy mahogany door, called in Jeanne and barked more orders to her than he had in months. "A small table and chairs, a mattress and make sure to get household linens while you're at it."

Jeanne took notes, nodding from time to time. Although she seemed perfectly composed, inside she was livid. *How could he?* As soon as Marcel had given her the address in the fifth arrondissement, she knew her suspicions had been right. *How could he make that child his mistress?* She bit her tongue and said nothing. There were not many jobs that paid as much as hers.

"By the way, Brigitte notified me that she found other employment. She won't be coming in anymore." His eyes avoided hers.

I'll bet she found a job, the oldest profession in the world. "After everything you did for her," Jeanne exclaimed, sounding outraged. "What an ungrateful girl." She had the small satisfaction of seeing Marcel Latreille look embarrassed for a moment.

"When I help someone, I do it for no other reason than for the deed itself. I don't expect anything in return," he answered virtuously.

You hypocritical little worm, Jeanne wanted to shout. Instead she said, "Monsieur Latreille you are an inspiration. I wonder if madame Latreille knows just what a gem she has as a husband." She smiled sweetly. "Will that be all?"

"Yes, that's all, thank you Jeanne," replied her employer, looking uncomfortable. "Just one more thing, keep this to yourself would you? I want a home away from home, somewhere I can escape. If anyone finds out about it, my privacy will be shot."

Jeanne nodded. "Don't worry, I won't tell a soul." She closed her steno pad and walked out. *I wouldn't want to be in his shoes when madame*

Latreille finds out, and one thing I am sure of, she will find out. The thought gave her great satisfaction.

* * * * *

Brigitte had no idea how painful it would be to go back to the rooming house. In her room the bed was still unmade, and although the bare mattress had been scrubbed clean, Brigitte could still see the faint traces of blood. *I almost died*, she thought, remembering the horror of that night. *If not for Marcel, I would have.* She quickly gathered her belongings, paid the landlady, and left.

Outside, she almost turned toward Richoux. It would have been nice to go back and see her friends. *I'll speak to Marcel about it*, she decided, and took a taxi back to her new apartment. Except for the new folding table and chairs in the kitchen and the mattress in the bedroom, the apartment was completely bare. Brigitte put her few belongings in the large walk-in closet and waited for Marcel.

Later that evening when he stopped by, Brigitte was surprised at the surge of happiness she felt when she saw him. Over coffee she broached the subject. "I don't care what the doctor says, I'm feeling well." She hesitated for a moment, glancing at him over the rim of her cup. He was in a good mood, enjoying a piece of rich chocolate cake. She gathered her courage, and continued. "I thought, maybe if I could go back to Richoux..."

"Under no circumstance," interrupted Marcel, explosively. "I don't ever want you to set foot in there," he told her. He put down his fork roughly and it clattered on the plate. "I know you miss having friends but I don't ever want you to go there, or for that matter, under no circumstances are you to any of Richoux's employees. Is that clear?"

"Perfectly," answered Brigitte, surprised at the vehemence with which Marcel had spoken.

"Believe me Brigitte. I'm only doing this for you."

His anger had been so quick and strong, Brigitte dared not insist. *I'll find other ways to keep myself occupied. After all, he is being so generous, how can I refuse him this one request.*

Suddenly Brigitte's days were filled with appointments. There were endless meetings and decisions to be made about the apartment. A decorator had been hired and he wanted to discuss every detail. "Before we do anything, we have to agree on what style you will feel most comfortable with. Then we go on to define a mood, choose colors and textures. And last, we select the furniture." Tony De Angelo was a short, balding man, given to grand arm gestures and an overly elegant style of dressing. Brigitte liked him instantly.

Style? thought Brigitte, overwhelmed with the number of decisions that she would need to make. *It would have been so much simpler if I had found a small apartment.* But as frightening as the whole process was, she found herself enjoying it.

Tony bubbled over with dozens of ideas. He walked around the apartment spitting them out so fast Brigitte could barely follow.

"...and over there." He pointed theatrically to the far corner. "A mass of tropical plants. This room, yellow. What do you think?"

Brigitte nodded. "I-I think so." She had never met anyone who thought, or for that matter spoke, so fast. "I like the idea of yellow. It would be like waking up in sunshine. We could choose a bright print for the bedspread and curtains, something happy and floral."

Tony threw up his arms enthusiastically. "That's great. A bright print will look wonderful here. I imagined something more classic but your idea is wonderful. Let's go for it."

Marcel walked out of Richoux at seven thirty. By the time he arrived at the apartment, he was tired and cranky. Brigitte rushed to great him and took his coat. She was eager to show him the preliminary plans. "Look. This is a sample of the fabric I chose for the upholstery. And here, this is what the living room will look like. What do you think?" She waited eager for his approval.

Marcel looked at them doubtfully. "A bit on the bold side, don't you think? What about something a bit more subdued? You know, something with a bit more class. This... Well it just looks so... common."

The next day, to Tony's great distress, Brigitte canceled all the previous day's plans. "I think your ideas are fresh and wonderful," insisted Tony. "You have a natural sense of style. I wish you would trust your instincts about those fabrics and colors. They suit your personality much better than a quiet and elegant look."

But Brigitte was equally adamant. She wanted Marcel to be pleased. After all, he was paying for everything. "I would have enjoyed bright colors but the decision is really not mine to make."

Tony did not insist. *The man with the checkbook speaks loudest*, he thought. He opened his notepad and jotted down the latest instructions.

Later when Marcel called from the office, Brigitte told him of her decision. "I'm glad you changed your mind about that fabric," he told her. "Don't worry. I'll teach you all about good taste. In no time, you'll be a proper young woman." He laughed as he said it. "By the way," he asked. "Did you call the adoption agency?"

Brigitte hesitated. "No, not yet," she answered. "I'll get around to it soon. I just haven't had the time." Afterwards Brigitte wondered why she kept putting off something she knew she wanted to do. *I still have plenty of time. The baby isn't due for months.* She quickly put the thought out of her mind.

Soon the renovations began. Carpenters and painters took over the apartment and for weeks the sound of hammering and sawing went on from morning till night. "Oops! Sorry lady. I didn't see you there." The man had almost hit Brigitte with a long piece of lumber.

"No problem. I'll just get out of your way." She carried her morning cup of coffee to the kitchen only to be disturbed again two minutes later.

"Sorry lady. Would you mind if I used the table here?" The burly man set his tool box on the table without waiting for an answer. Coffee splashed all over the table.

"No problem, I'll just get out of your way." But no matter where she was, she seemed to be in someone's way. *I'm getting out of here*, she decided, moments after brushing against some wet paint in the hall and earning herself a dirty look from the painter. She grabbed her coat and fled. From that day on, Brigitte left as soon as the first workman arrived, and only returned when she was sure the last one had left. Then, with no one around, she leisurely walked through the apartment and inspected the day's progress. So much work had been done, yet there was still so much to do. New plaster moldings were going up throughout the apartment. A new marble floor was chosen for the entrance. Walls were being painted with a faux-marble effect. The entire project was taking on ridiculously large proportions. *This is crazy. I never wanted anything so elaborate. I would have been happy with much less.*

* * * * *

Marcel had had a long, hard day at the office. For months now, the sales figures had been slipping. He had tried a new, more aggressive advertising campaign but the response had been disappointing. And today, Hélène had stormed into his office demanding to know what he was proposing to do about the situation. Half a dozen aspirins later, his head was still throbbing.

He drove slowly. The thought of Hélène waiting for him at home was anything but enticing. On the other hand Brigitte was always a joy to be with. He made up his mind suddenly, pulled a sharp turn and drove off in the opposite direction. Fifteen minutes later, he let himself into Brigitte's apartment. "Brigitte, I'm home!"

Brigitte appeared from the kitchen. "Marcel! What a nice surprise," she exclaimed. "How did you get in?"

He lifted the key for her to see. "I kept one. Do you mind?"

"Don't be silly. Of course not. I'm here all by myself. I feel safer knowing you have a key. Can I get you something to drink?"

Marcel collapsed onto the couch and patted the seat next to him. "First I want a kiss then you can make me a scotch," he said.

Brigitte ran over and threw her arms around him. "Marcel, you are the dearest person in the world."

Between sips of his drink he told her of his problems with the dropping sales at the store. "I've tried everything I could think of and nothing seems to work."

"Are you worried about money?" asked Brigitte, concerned. "Marcel, all I need is a bed, a table and a roof over my head. I don't need to live in this expensive place."

"Don't be silly. I am not having financial difficulties. It makes me happy to do this for you. The least you can do is enjoy it."

Brigitte hesitated. "It's only that I'm not used to such luxury." In the back of her mind was the growing feeling that she would forever be indebted to Marcel.

In time the apartment was finished. All the bold, exciting ideas Brigitte and Tony had dreamed up had been replaced by quiet, graceful elegance. Although it was not what she would have preferred, Brigitte had to admit that the apartment looked wonderful. She walked through the rooms and familiarized herself with her new home. But somehow, the formal beauty and obvious wealth of the place made her feel uncomfortable.

Marcel, on the other hand, was pleased. "Beautiful," he pronounced after inspecting it. "Much better than what you had originally wanted, don't you think?"

"It is beautiful. Thank you." Brigitte was happy that he liked it. She hesitated for a moment. "How would you like me to cook you dinner? You've done so much for me; I want to do something for you."

"Cook? You?" Marcel looked at her, mildly amused. "What are you planning to serve, something out of a can?"

"Absolutely not. I can cook. Come over one night next week and I'll prove it to you," answered Brigitte, laughing. *He is such a dear, and I owe him so much.*

For days, Brigitte searched through cook books until she had the perfect menu. On the day of the dinner, she got up early and made the list of everything she needed. At the market she went from stall to stall, looking, touching, and smelling. She wanted everything to be just right. Asparagus, fresh Boston lettuce, cherry tomatoes, all were carefully inspected until she was satisfied they were of the finest choice. At the butcher's she asked for their most expensive cut. She almost fainted when she heard the price. *That's more than I made in a day's work.* She could hardly wait to see his face when he saw the feast she would prepare. She hurried home and went to work.

At seven o'clock, everything was ready. The *boeuf en papillotte* was nicely golden. The salad was tossed and waiting in the refrigerator. The cheeses were mellowing on the counter and the wine was breathing on the coffee table in the living room. The only thing missing was the guest of honor. Minutes ticked by.

Brigitte looked at her watch impatiently. It was eight o'clock and still she had not heard one word from Marcel. The beef in its blanket of puff pastry was over cooked. The salad had wilted and the cheese was over ripe. Dinner was ruined. At nine o'clock, Brigitte took her carefully prepared meal and scraped it into the garbage. Later, as she climbed into bed, she forced herself to be calm. *The man is running one of the largest chains of stores in the country. There are bound to be times when he will have to cancel social plans.* But why he had not bothered to call.

* * * * *

Brigitte stepped into her obstetrician's office. Doctor Beaulieu was reassuringly old and gray.

He looked at Brigitte over his gold rimmed bifocals. "*Alors.* How far along are you?"

"About five months," Brigitte replied nervously. "I- I'm not exactly sure."

"Well. Let's take a look at you." He instructed her to take everything off and handed her a white hospital gown. Brigitte lay on the cold table while the doctor performed his examination.

"I expect that you are closer to six months than five and from what I can determine you are going to have a healthy baby. From now on, you should supplement your diet with vitamins." He wrote out a prescription and handed it to her. Still, Brigitte did not move. "Was there anything else?" he asked.

"I- I was wondering if I could have harmed the baby when..." She did not finish the sentence.

The doctor leaned over and patted her arm reassuringly. "From what I could see, everything looks normal. Right now what you have to do is stop worrying. That won't do anybody any good." He smiled cheerfully. "Aren't you going to ask me whether it's a girl or a boy?"

"I didn't know you could tell," she said, surprised.

"Science claims I can't, but just between you

and me, I'm never wrong. It's a boy," he said with a twinkle in his eye.

Brigitte felt a strange sense of wonderment. She thanked the doctor and left. On the way home, the same thought kept dancing through her mind. *A boy! I have a real live baby growing inside of me. A baby boy.* At that moment there was a sudden fluttering in her abdomen. *Can it be? No. I must be having some indigestion.*

A few days later there was no question about it anymore. The flutters had grown to kicks and jabs. *Active little fellow*, she thought. Almost against her will, as she felt the child moving in her womb, she began to feel emotions stirring deep inside of her. *I must make that call. It's ridiculous for me to keep putting it off.* But the telephone number on the piece of paper remained under the telephone, where she had put it.

Gradually Brigitte settled into her new life. T*his is not so bad*, she told herself repeatedly as she walked through her beautiful, apartment. *Millions of women would give their eye teeth to be able to live the way I do.* But slowly, loneliness and boredom were setting in. Because of Marcel's objections, she had cut contact with all of her friends. The only person she saw was him. She felt so desperate for company she thought she might go crazy.

Marcel called. "I'm sorry I missed your dinner. Hélène pulled a tantrum. I'm afraid I couldn't get away."

"Marcel, wouldn't it be simpler if Hélène and I met. That way we could all..."

"Don't be ridiculous!" Brigitte listened, subdued, while Marcel went on. "What do you think she would say about us? What do you think anybody would say for that matter? I pay for all of your expenses. If that doesn't look like a cozy little set up, I don't know what does. Instead of pressuring me, why don't you try to show me some understanding?"

Brigitte was stunned. The conversation ended on a sour note. She put the telephone back in its cradle and sat down suddenly exhausted. *What was that all about? Why would anyone think her and Marcel...?* The thought was ridiculous. Or was it? She looked around at the expensive furniture that surrounded her. Marcel's money had paid for all of it. The reality of her situation suddenly hit her. If she ever did anything to anger him, he could very easily kick her out. The thought sent chills down her spine. Nothing here actually belonged to her. She was nothing more than a charity case, a beggar in this apartment. There, as long as Marcel allowed.

I would not be in this position if I wasn't pregnant, she thought, and immediately felt guilty. Although she had no more than a hazy recollection of most of her stay in the hospital, she could recall every detail of her attempt to end her pregnancy. She reminded herself of the doctor's last words to her before her release. *The baby will be fine.* Repeating those words like a mantra, she climbed into bed.

* * * * *

CHAPTER 9

It was mid-summer in New York and the temperature was 90° in the shade. It was the hottest 24th of July in recorded history. On 42nd Avenue, a fire hydrant was illegally turned on and children frolicked in the cool rushing water until the police chased them away them. All along Madison, traffic was stalled. Impatient drivers waved their fists and honked their horns. From a distance, the noise was like one long plaintive wail, the sound of a city crying.

Alex lay on his bed, perspiring. The open window brought no relief from the unbearable heat, only dust and noise from the traffic below.

This was Manhattan, the city of his dreams. Somewhere along the way, the dream had turned into a nightmare. For three years, he had worked harder than anyone would have believed possible — and for what? Since his graduation, a year ago, he had applied for twenty-three different jobs. At every one of them, the answer had been the same. Sorry but we're not hiring at the moment. He was near despair.

His ambition of someday designing skyscrapers was beginning to fade. He was lucky to have a job, any kind of job. Half the people with whom he had graduated were unemployed, or worked in an area totally unrelated to architecture. At least he was still at Durring & Durring. He wiped the beads of moisture from his forehead. A frightening thought, one he had vainly tried to brush away for months, now crept into his mind. *Three years of studying and working, could they really have been for nothing?*

The phone rang and Alex was startled out of his morose thoughts. He hesitated and glanced at the clock on the table. It was nearly 5:00 o'clock. In another hour, he would be leaving for work. He let the phone ring again. The last thing he wanted was to listen to some girl demanding to know why he had not called her back. The ringing continued. Exasperated, he picked up the receiver. "Yes," he answered gruffly.

"This is the Frost Placement Center," the voice

said. "There is an opening for a junior at William Brandon & Company. Would you be interested in applying?"

Interested? What an understatement. His fears of a moment ago quickly disappeared. "Of course I'm interested." He scribbled down the details and hung up the phone. *This is it. I just know it*, he thought as he did every time he had an interview. *I don't care what kind of architectural work they do. Just let me get in.*

* * * * *

The brass plate on the outside of the elegant brownstone read 'William Brandon & Company, Architecture & Design.' Alex wiped his palms against his trousers and pushed open the door.

The reception area was luxuriously decorated. High white ceilings with ornate moldings contrasted sharply with the deep sable of the silk covered walls. The gentle strains of a Beethoven concerto played softly from the large Marconi radio-cabinet in the corner. Alex noticed every opulent detail. He closed the door quietly and walked in.

At the front desk, the receptionist called Brandon's secretary. The stunning young blond arrived a moment later and greeted Alex with a pleasant smile. "May I help you?" Her crisp blue linen dress, with the fitted waist and flared skirt, looked expensive. Alex wondered if the gold and diamond pin she wore was real. She discretely looked him up and down and he became aware of his own well-worn suit, which he'd bought years ago.

"I have an appointment with William Brandon," he said and wondered if he looked as nervous as he felt.

"Please be seated. I'll let him know you're here." She disappeared down the hall, her high heels silent in the thick wall-to-wall carpet.

Alex sank into one of the leather chairs and inspected the rest of his surroundings. In front of him, a row of shelves held an assortment of plaques for various honors in architectural design. On the coffee table was a miniature scale model of a large residential development project and on the wall facing the entrance was a large original by Monet. *William Brandon must be a rich man.*

The blond reappeared. "He can see you now."

Alex followed her down a long and narrow hall. Through open doors along the way, he caught glimpses of countless house plans. Some were pinned to walls. Some were rolled and stacked in corners. Others were spread open on drafting tables. Workers leaned over sketches, drawing and measuring. *Hell, there must be a hundred projects going on here. There is bound to be something for me.*

"Right in here." She stopped and gestured him into a luxurious mahogany paneled room.

Alex walked in and found himself facing a florid, heavyset man sitting behind an elegant partner's desk. His suit was expensive looking but did not entirely conceal the thick waistline. His hair was graying, the hairline receding and the hair combed from back to front and back again in a vain attempt to hide the bald spot. His jaw was set, betraying a lifelong habit of being in control.

Alex felt his anxiety rise.

"I'm William Brandon. You wanted to see me?"

"I'm pleased to meet you Mister Brandon. I'm Alex Ivanov." He paused. The man looked at him with a blank expression on his face. "I'm here for the job interview?"

The jaw softened and the lips parted in an apologetic smile. "I'm terribly sorry, but we've already hired someone." The man shook his head in dismissal.

Alex wanted to cry. For a moment, his expression betrayed his disappointment, and then he forced himself to look composed and confident. "As long as I'm here, would you mind taking a look at my resume? You never know; you'll probably be hiring again soon."

"I'm sorry, I forgot about your interview. The agency should have called and canceled your appointment." There was no stop between comments, no invitation to shake hands. Brandon continued in a rush. "I'm afraid I won't be able to give you any time. Miss Turner, don't I have another appointment?"

Alex held his breath and threw Miss Turner a pleading look.

"You have a meeting with the building committee, sir." Her eyes met Alex's and she hesitated. "But that's not for another half hour," she added innocently.

"Thank you. That will be all Miss Turner." The door closed behind her. William Brandon took a cigar from the silver box on his desk. He rummaged for a moment through his pocket, pulled out a heavy gold DuPont lighter. The flame shot up and he took a series of short puffs. The entire procedure took a minute, during which the young man waited patiently. Brandon tapped the end of the cigar in the ashtray. "Is that your resume?"

Alex had rarely been greeted so unenthusiastic. He handed his C.V. to Brandon, who skimmed through it.

"I see you have no experience."

"True, but if you look at my college grades, you'll see that I was consistently at the top of my class."

Brandon's eyebrows furrowed. "That's not experience," he insisted.

"Experience has to start somewhere." Alex spoke calmly, an easy manner covering his nervousness.

"What kind of architecture are you most interested in?"

"I'm interested in every type of architecture. I'm good, I'm bright and I'm willing. Whatever I don't know, I'll learn."

William Brandon closed the C.V. and handed it back. He looked at this Alex Ivanov more closely. The young man was obviously intelligent. His grades certainly attested to that. He had strength about him. Brandon guessed that along with his obviously strong will, the man also had ambition.

He liked that. It almost made him rethink his decision to hire the other candidate.

"Mister Ivanov you strike me as a good candidate. If I needed another employee in my firm, I would hire you. Truth is, I am a businessman and I cannot logically hire and pay for an employee I don't need. Leave your name and number with my secretary when you leave. Next time there's an opening, I'll make a point of asking for you."

Alex saw his chance disappearing. There had to be a way of turning things around. "Sir, if you're a business man, then let me make you a deal."

Bill Brandon leaned back in his chair and chuckled. "This I have to hear."

Alex took a deep breath and plunged ahead. "Let me work here for two weeks without pay. At the end of that time if you still feel that your company does not need me, I will leave. If you like the work I do, hire me at whatever level you choose."

William Brandon burst into laughter. "I've got to hand it to you; you really have a lot of guts. I could take your offer and work you like a dog for two weeks, without any intention whatsoever of keeping you."

"That's a chance I'm prepared to take."

William Brandon picked up his cigar again and took another series of short puffs. "I think you ought to know that I demand a lot from my people," he said. "The hours here are long and the pay isn't great until a man proves himself."

"Sounds fair to me, sir. I'm not afraid of hard work."

"On the other hand, when someone does good work, I don't hold him back. Hell, I built my company on the talent of good men. Talent is the foundation of this company, talent and honest to goodness hard work."

"I don't mind sir. I can work hard and I know I can do well." He felt like a schoolchild, repeating the same thing over and over.

"...next Monday morning at eight," Alex heard Brandon say. Suddenly the interview was over and Alex was shaking the older man's hand.

"Do you mean I'm hired?"

"Hell yes," replied the big man is his booming voice. "How can I refuse free help?"

I'm hired! He could hardly believe it. He had barely said three words. Brandon was obviously impressed with him. Outside Brandon's office, he gave Miss Turner his most glowing smile. "I'm hired," he told her.

She laughed and gave him the thumbs up sign.

He walked out into the sunshine, filled with a sense of euphoria. He could already imagine himself a full partner. *Brandon & Ivanov, Architecture & Design*. There was a certain ring to it.

* * * * *

The first wave of pain came suddenly. She looked down at herself and noticed a fine thread of crimson snaking its way through the warm sudsy bath water. Horrified, she jumped up. Mon Dieu! Blood streamed down her legs. Again, a stab of pain went through her body, this time followed by an overpowering urge to push. Push! Push hard! Harder! *The voice seemed to come from inside her head. Slowly, in a wave of agony, the baby made its way through the birth canal until it slipped out from between her legs. Brigitte plucked it out of the water quickly and looked down at it. In her arms was a pulsating mass of bleeding tissue.* You did this to your child... You did this... *The voice echoed in her mind, while from far away, she heard a child crying.*

Brigitte woke up with a start. For a moment she could still hear the child crying, and then she realized that the strangled sound came from her own mouth. *It's a nightmare, just a nightmare.* Yet it had seemed so horribly real. She huddled under the blankets and closed her eyes. Immediately her mind wandered back to the deformed creature of her nightmare. Minute by minute, the dark hours ticked by while she lay awake trembling. Over and over she repeated the same prayer. *Please let this child be healthy. If there is a God in heaven, please let my baby be all right.* There was no question about it anymore. She loved her unborn child, more than she could ever have believed possible. *How will I ever find the strength to give my child away*, she wondered suddenly frightened.

Morning came, gray and rainy. Brigitte watched from her window, as the people rushed about on the wet streets below. *Everybody seems to have things to do and places to go except me. What kind of a life do I have? I'm living in a cage. I am still a prisoner.* Then she thought of Marcel. She had to give him credit for coming to her rescue, and although she regretted not being able to see her friends, it was a small price to pay for his help. Rather than sit here and worry about my future, *I'll just have to find ways to occupy my time. Otherwise, I'll just go crazy.*

She grabbed her raincoat and umbrella from the closet and set out for a walk. For hours, she walked around without direction with the rain beating down on her. She wandered on until she found herself in front of the Louvre's.

* * * * *

The Louvre, was Frances most famous and venerable museum. Among the thousands of priceless art works on display, were paintings by Michelangelo, Rembrandt, Degas, Monet, Picasso, Renoir and countless others. Brigitte stood in front of the portrait of l'Enfant Marguerite by Velsquez, awestruck. Every detail was perfection, from the luster of the rich brocade, to the detail of the child's hands. Never in her life had Brigitte seen anything so magnificent and so touching.

Hours later, Brigitte was roused from her spell when a guard came by. "*Madame*, visiting hours are over," he said.

Brigitte looked up, startled. She had never been addressed as Madame before but with her lightly swollen belly, it was normal she realized. "I'm so sorry. I didn't realize how late it was." She stood and pulled on her coat.

"No apology needed. Have a good evening." The guard tipped his hat to her and watched appreciatively as the attractive, young red head left.

That night Brigitte's dreams were filled with images of the many wonderful paintings she had seen. In her dreams, she felt peaceful and happy. The next morning, when she awoke she felt an irresistible urge to go back to the Louvre, and when it opened that morning, she was the first in line. "Bonjour *Madame*," called out the burly security guard as Brigitte rushed through the entrance and up the stairs.

"Bonjour *monsieur*," she called back and waved.

"You're here again today. Don't tell me there are still some paintings you did not see."

Brigitte laughed. "Maybe I'm planning a robbery. You'll have to keep your eye on me."

"Keeping an eye on you, *Madame*, will be a real pleasure," answered the guard. He watched as Brigitte rushed ahead, in a hurry to get to the impressionist wing. Though in her sixth month of pregnancy, her skin glowed and she looked radiant.

Within minutes Brigitte was once again transported into a world of beauty. This time a garden scene by Monet captured her fancy. For hours she stood entranced by it. *Just imagine, she thought, the joy an artist must feel, being the creator of such beauty. How I would love to be able to produce something as magnificent as that.* She remembered the joy drawing used bring her so many years ago. *Perhaps I could pick up painting as a hobby.*

* * * * *

Hélène Richoux walked into Richoux's department store like a general inspecting his troupes. She wore a brown Christian Dior front-buttoned dress for which she had paid a small fortune. On her ears, she wore a pair of drop pearl earrings worth a king's ransom, and on her shoulders was a sable mink wrap, thrown on with what she had hoped would appear to be casual chic. Instead, Hélène Richoux looked frumpy. It was one of the tragedies of her life. No matter how much money she spent, she always managed to look like a maid in her employer's finery.

"*Bonjour madame Richoux*," called out a sales girl.

As the woman marched through the cosmetics department to the elevator, the greetings continued. *"Madame Richoux, bonjour."*

She walked briskly, nodding occasionally to a few of the senior employees. She stepped into the elevator. The uniformed operator, a pleasant gray-haired man, greeted her politely and immediately pushed the button to the fourth floor. The brass cage climbed slowly until it came to a bouncing stop on the executive floor. She glared at the old man and stepped out hurriedly. Moments later she stormed into Jeanne's office.

Jeanne looked up from her Olivetti. *Uh, oh, trouble.*

"Where is Marcel?" demanded *madame* Richoux in a tone meant to intimidate. Instead she sounded nasal and whinny. "I have just had the most frightening experience in my life. Tell me why in the world is Simon still working here? He should be retired. Hasn't anybody complained about the way he operates the elevator? Where is Marcel? I want him to fire that man immediately."

"Simon has been with the store for thirty-three years. He is almost an institution by now. He knows all of our better customers by name and people expect to..."

"Oh for goodness sake, if I'd wanted a speech I would have asked for one. Where is my husband? He left the house at six thirty this morning. Don't tell me he's not here yet."

"He's probably somewhere in the store. He likes to make his rounds and check every department before he comes upstairs."

"You mean to say he hasn't even set foot in the office yet?" Hélène Richoux screeched. "For goodness sake, how long are his inspections supposed to take? When he bothers to show up, tell him I'm waiting." She dismissed Jeanne with a wave of her suede gloves and opened the door to her husband's office.

Jeanne groaned in despair. There would be an argument, and she was sure to be caught in the middle. Hélène Richoux had a habit of pulling everything and everybody into her private affairs. A few minutes later, still wearing his overcoat and carrying his briefcase, Marcel walked in.

"Your wife," Jeanne whispered and she pointed to the door of his office. He looked stricken for a moment. He was guilty of nothing more than an early breakfast meeting with an advertising agency executive but he knew from experience that Hélène would never believe him. She was insanely jealous. He hurried back out. A moment later he reappeared without the coat and briefcase.

"Jeanne," he said loudly. "I've just been through the designer department and I've noticed that..." Before he had a chance to finish, the door flew open and Hélène stepped out.

"Where were you? I've been waiting for hours."

"You couldn't have, my dear. The store hasn't been open for more than a half hour," replied her husband. He walked into his office and closed the door behind them.

Through the wall, Jeanne could hear voices arguing but the words were muffled. *I hope she nails the bastard*, she thought. She turned back to her work and soon the sound of her typewriter drowned out the voices.

* * * * *

The next morning Marcel walked into the formal dining room and was greeted by the pleasant aroma of freshly baked scones and percolating coffee.

"*Bonjour Marcel*," his wife called out to him from across the room.

Marcel forced himself to smile. "Good morning Hélène." He walked over to the sideboard, poured himself a cup and sat down.

"Is that all you're having? Agnès made those from scratch for you and you won't even touch them?" She spoke with her mouth full and waved her jelly covered knife toward the basket of croissants. After a lifetime of being one of the wealthiest women on the continent, Hélène Richoux prided herself on the fact that she did not need to stand on formality and etiquette. Manners, she was fond of saying, are for the poor. With my money, people will damn well love me as I am.

Marcel felt himself tense up. It was amazing how even the sound of his wife's voice had that effect on him. He thought wearily of how he would rather be working. "No," he said. "I'm not hungry." He sipped his coffee under the watchful eye of his wife.

Fifteen minutes later when he drove off in his Citröen, Hélène watched discreetly from behind the velvet drapes. She looked at her watch. Eight o'clock. *We will see at what time he arrives at work this morning.* She walked over to the telephone and picked up the receiver.

Hélène put on her buttery voice. "Jeanne? I'm

sorry to be calling you at home. I want you to do me a favor."

* * * * *

It was nearly nine o'clock. The coffee was cold in the percolator and the fresh croissants had long dried out in the oven. Marcel had not stopped by. Brigitte picked up her breakfast plate and scraped off the crumbs into the garbage. At that moment, the telephone rang and she picked it up. "Hello," she answered breathlessly.

"Brigitte, I'm sorry I wasn't able to stop by this morning." Marcel sounded contrite.

"Is there something wrong?" she asked.

"No, no. Don't worry; I'll be there tomorrow morning I promise." Marcel said a quick good-by and hung up. For a long time, he sat in his office and stared at the telephone. Lately Marcel had realized how difficult he found it to be in Brigitte's company. Brigitte was young, beautiful and desirable. Although she was in an advanced state of pregnancy, he still found it difficult to keep his hands to himself. Until the baby was born, he knew he had no other choice but to wait. The frustration was driving him wild. Be patient. *Only a few more months*, he told himself. It felt like an eternity.

* * * * *

Jeanne Leblanc looked down at the notes on the desk in front of her. Neatly typed on two sheets of paper, was her report of Marcel Latreille's comings and goings over the last few weeks. She sighed deeply and wondered what to do. After all, as Hélène Richoux had pointed out, Jeanne was her employee. If she gave Madame Richoux the information, she would only be doing her job. Besides, although the notes showed a pattern of late arrivals and early leavings, the information on its own would prove nothing. She picked up the sheets of paper, folded them neatly and slid them into the envelope.

* * * * *

The next morning, Marcel arrived at Brigitte's apartment carrying three large gift-wrapped boxes. "I have a surprise for you," he said.

"Marcel, *vraiement*, you shouldn't. What is it?" asked Brigitte, curiosity getting the better of her.

"Open them and you'll see. "Marcel put the boxes down.

Brigitte tore off the paper. She lifted the cover off the largest of the boxes. Inside, was a bunch of long wooden sticks and a bag of nuts and screws. She looked at Marcel, puzzled.

"Open the rest," he said sounding like an excited child.

In the second box, Brigitte found what looked like a wooden briefcase. Finally, in the third she found a complete set of Grumbaker oil paints, brushes, linseed oil and paint thinner. "It's an easel and paint box," she exclaimed. *"Pour l'amour de Dieu* Marcel, what do you think I'm going to do with all of this?" asked Brigitte.

"Paint," said Marcel, laughing. "I can't stand to see you so lonely all the time. I've been trying to think of something you can do to keep yourself busy. Since you enjoy visiting the Louvre so much, art supplies seemed like a good idea." He shrugged his shoulders. "If you think it's silly..."

"You read my mind," exclaimed Brigitte, excited. "The same idea had occurred to me..."

For lack of a better place, the easel and the paint box were set up near the window in the living room. *The light is good here*, thought Brigitte. *It's the perfect spot.*

Over the next few days, every time she walked by the living room, there was the easel, waiting, beckoning. A few times Brigitte went so far as to pick up a brush or a tube of paint, but the thought of putting color on a canvas and of trying to create something from her own hands filled her with apprehension. Images of the magnificent paintings she had so admired in the Louvre kept filling her mind. *How can I even think of doing this? I don't know the first thing about painting.* At first tentatively, then with growing confidence, she began.

"You did this?" exclaimed Marcel when he saw Brigitte's first tableau. It was a landscape, with softly rolling hills, cows grazing peacefully in the background and big puffy white clouds in a blue sky. "This is pretty good, not bad at all, considering this is your first effort," he said. "You have a good sense of form and color."

"I don't like it all," pronounced Brigitte. "Something is missing. I don't know what. I was trying to remember a place I once saw as a child. It would have been easier if I'd had the picture in front of me." She picked up a drop cloth and covered the painting. "Enough of that. Have you had any breakfast?"

"Maybe this painting idea wasn't so good after all," said Marcel as he followed Brigitte to the kitchen.

"Why not," she asked, surprised.

"Do you realize, this is the first time you haven't had breakfast ready and waiting for me when I got here?" He was laughing as he said it, but Brigitte saw the disappointment in his eyes.

* * * * *

Hélène Richoux was in her office, a large sunny room with brocade draperies and Louis VXI furniture. She threw the financial report across the room. For the last half hour, she had read and re-read the damn thing and she was not pleased. The problem was Marcel. He was simply not doing his job. It was obvious to her lately that he was up to something. He had been leaving the house early and coming home late for months. His excuse was always the same. Work! Yet, when she called the office to speak to him, he was rarely there. With the amount of hours he claimed to be spending at the store, business should be thriving, but this financial report said otherwise. Sales had fallen by four percent. Her mind wandered back to the report Marcel's secretary had sent her. It proved nothing. In view of the fact that all she had were suspicions, Hélène had chosen to say nothing until she had hard proof. *If the son of a bitch is cheating on me he will pay for it dearly. Nobody makes a fool of Hélène Richoux and gets away with it.*

Hélène Richoux looked at the number on the old, decrepit building. *333 rue de La Commune. This is it.* Hélène Richoux crumpled up the piece of paper and threw it back into her purse. On the door the sign said Investigation Rosaire. She snapped her purse shut and walked in. The office was small and dusty. She sniffed the air disdainfully and slammed the door shut behind her.

"Anybody here?" she called out. She rapped her knuckles against the reception desk. "Anybody here?" she called out again.

A moment later a pudgy middle-aged man appeared from the other room. "My secretary is out. Are you the two o'clock?"

"From the looks of this dump, your secretary has probably been out for a few years," quipped Hélène arrogantly.

The disheveled man did not appear to be offended. He chuckled. "Hey, that's a pretty good sense of observation you got there." He let Madame Richoux lead the way into his office. "I'm Rosaire. What can I do for you?"

She waited for him to close the door and told him.

Rosaire listened while carefully appraising his new client. Although her clothes were mismatched, they were of the finest quality. *This lady has bucks.* As Hélène spoke, Rosaire's smile grew. "Trust me; I have a lot of experience in those matters. It might take a bit of time but you can count on me. Of course, it will cost some money."

His client opened her purse and pulled out a thick roll of bills. "How much do you need?" she asked. And when Rosaire quoted the amount, she did not even blink.

This is one investigation I won't finish in a hurry, the rumpled man told himself as he counted out the money. *I'd be a damned fool not to bleed this one for a long while.*

* * * * *

Jeanne sat in her office, lost in a daydream. Lately it had become more and more apparent to her that Marcel Latreille was completely unnecessary at Richoux. There was nothing he did, that she couldn't do herself. *All he does is give the orders. I'm the one who does all the real work.* If only she could get rid of him somehow, then maybe she could persuade madame Richoux to make her the new director.

She opened her drawer and pulled out Brigitte's address on the rue George V. For some reason she had kept it. Instinctively she had always believed that it might come in handy some day. Now she knew exactly in which way she could use the information. She pulled out a new sheet of typing paper and rolled it into the Olivetti.

Dear madame Richoux,

I think it is my duty to inform you that...

Five minutes later she signed it anonymously, 'a friend,' pulled the paper out of the typewriter and folded the letter into a plain white envelope. She could already see herself sitting behind Marcel's mahogany desk.

* * * * *

Brigitte sat by the living room window, absorbed in her new art book. She had just finished reading a wonderful section about Montmartre, the small, humble area of Paris which had been home to so many great artists. The photographs fascinated her. *Now, there is a place where I would love to live*, she though and immediately felt foolish. Why should she be tempted by such a run-down area when she was living in a luxurious apartment?

She sighed and flipped to the next chapter, which offered a study of many different types of photographs. There were portraits and still lives, black and white shots and colors photos. Every picture was stunning. For a long time, she studied the way groupings of objects created interesting shapes and forms, the way juxtaposed colors looked brighter and stronger, the way light and shadow were used to give illusions of depth. Ideas crowded her mind. She closed the book and stood up. Suddenly the baby kicked sharply. She stopped and patted her swollen belly. "My...my. We are active today aren't we?" From the window, she noticed a man standing on the street below. He looked so sad, standing there by himself. *I guess other people are lonely too.*

* * * * *

From across the street Rosaire pulled out a camera. *A picture is worth a thousand words. This one will be worth a thousand francs.*

* * * * *

On her palette Brigitte mixed the colors, thinning them with oil and turpentine until she had the shade and consistency she wanted. Then she dipped her brush in the paint and with a steady hand applied it to the canvas.

"You're taking this painting business much too seriously," commented Marcel from behind her.

Brigitte's heart nearly stopped. She'd been so engrossed in her painting, she hadn't heard him come in. "Marcel, please don't do that. Tell me when you're coming over. You nearly scared me to death," she said when she managed to catch her breath. She wiped her hands on the cloth and gave him a quick kiss on the cheek. "Would you like some coffee?"

"No, I just stopped by for a minute."

Brigitte stood waiting and Marcel had the uncomfortable impression that she wanted him to leave. "Maybe this wasn't such a good idea after all," he said.

"What are you talking about?"

"This! The painting." He looked exasperated.

"It was a brilliant idea, Marcel. Look at me. Don't I seem happier these days?"

It was true that she looked well, thought Marcel. Brigitte's face was rounder, filled out by the weight she had gained. Her eyes shone and her skin glowed. Her pregnancy was now advanced and obvious. Her stomach was large and protruding and her breasts full and heavy, yet even dressed in her splattered painter's overalls she was attractive.

Marcel felt a rush of desire run through his body. He felt an almost uncontrollable urge to hold her in his arms, to let his mouth cover hers. *Christ she is beautiful!* "Do you know that you are a very desirable young woman ma chérie?" he asked, his voice strangled with emotion.

Brigitte put down her paint brush, suddenly afraid. *I'm being ridiculous. This is Marcel, my friend.* "*Voyons*, Marcel. Look at me. I am fat; my hair is a mess..."

"... and you have never looked so lovely." He walked over and pulled Brigitte into his arms. "Brigitte, you must know by now the way I feel about you."

Brigitte pulled away from him, shocked.

Marcel continued, almost begging. "For months now, you have been driving me crazy, playing with me, teasing me, and always keeping me at arm's length. I can't take any more. I want you and I'll be damned if I'll wait for you any longer."

Brigitte felt dizzy. "Marcel, please. Marcel..." She felt his hands on her breasts, his mouth on hers, his tongue pressing into her mouth. *Oh Mon Dieu, this can't be happening.* His hands were all over her, touching, feeling, fondling. She pushed him away again. "Marcel, please. What are you doing?"

"I'm doing what I've wanted to do for a long time. Oh Brigitte. Come here *ma chérie. Juste une petite caresse*," he said his voice strangled with desire.

Brigitte listened in horror. She had heard those same words a hundred times, a thousand times. They were Lucien's words, now coming out of Marcel's mouth. "No!" she screamed. "Go away. Just go away and leave me alone." Panicked, she ran to the bathroom and locked the door behind her.

Furious, Marcel grabbed his coat and stormed out. At the door he turned angrily. "Listen you conniving little bitch, don't tell me you didn't know what the deal was. After everything I've done for you, you owe me. You better realize that I mean business, and you are going to pay up." A moment later, still cowering in the bathroom, Brigitte heard the front door slam shut.

For a long time, Brigitte stayed huddled in the bathroom, weeping. *Now what?* she asked herself desperately. What she had feared most had finally happened. She was alone again. There was nobody she could rely on but herself. She looked down at her protruding abdomen. *Don't worry little one. I'll take care of you.* Wearily, she picked herself up, picked up her purse and pulled out the wad of remaining Francs from the last amount Marcel had given her. At least enough to last six months if I am careful. She went to the closet, grabbed her coat and walked out. Fifteen minutes later she was back with the newspaper. She spread it open and with a red pencil began to circle the apartments for rent.

Later that evening, she looked at the three suitcases lined up against the wall. *How appropriate*, she thought. *I came here with almost nothing, and now I'm leaving the same way.* She picked up the telephone. "Hello. I'd like a taxi please..."

Half an hour later, the cab was there. The driver helped her put the suitcases into the trunk and held the door open for her. "Where to lady?" he asked when she climbed in.

"Ninety-nine *avenue du Seigneur*," she told him and leaned back in her seat.

"That's in Montmartre, isn't it?" he asked.

"That's right, in Montmartre." She leaned back into the worn vinyl seat, completely exhausted. As the car pulled away, she turned for a last glimpse of the luxurious building she was leaving behind.

* * * * *

Secure in the knowledge that she needed him more than he needed her, Marcel waited for Brigitte to call. *She's pregnant and I am her only source of income.* She'll call, he told himself. Every morning, he hurried to the office and asked Jeanne for his messages. There were messages from suppliers, from the store managers, from clients but none from Brigitte. H*ow long is she going to wait,* he asked himself in dismay. Days went by and still there was no call. Slowly, it dawned on him that she might never want to see him again. *If she thinks I am going to continue paying for that apartment forever, she's dreaming.*

One week later Marcel had had enough. After work one night, he drove over and burst into the apartment in a rage. "Brigitte," he called out. There was no answer, only an eerie silence. Then he noticed that the easel was gone. He stood in the entrance in shock, refusing to believe the obvious. He ran from room to room, flinging open closet doors. They were all empty. "Brigitte!" he called out, his voice almost a roar.

"Are you looking for someone?"

He turned at the sound of the familiar voice. In the doorway stood Hélène, a small bitter smile on her thin lips. "I hope the screwing that whore gave you," she said, sounding victorious. "Was worth the screwing I'm about to give you."

Marcel felt the blood drain out of him. "Hélène, I can explain."

She laughed and her joy sounded ominous. "Don't bother Marcel. I have all the explanation I need."

Helplessly, Marcel watched as Hélène turned and walked out of his life, taking with her, his entire future as director of Richoux.

* * * * *

In her office one week later, Jeanne was reading the business section of Le Monde. The headlines that morning were 'Hélène Richoux becomes CEO of Richoux stores.' Underneath, in smaller letters the story went on to tell of Marcel Latreille's dismissal after years of service and of the couple's sudden break up.

Jeanne crumpled up the newspaper and threw it into the garbage. "Serves him right!" she muttered to herself. "Now if that old bag has any brains, she'll put me in charge of this store."

"Did you say something dear?" From the doorway madame Richoux watched her with a small, self-satisfied smile. Jeanne froze. Hélène continued, her voice saccharine sweet. "My dear, would join me in my office? I'm afraid I have some bad news for you."

Numb with sudden fear, Jeanne followed the woman into the mahogany paneled office.

Hélène pulled out an envelope from her briefcase and abruptly handed it to Jeanne.

"Wh-what is this?" asked Jeanne.

"That is your severance pay. You have been with the company for a long time, and that is why I'm generously giving you two month's salary as compensation."

Jeanne was aghast. "B-but.." she stammered, trying to think of something intelligent to say. "I-I'm invaluable to..."

Hélène shrugged. "Everybody is expendable my dear. I suggest you leave now. You have just been fired."

* * * * *

Brigitte's new apartment in Montmartre could not have been any more different form the one she had just left. The main room was the size of the kitchen she'd had on George V. In it were an old ice box and a double burner, a couch, a small table and a few wobbly chairs. The only other room was what would have been the bedroom... if she could have afforded a bed. *I don't need more than this*, she thought. *I can sleep on the couch.* Since she had moved into her new home, she felt stronger and happier than ever. Life would not be easy, she knew, but she also knew that she would manage somehow.

She threw herself into her project. She had a home to make for herself and after paying for the first two months rent, she only had a few thousand francs left. It was more than enough to live comfortably until her baby was born. *After that...* God only knew how she would survive. *I'll find a way*, she told herself optimistically. She used her imagination and came up with dozens of inexpensive ideas to decorate the apartment. A lace table cloth from the flea market dressed the small window, hiding from view the battered brick wall from across the alley. She painted the walls a sunny shade of yellow and covered them with her own paintings. On the old couch, she threw a bright floral sheet, then stood back to study the results. The small room looked warm and inviting.

As soon as she had settled in, Brigitte set up the easel in a corner of the main room and began to paint. More and more lately, the baby moved inside of her, kicking sharply at a spot just under her ribs. Somehow, as uncomfortable as it was, the sensation felt oddly reassuring. "You're a healthy little one, aren't you?" she asked the child within her. She dreaded the moment she would have to give him over to the adoption agency. For months now, she had kept the number of the agency director Swanson had given her. But she still kept putting off making the call.

Standing in front of her easel, she carefully leaned forward as much as her protruding stomach would allow. She picked up her palette and dipped her brush delicately into the vermilion red, then lathered it into the ochre yellow. She cautiously applied the resulting color to the canvas.

"Merde!" she exclaimed impatiently. No matter how she tried, the results were not what she wanted. In a sudden surge of anger she struck out at the canvas with her brush. Again and again she slashed on the paint. Then, her frustration relieved, she threw the brush into the jar of cloudy turpentine.

This is absolutely crazy, she told herself. She wiped her hands on the paint covered rag reserved for that purpose and strode away. *I am not an artist. Whatever possessed me to think I can paint?* From across the room she glared at the ruined painting. From where she stood, the angry streaks on the canvas seemed to jump out. Those few splashes of color looked more alive than anything else she had ever painted.

She stared in amazement. *That's the kind of vibrancy I want to put into my work*, she thought. Slowly, she walked back to the easel. *Maybe that's what I'm doing wrong. I'm being too careful, too timid.* She picked up her brush again, wiped off the turpentine and this time purposely slashed the paint onto the canvas with strong, bold strokes. *This is more like it!*

Brigitte's brush flew across the canvas. In minutes, flowers sprung to life, blooms exploded with color. This was no longer an insipid little still life. Instead, the result was exciting, wildly live foliage. Almost drunk with the thrill of discovery, she worked for hours. Only long after the light from the window had disappeared, did she notice it was night. Exhausted, but exhilarated, she stepped away from her finished work. At last she had a painting she was proud of. At that moment, the first contraction came. It shot through her like a knife and left her breathless. A few moments later she felt another and she thought, *it's time*.

* * * * *

Chapter 10

The following Monday, promptly at eight, Alex arrived at work fresh and eager to start his new career. At the entrance, another young man greeted him. His name was Andrew McGregor. He was short, no more than five feet six, but built like a brick wall. His brown hair was curly and a multitude of freckles covered his face.

"So you're the new guy. I don't know what you said during your interview but you sure made some impression."

"Why do you say that?" Alex asked, his interest awakened.

Andrew McGregor looked at him intently. "The word is out you got your job by offering to work for free. So for the next two weeks, you are going to bust your ass making a good impression and at the end of that time, there is a good chance Brandon will hire you. Then what will you do? Don't even think of going after my job." Andrew's handshake was crushing. "Welcome to William Brandon & Company," he added, his tone only slightly friendlier than his words.

They went down a flight of narrow stairs to the basement and Alex found himself in a large, cavernous room. There were building plans everywhere. A dozen or so cafeteria-type tables lined the walls. At each one a worker sketched, hunched over a drawing, under the glare of large fluorescent lights.

"The guys call this purgatory," McGregor said. "But maybe it would be more realistic to call it hell. All the boring work gets done down here." At Alex's expression of surprise he explained "That's what you'll do, drudgery, until God," he pointed to the ceiling, "decides you're worthy of more important work."

"I take it William Brandon is God."

"You're a fast learner," he replied with a glint of sarcasm in his eyes. "Maybe you'll move up fast. Hey everybody, this is Alex Ivanov."

"Hi Alex. Nice to meet you." A thin man in horn-rimmed glasses introduced himself as Joey.

"Welcome to the group, I'm Ben..." The introductions continued.

Alex shook hands with everyone, and then Andrew directed him to a corner of the room. There he picked up a stack of plans from a table and piled them onto a chair. Alex's eyes lit up.

"This is where you'll be working. Your job will be to go through this." Andrew pointed to the stack of mail at the other end of the table. "Sort these. Go through the junk, keep whatever might be useful, and deliver the letters to whomever they are addressed. If you need coffee, the percolator is over there. Lunch is at twelve, you can take forty-five minutes, and at five you're out of here." He turned to leave.

"Wait a minute," said Alex. Andrew turned back. "This isn't what I was hired for. This is secretarial work."

"Hey, if I remember correctly, there was no job description attached to your offer. Shall I tell Brandon you don't want to do it?" A few of the men chuckled. Andrew walked away and a few steps further he called out, "Like I said. Welcome to purgatory."

Alex sat down and pushed the mail to one side of the desk. For the rest of the morning he sorted flyers and catalogues from countless construction supply companies, and carefully filed them under various categories. There were files for lumber, files for plumbing, others for electrical wiring. The list was non-ending and Alex had to decide which information was worth keeping and which was not. In the end, he relied on an infallible method. *Eenie... meenie... minie... mo... Shut up and work*, Alex admonished himself. *Two days ago, you were willing to take anything. Well, looks like anything is what you got.*

At twelve o'clock, all work stopped instantly. Workers put away their pencils, rolled up their plans and stacked them, then disappeared as if by magic. Within seconds, the place was empty.

"Want to go for lunch?" Andrew McGregor stood beside Alex, a smirk on his freckled face.

The cafeteria was a crowded room with one long narrow table and a shortage of chairs. People sat on the floor, on windowsills, wherever they could.

As soon as Andrew walked in, a few men stood and walked toward the back of the room. "Have a seat," said Andrew motioning to two of the unoccupied chairs. "Did you bring your lunch?" he asked as he opened a brown paper bag and pulled out its contents.

Alex's stomach rumbled. "No, I didn't think of it."

"Don't worry about it. Here." He grabbed one of his own sandwiches and set it on the table in front of Alex. "I always bring too much food anyhow."

"Thanks." Alex bit into the thick chicken and lettuce sandwich with appetite. He watched the way the other men seemed to defer to Andrew. "So how long have you been with the company?"

"Long enough," Andrew replied. "How are you enjoying it so far?"

"I didn't go to college to learn filing. But I'll do it for as long as I have to."

"Listen Alex; let me give you a piece of advice. Don't go expecting any big projects to land in your lap. Even if you stayed with the company, which you may not, you're going to be staying right where you are for a good long time." There was a hint of the earlier edginess in Andrew's voice. "Let me put it to you this way. If there's any promotion being handed out, there are a few people in line before you."

"I guess that's up to Brandon to decide, don't you think?" asked Alex. Andrew glared at him and Alex decided it was time to change the subject. "Want another coffee? I'll get it for you."

Back in the office, Andrew made a point of repeating, word for word, his conversation with Alex. "So what do you think guys? Maybe we should place a bet on how fast Alex takes over this company." A few of the men chuckled. Alex did not. *Go ahead, laugh. While you go around wasting time trying to intimidate me, I'll be working on more important things.*

Halfway through the afternoon Alex finished sorting the mail and asked for something else to do. "Go see Anne Turner. She has tons of files that need sorting."

Alex found her in the small office adjoining William Brandon's. It was a pretty office. The walls were a soft shade of blue. On her desk was the picture of a woman and two children. *Her sister*, thought Alex, noting the resemblance. African violets were blooming in a white ceramic pot on the windowsill. Anne looked up at him expectantly.

"I was told you have files that need to be sorted."

"You're filing?" She sounded surprised. "Does Andrew McGregor have anything to do with this?"

Alex nodded.

"Well, I'm sure it won't last forever. Sometimes Andrew can be a jerk. He likes to think he's the boss." She led him to large file cabinet and pulled open the top drawer.

"What happens if I tell him to fuck off?"

"Have you ever heard of Daniel McGregor?"

Alex recognized the name as one a well-respected architect. "Sure, who hasn't?"

"Andrew is his son." She pulled a thick stack of files and handed them to Alex. "Brandon and Daniel McGregor have been friends for a long time."

Alex shrugged. "Hey, I love filing, right?" The rest of the day went by in a blur of envelopes.

The next day, Alex went to the accounting department to fill out his employment form. The accountant, a bored looking man with glasses thicker than the bottom of coke bottles, took back the sheet of paper Alex handed to him and jotted down a few words. "Mister Brandon told me to let you know that you are on salary as of now," he said.

Great! Alex cleared his throat. "Can you can tell me what my salary will be?"

"Sure. Let me check your file." He came back a moment later with another form. "Here you go," he said and handed the sheet to Alex.

Alex looked at the figure on the sheet. *What? This is less than I make at Durring & Durring.* He had been working the night shift with the company for nearly four years and his salary, already high because of the time-and-a-half nightshift rate, had grown to comfortable wages. *I definitely have to get a promotion. I can't afford to work for so little.* In the meantime, he had no choice but to keep his night job. *At least I can bank my entire Brandon & Brandon salary.*

Since leaving Brooklyn four years ago, he had sent a check to his mother every month. Not once had he ever heard a word of thanks or even received a note from her. *The day I stop sending her money, is the day she will call.* In the meantime, slowly, gradually, through careful spending and consistent thriftiness, his savings had grown to a sizable amount. Now with the extra income, his bank account would grow even faster. And someday, when he had enough money...

Later that same afternoon Sol Goldstein, one of the senior architects, came downstairs. He looked around until he spotted Alex and walked over. "Brandon asked me to give you this. He wants you to work on these revisions. Do you think you can handle it?"

"Can I handle it?" Alex exclaimed. He grabbed the roll of plans and spread them out on the table.

A few tables away, Andrew looked up from his work. "Hey, what's that?"

"A project for Alex to do," replied Goldstein firmly.

Andrew shrugged in a futile attempt to appear indifferent.

Alex studied the plans carefully. The revisions were simple. He needed to move a bathtub to the opposite side of a bathroom. He was to add a powder room near the entrance. He set to work with enthusiasm.

Within an hour of bending over the sketches, his back was aching. He would have cheerfully given an entire week's paycheck for a comfortable chair and a proper drafting table. *I do not want to create trouble for myself by asking for special treatment*, he thought. *However, I will be damned if I have to work under these conditions.*

Saturday, his first day off, Alex got up early. An hour later, he walked into a drafting supply shop.

He looked through the store until he found what he wanted. At the cash, he pulled out his wallet and counted out the money. This was one purchase he knew he would not regret. *How can I expect to do a good job if I have to work on a wobbly old table?*

Monday morning, Alex was sketching away busily when Andrew McGregor walked in. "Nice table. Where did you get it?" he asked a dumbfounded expression on his freckled face.

"A gift from God," answered Alex calmly, knowing Andrew would go crazy wondering why Alex got a new drafting table and he did not. Alex went back to work whistling happily.

A few days later, another drafting table suddenly appeared at Andrew's end of the room. Alex waited for a moment when nobody else was around. "Hey! Andrew! How much did you pay for yours?"

It took a moment for the meaning to sink in. Andrew looked at Alex in surprise. "You mean you...? " He burst out laughing. "You bastard! You got me. You really got me."

* * * * *

CHAPTER 11

After an exhausting twenty-two hours labor, the eight-pounds baby boy made his appearance shortly after midnight. *He's beautiful*, thought Brigitte as he was handed to her still slippery and wet. She lay on the hospital bed, tired but ecstatic and gazed down at her son in wonderment. He had a fuzz of bright copper hair on his head and his unfocused eyes were a deep shade of jade. She scrutinized his small face and was infinitely relieved to find no resemblance to Lucien. More important, he was pink all over; he had all his fingers and toes; and judging from the way he was screaming, he had a good pair of lungs. *You look just like me.* Her reaction was unexpected and immediate. *I love you. Don't worry, I won't leave you.*

Her baby was healthy. *David, that's what I'll call you, because you are so small and I want you to be strong and face life without fear.*

The next day Doctor Beaulieu stopped by Brigitte's room during his hospital rounds. "How is our new mother doing?" he asked as he palpated her abdomen. "Looks like you're doing just fine," he said after completing his examination. "And how is your son?"

Brigitte's smile lit the room. "How did you know?" she asked.

The doctor looked puzzled. "Know what?"

"You predicted I would have a boy and you were right. How did you know?"

"Is that what I predicted?" He chuckled. "Let me tell you my little secret. It's really very simple. All pregnant mothers want to know the sex of their baby. I always tell them the same thing, that they're expecting a boy, but I write down in my book that they're expecting a girl. I have a fifty-fifty chance of being right. When I'm right the mothers don't question it. When I'm wrong, I just open my book, show them my notes, and tell them they must have misunderstood." He chuckled again. "One way or another, I'm never wrong."

Scorpio Rising

When he was one week old, Brigitte took David home. As soon as she was strong enough, she bought a crib at the flea market. For his blankets and sheets, she used the Porthaux and Descamps sheets Marcel had purchased for her. *This is what I think of your fancy sheets.* She tore the expensive linen into crib-size pieces of fabric. Then she painstakingly hand-sewed the hems on each piece and put her baby to bed in his new crib. Suffused with love and happiness for her child, she stood watching while he slept. *Thank you God for keeping him healthy.* At last she could put her fears behind her.

* * * * *

What Brigitte wanted most, was to be a good mother. *I want to give you everything I never had*, she cooed into her baby's ears. *I will love you and protect you and never, ever abandon you.* And she took her new role to heart. Every time David cried, she panicked. Was he hungry? Did he have colic? Or did he simply need a diaper change? She consulted her child-care book constantly. Sometimes in the middle of the night she would wake up with a start, convinced that he had stopped breathing. She would rush over to his crib only to find him sleeping peacefully.

"Don't worry so much. He's fine," Réjeanne Sauvé, Brigitte's landlord and downstairs neighbor, told her repeatedly. Although Réjeanne Sauvé was not an attractive woman, nobody noticed. What people saw was a short, comfortably plump widow, with a heart of gold. Although her deceased husband had left her a duplex with a large mortgage and a miniscule income, she was always willing to help others in need. When Brigitte first rented her upstairs apartment, Réjeanne Sauvé adopted her the same way she adopted everyone in her life.

Réjeanne sat at Brigitte's small table drinking another cup of *café au lait*. "I don't see what you're so worried about. Look at him. I've never seen such a healthy looking baby," she said, laughing fondly. "Everybody knows you should let a baby cry. It's good for their lungs."

"How can you even say that?" asked Brigitte horrified as she cradled her son in her arms. *Never, not even in a million years.*

But soon, she learned the difference between David's many cries. Loud, frantic screaming meant hunger. The milder wailing meant he needed a diaper change, whimpering meant he wanted to be picked up. As Brigitte became a more confident mother, David became a more contented baby and his crying all but disappeared.

Brigitte settled into a calm if somewhat solitary life and soon was painting again. Now, there was a new urgency to her efforts, a new purpose to her art. Foremost on her mind was the fact that she had a child to support. She could not afford the luxury of painting for pleasure. She needed to sell her work.

With this in mind, she chose to paint bright and vivid still lives. She used everyday objects—cracked vases, fruit, bits of ribbon and lace—and created interesting compositions of diametrically opposing shapes, colors and textures. Every one of her paintings was arresting, bold and interesting. Still, she was never satisfied. It seemed to her that the effect she wanted to create was always just out of her reach.

She needed to have a few good paintings before she could even dream of selling them. Like a woman possessed she began early in the morning and stopped only when daylight faded. Her only breaks came when David needed attention.

"What I need is better lighting in here," she told Réjeanne one evening as she put away her paints, carefully making sure each tube's cover was tightly twisted on. Good quality oils were horrifyingly expensive and tended to dry out quickly. "If I had proper lighting..."

"...you work day and night," interrupted Réjeanne. "It's nearly nine o'clock now and I know you've been working since six o'clock this morning."

Brigitte looked up from her paint box.

"I can hear you from downstairs when you walk around," explained Réjeanne.

"I'll try not to make so much noise."

"My goodness! You are in a mood. The noise doesn't bother me. I'm only worried for you. You've just had a baby, Brigitte. When are you going to take proper care of yourself?" She went to the ice box and opened the door. "Look at this. There's nothing in here." She picked up a limp carrot. "This isn't even good enough to use as a model for a painting. It looks sick. I bet you haven't had a bite to eat all day, have you?"

"I-I guess I got so carried away with my painting, I forgot."

"You forgot! How can you forget to eat?"

"Don't worry. I make sure David is fed."

"That's not what I'm worried about." She hesitated. "Brigitte, what are you doing for money?"

"I-I'm sort of short right now but..." Brigitte voice quivered and she turned her eyes away.

"Brigitte, if you like..."

"No! I don't want to owe anybody anything."

"Who said anything about borrowing? I was just going to say, you should think about meeting a man. There's this man I know who'd be perfect..."

"Réjeanne, finding a man is not the answer to everything. I don't want to hear about meeting anyone right now."

Réjeanne sighed. "I'm only trying to help. You're so young and so pretty. You could make someone happy, and you could be happy too. Besides, I don't know about you but I think life without love is very empty." Réjeanne poured herself another cup of coffee. "O.K. so back to your financial situation. Your paintings are really good. Why don't you go the *carré* and try to sell to them there?"

Brigitte hesitated. "That's what I'm planning to do but I don't think I'm ready."

"Ready! Ready for what? For someone to come knocking on your door to discover you?"

"I just don't like the idea of David being outside all day. He's still so young."

"Seems to me like you don't really have a

choice. You have to feed him. How else are you planning to make money?"

"I know you're right," answered Brigitte hesitantly. "I don't have a choice." She bitterly remembered another time when she'd had no choice, as Marcel had pointed out.

Réjeanne smiled reassuringly. "One thing I have learned, *chérie*, is to trust life. Things always work out somehow. I'm free tomorrow. If you want to stop by the *carré* and give it a chance, you don't have to take David with you. I'll be happy to mind him for you."

After Réjeanne went back to her own apartment downstairs, Brigitte put David back to bed and stayed with him until he slept peacefully. Then she went back to the living area and poured the contents of her purse on the couch. A quick count told her there was barely enough money to carry her through the next few weeks. *Things always work out somehow*, she reminded herself. She put the money back into her purse and lay down on the couch for the night. As she tried vainly to sleep, she thought of Réjeanne's offer to find her a boyfriend. Although she had not said as much, Brigitte was convinced her friend was hoping she would find a man and that would solve her financial situation. *I won't make that mistake again. I was so eager to be saved, I would have believed anything Marcel told me*, she thought as she remembered the apartment on the *Avenue George V* and the life of luxury she had enjoyed for such a short time. *Dear God*, she asked bitterly in the night. *Tell me; what makes you decide someone like Marcel Latreille should have so much money, while I have to worry about every sou?*

She buried her head into her pillow and began to cry softly.

* * * * *

"Come here," the man said. He was blond, with deep blue eyes and Brigitte felt herself drawn to him. He smiled and lifted his hands to her breasts.

She moaned.

"You like that don't you?" His voice was low and caressing.

She squeezed her eyes shut. "No, no I don't."

"You won't tell anyone about this will you? This is our little secret."

The voice sounded familiar, horrifyingly familiar! Brigitte's eyes flew open. Inches away was her step father's mean face grinning down at her.

Brigitte screamed. She sat up in bed, startled, the sound of her voice still echoing in her ears. Just a dream, she told herself and hugged herself tightly under the covers. *Just a bad dream. Lucien is out of my life. He can't hurt me anymore.* But it was hours before she went back to sleep.

The next morning she got all of her things together, gave Réjeanne dozens of instructions, kissed David goodbye and set off for the *carré* with her son's cries ringing in her ears. She walked resolutely on. Over and over again, she repeated to herself. *What else can I do? I have no choice.*

* * * * *

Sometimes it seemed to Brigitte that her life would forever be filled with difficulties. Exhaustion followed her twenty-four hours a day. There were always a million things to do. In the mornings, there was David's formula to prepare, his diapers to rinse out in the toilet, wash by hand in the sink and hang on the line out back. There was the dusting and cleaning of the small apartment, dishes to wash and clothes to mend. After housework and a few short moments with David, she would run off to the square and spend the rest of the day trying to sell her paintings. No matter how hard she worked, there was never enough money.

The worst was the guilt. *Poor child. He has a mother who loves him, but I'm never there for him. What kind of life am I giving him?*

"You won't believe it," Réjeanne told Brigitte when she came home one evening. "Today, David crawled for the first time."

"What a good boy," Brigitte cooed to her son. "*Maman* is so proud of you." *And I wasn't there*, she thought sadly. *As long as he's happy and healthy, that's all that really counts. I only wish I didn't have to miss his childhood. I'll try to spend more time with him. Money isn't everything.*

At the end of the day when Brigitte, exhausted, tried to find sleep, it often evaded her. And when it did come, it was filled with nightmares of Lucien. The next morning, still exhausted from the day before, she would drag herself out of bed to begin another demanding day. *As long as I have David, and he has me, that's all that matters.*

When David spoke his first words at eleven months, they were spoken to Réjeanne. When he sang his first song, Brigitte heard about it in the evening when he was already in bed. Because her time with David was scarce, it became ever so precious. After finishing her housework, she tiptoed into his room and watched him sleep. *My beautiful baby, I don't know what I would do without you. I love you David.*

* * * * *

Brigitte walked briskly in the mid-morning sun. It was not yet noon and already small beads of perspiration were gathering at the nape of her neck. This June day promised to be a hot one. Her arms ached from carrying her easel folded under one arm and her stool and paint box under the other. Still, she hurried on. As she turned the corner of the Avenue Junot, a flock of pigeons flew off. Dozens of wings flapped in the air, a faint cloud of dust lifted from the sidewalk and settled down again. Brigitte squinted. Down the street a few hundred meters she could see the square.

It looked the same as it did every morning since she had become a regular nearly three years ago. Still, she felt her breath catch in her throat. Imagine, she told herself. Many of the world's greatest artists began there. In her mind she could see them all, Picasso, Toulouse Lautrec, Renoir and countless others, standing before their easels, capturing genius on canvas.

In reality, the small park in Montmartre had long ago lost its charms. It was now no more than a grassy knoll overtaken by weeds and patches of dry earth. Its outline was fenced in by rusted iron pickets along which a trove of mangy looking artists eagerly displayed the fruit of their indifferent to terrible talent.

Brigitte saw none of that. To her, the square was a wondrous place where every day her soul was allowed to soar. In her eyes, every haggard painter was another colorful character destined to become one of the great artists of tomorrow. Apart from David, who was now a bright and cheerful three year old, and Réjeanne Sauvé who had become family to her, these people were her only friends.

"*Bonjour* Brigitte. You're late this morning. I saved your spot for you."

"Thank you Julien. David wouldn't let me leave this morning. He wanted to read me his new book."

The skinny young man in the loose white shirt and black *béret* rushed over to help her unfold her easel. Julien embraced his role of artist with passion and dressing the part was a responsibility he enthusiastically performed. "Read? What do you mean read?"

"Well, he doesn't really. I've read David some books so often, he has memorized the words. He loves to pretend he can read and I play along with him." Brigitte opened her paint box and pulled out a dozen small, colorful still lives and set them up along her small piece of sidewalk.

"What else is new?" asked Julien as he picked up his charcoal and resumed his sketch of the café across the street.

"Don't ask. My rent is due tomorrow and I don't have a single franc!"

"Rough times lately?"

Brigitte sighed. "Rough times lately," she admitted.

"Tell me about it." Julien grinned suddenly. "Hey, that one is good." He was looking at the painting Brigitte had just set up on her easel. "Hate to tell you, but you'd make a lot more money if you painted more of these. That's what tourists buy." He pointed to his own, a series of scenic drawings, similar to those popularized on postcards.

"I know. I just don't seem to have the knack for them the way you do," answered Brigitte, generously. "I'll only try them if I get absolutely desperate."

"And you're not desperate now, with your rent due tomorrow?"

Brigitte said nothing for a moment, and then shook her head, her mane of red hair bouncing. "I want to do something different." She could not tell Julien that his work was no different than every other artist's in the square any more than she could tell him that what she created was special. As long as she was the only one who liked her own work, she was as much a failure as any other artist struggling to eke out a living.

"If a lot of artists do it, it's for a good reason. It sells!" Lucien put on his most charming smile and called out to the tourists swarming the square, switching effortlessly from his native French to a heavily accented English or German. *"Bonjour Madame.* That is a pretty hat you're wearing. *Komen zie hier ein moment, bitte."*

The tourists stopped and looked. A few charcoal sketches sold and a client accepted to pose for a quick pastel drawing. If the picture was flattering, Julien was rewarded with a generous tip.

Meanwhile, Brigitte painted on quietly, carefully hiding any envy she might have been feeling for her neighbor's brisk trade. Her own business was not good today, but it was not always so. Some days, people stopped by her easel and bought her paintings. Even though they were more expensive than any others on the square, she sold enough of them to pay the bills. And when she did sell one of her paintings, she would pocket the money reverently and hand over the canvas with mixed emotions. As much as she needed the money, parting with one of her oils was like giving away a small piece of her heart.

By the time the day began to fade, Julien had sold two pastel drawings, one small charcoal and had extracted a promise from another customer to come back the next day for one of his oils. All in all, he'd had a great day. "Hey! Brigitte, how did you do?" he called out as he put away his paintings.

Brigitte shook her head. "Nothing." She folded up her easel, put away her paints into their wooden case and picked up her paintings. "Tomorrow will better. The rent will just have to wait. God bless my landlady. She is the most understanding person in the world." She waved to Julien and hurried off.

In her rush to leave, she did not notice the small oil she left leaning against the fence. Moments later, Julien found it. He looked off in the direction Brigitte had taken and decided she was already too far. *I'll give it to her tomorrow*, he told himself and threw it in among his own.

What am I going to do? Brigitte asked herself as she walked home. Although Réjeanne was the most patient landlady she could ever hope for, she hated to make her wait. Also, there was dinner to worry about. She mentally reviewed the contents of the icebox. There were a few carrots and potatoes, and a small piece of leftover meat from last night's meal. She could throw it all together and make a soup. She sighed and walked on. There wasn't much, but it would be enough for a frugal dinner.

A few blocks later, just a hundred meters from the church of St Pierre, was the small apartment she called home. She ran up the rickety stairs and flung open the door. "Here I am Réjeanne."

A moment later Réjeanne Sauvé appeared. "David is sleeping," she said. "I gave him his dinner just a half hour ago. He seemed a bit tired."

"Thank you," replied Brigitte, keeping the disappointment from her voice. She had so looked forward to giving David his dinner and putting him to bed herself.

"So how did you do today?"

"Not so good," answered Brigitte with a grimace.

"Well, don't worry about the rent. Pay me

whenever you can. But there's something else I want to talk to you about. There's this man I know. He's a very nice man. He owns a small restaurant down the street. He'd be perfect for you. Why don't you let me introduce you? We could go out some time and have dinner there..."

Brigitte interrupted. "Réjeanne please. You know how I feel about that."

Réjeanne shook her head. "It's been three years since David was born. Don't you think it's about time you got on with your life? You need a man in your life. It's just not healthy for a grown woman to stay by herself all the time."

Brigitte sighed wearily. She had heard all of this a hundred times before. "Réjeanne, I love you dearly, but this is my life." Before she could go any further, a cry, followed by a loud, repeated banging came from the other room. "What is going on?" asked Brigitte puzzled. She rushed over to the door and tore it open. "Oh my God! David!"

Inside his crib, David was thrashing around, his small body seized by a series of convulsions. With each contraction of his limbs, the crib banged against the wall.

"Nooo!"

From the other room Réjeanne heard her cry

and ran over. "What is it? Brigitte, what's wrong? Dear God! What's happened?"

Brigitte was holding David's body down, trying to prevent the pudgy little arms from flailing about. "Quick, get help."

Réjeanne turned about and hurried to the telephone.

* * * * *

The hospital waiting room was filled beyond capacity. In a small area meant to comfortably seat a dozen people, nearly forty, tired and cranky people waited impatiently. They crouched on the floor, leaned against the walls and sat two to a chair. From far away came the sound of a baby crying.

"What do you think is taking so long?" asked Brigitte, her voice quivering. It had been over three hours since David had disappeared behind the emergency doors. It felt like a life time. "I don't think I could bear it if anything happens to him."

"Don't worry. I'm sure it won't be too long now," replied Réjeanne reassuringly. But the memory of David thrashing about in his bed sent shivers down her back.

At that moment the physician appeared. "*Madame* Dartois?"

"Yes!" both Brigitte and Réjeanne replied in unison.

He looked from one to the other.

"I'm *Madame* Dartois," said Brigitte.

"Your son is fine," said the doctor, flatly. "From now on, he will have to be on medication to control the seizures..."

"What seizures? You mean this will happen again?" Brigitte was frantic.

"Madame Dartois, your son has epilepsy. He has just suffered what is called a grand-mal seizure. There was loss of consciousness, severe convulsions and urinary and fecal incontinence. At the moment he is sleeping. When he wakes up he will most likely have some muscle soreness and be quiet and disoriented for a short time. If we do not take preventative measures, he most likely will have this kind of epileptic attack again."

"Oh my God," said Brigitte, tears welling in her eyes. "Is it dangerous? Can he..."

The doctor averted his eyes. "Rarely, but it can happen. Sometimes one seizure follows another with no intervening period of consciousness. Such an attack could persist for hours or days and can sometimes be fatal. But with medication it is not likely to happen. What we will have to do is try different types of medication until we find the right drug and the right dosage."

Brigitte was no longer hearing anything the doctor was saying. The same words kept playing over and over in her mind, 'and can sometimes be fatal'. This was a mistake. It could not be happening. Not to her David. *Please God, not to David.*

For the next few weeks, Brigitte did not let her son out of her sight. She watched him like a hawk.

Réjeanne watched as Brigitte in her panic to keep her son safe, abandoned her painting. "If you want to go to the square I can take care of him..."

Brigitte was adamant. "Thanks Réjeanne, but I don't want to leave David right now."

Réjeanne hesitated. "You'll have to go back sometime."

"Yes, yes I know. But not just now. Not until his medication is stabilized. Then I'll go back. I'm sorry. I won't be able to pay you the rent until then."

"Don't worry about the rent. I really don't mind. If you need anything..." She paused for a moment. "I guess now is not the time to tell you about this man I thought you might..." She saw the look on Brigitte's face and blushed. "I'm sorry, *chérie*. I just wish you would allow some man to make you happy, but if you don't want me to say anything more, I won't. I'll go on downstairs. If you need me for anything, just call."

* * * * *

CHAPTER 12

During the next few months Alex put in eight to ten hours daily at William Brandon & Company, then he rode the bus across town to Durring & Durring where he worked another eight hours. In the morning, after a few hours of sleep, a quick shower and a shave, he hurried back to William Brandon & associates and started all over again. *I cannot take the risk of quitting Durring & Durring until I feel secure at the firm.* Although he had been on salary from the first day, Brandon had never officially told Alex that his position was firm.

In the morning, Alex was always the first to arrive, and by the end of the day, he had completed more work than anyone else had. He rarely stopped for coffee and his lunches usually consisted of a fast sandwich at his drafting table. Alex's plan was simple. He would keep working harder and producing more than anyone else. In time, surely it would come to the boss' attention.

"Good day Mister Ivanov. You sure are getting here early every morning. Don't you sleep nights like normal people do?" The old cleaning woman paused in her vacuuming and greeted Alex.

"Good morning Hazel. Got important work to do." *Who am I fooling? There is no important work. Moreover, the only person who is impressed with my diligence is the cleaning lady!*

One person did notice. It was a non-ending source of irritation to Andrew McGregor that every morning when he arrived, Alex was already there; that every afternoon when he left, Alex was still at work.

Damn jerk! He's only trying to make the rest of us look bad, he muttered to himself one night as he left the building and walked into the parking lot. He hopped into his new car, a 57 red Corvette with white inserts and turned the ignition key. The motor growled to life. He threw the gearshift into reverse and backed out in a spray of gravel. Forty minutes later, he pulled into the driveway of his parents' house, a modern concrete structure with huge expanses of windows. Automatically he reached into the glove compartment for his Rolaids. A moment later, he opened the front door and walked into the marble foyer.

"Andrew is that you?" his father's voice called out from the den.

Andrew felt the familiar burning sensation of acid flaring up in his stomach. He popped a second Rolaids and hoped it would take effect soon. "Yes sir," he called out.

Daniel McGregor appeared. He was as tall as Andrew was short and as frail as his son was muscular. "Where are you going?"

"Just thought I might go and exercise a bit before dinner." Andrew headed for the long curving staircase.

Daniel McGregor watched his son walk away. "Don't imagine for a minute that you're fooling me."

Andrew stopped one hand on the railing and turned to face his father. "How exactly am I trying to fool you?"

"Every time I try to talk to you, you lock yourself in your room and tell me you're lifting weights."

"That's because I am lifting weights."

"That's not the point. The point is you avoid me."

Andrew hesitated. "Give me fifteen minutes to freshen up and I'll join you in the den."

Half an hour later Andrew walked into the small wood paneled room. His father motioned him toward the leather wing chair across from his.

"How is everything going at work?" the old man asked the expression on his face unreadable.

"Everything is going fine. You don't have to worry about anything. I've been there nearly one year now and I'm doing all right."

"That is just what worries me." The old man sounded exasperated. "All right, might be good enough for you, but it isn't good enough for me."

Andrew grimaced. *Here we go again*, he thought.

"Don't make that face when I'm talking to you. Your grandfather was an internationally respected architect and so am I. With the connections we have, you could already be on your way to a world famous career. But does my son want any help? No! He wants to do it all by himself. Well, that's what you want, that's fine with me, but from what I can see, you're getting nowhere fast."

"Dad!" It had been years since he had last called him so informally. His father stopped, surprised. "Maybe it's time you accepted it," Andrew said wearily. "I'm just not as good as you and grandfather. I do not have your talent. Don't you understand?"

The truth of the simple statement hit Daniel McGregor like a punch. Years of hope and ambition dissolved. He had always hoped his son would someday take his place in the annals of world-renowned architects. All of his son's life, he had pressured him to share these ambitions, but to no avail. Daniel McGregor suddenly felt old. "You could if you tried," he said weakly.

Andrew shook his head. "No, I can't. And you know it."

The old man nodded sadly. "I only wanted you could take my place." In his disappointment, he looked older.

"I'm just not cut out to be an architect."

Daniel McGregor was confused. How could anyone not want to be an architect? "So what is it you want to do?"

Andrew hesitated. "I don't know. I just don't know." He watched as Daniel McGregor held himself from comment, but the look on his face spoke loudly. Andrew walked over to the bar and poured himself a double scotch. "Now, why don't you tell me again what a disappointment I am to the family?"

* * * * *

Andrew watched Alex as he calculated and measured the plan in front of him. He could see the concentration on Alex's face, the excitement in his eyes. *Why can't I feel that way?* In the last few months, working with Alex and seeing the dedication his coworker brought to his job only made him more aware of his own unhappiness.

He walked over to the percolator in the corner and poured himself a cup of coffee. "Want one Alex?" he called out. There was no reply. Andrew shrugged and came back. He sipped quietly and watched as Alex studied the drawing before him. He tried again. "Hey Alex, how is everything?"

"Same as usual," Alex answered distractedly. All of his concentration was on the plan before him. He tore off the sheet of paper from the wall and looked at it more closely. It was another budget house plan, one like hundreds of others he had seen since joining the company. This particular plan showed a small two-story house with a living, dining, family room and breakfast nook. The rooms were small, the layout uninspired. He could think of at least a dozen inexpensive changes that would greatly improve the esthetic and practical aspects of the house. *I could design a better house than this.*

"What are you looking at?"

Alex looked up startled. He was so immersed in his work that he did not notice Andrew standing there. "I was just thinking about something." He hesitated for a moment. "Come and take a look at this. Not too bad, but not too good. Right?" Andrew looked at the laid out plan as Alex continued. "Anybody can come up with designs way better than this one. Have you ever visited a Brandon house?"

Andrew laughed. "I see enough of them right here at work. I don't think I need to go and visit any."

"If we want to move up in this company, we might have to do just that," replied Alex.

"You're nuts, you know that?" Andrew walked away shaking his head and muttering under his breath. *Great! Now he's going to start doing house inspections on weekends.*

* * * * *

The idea of visiting Brandon-built houses stayed on Alex's mind and the more he thought about it, the more it seemed like a good idea. The only problem was that with the closest project being miles out of the city, Alex had no way of getting there. In the meantime, he still studied every Brandon plan that came his way. He analyzed the average square footage of the houses, their typical layout and determined what he felt were the strong points and the weak points of each design. Then he went to work.

Every spare minute he had, he devoted to his new project. Instead of napping during his night shift at Durring & Durring and going out on weekends, he planned and sketched. *I don't know how long I can keep this up.* Somehow, he was not tired. Rather, he felt more energy than ever. It seemed that the more he pushed himself, the happier he was. *As long as I work this hard, I'm bound to get somewhere.*

Andrew, a silent witness to Alex's efforts, watched from afar, and with grudging admiration. *Have to give the guy credit. He's a determined bastard.* Slowly, Andrew's curiosity was getting the better of him until one day, feeling particularly indulgent, he approached Alex. "I hear Brandon has a residential development going up about twenty minutes out of the city. I thought I might drive out to see it on Saturday. Want to come along for the ride?"

"Sounds good," Alex answered, wisely choosing not to show his eagerness.

"Fine. I'll pick you up around one. What's your address?"

The following Saturday Andrew arrived on schedule. Alex climbed into the Corvette and the two drove off.

Alex noticed every luxurious detail of the sports car, the leather seats, the high-gloss steering wheel, the multitude of dials on the dashboard. "Nice car," he said his voice full of admiration.

"A gift from my parents," explained Andrew. "Believe me, I pay for it. I pay very dearly for it."

Alex did not understand, but nodded all the same.

It was a beautiful day for a drive. The autumn sun was shining in a clear blue sky and the air breathed a chilly hint of the winter ahead. As they left the city and drove further into the country Alex was awed by the scenery. Everywhere the trees were aflame with yellow, orange and red foliage. Such colorful leaves he had never seen before. He sat back and relaxed, enjoying the purring of the powerful engine and the breathtaking scenery along the road.

The car turned into a rough dirt road and bumped along for a few miles before the construction site came into view. The development was huge. It covered nearly a thousand acres of land. Toward the north end of the property were rows of completed houses sitting on bare land, no trees, not a blade of grass around. At the south end, construction was just beginning. Huge mechanical cranes bit into the earth, belching clouds of dust. Bulldozers pushed away at mountains of earth, stirring up yet more dust. There was dust everywhere. It rolled in like thick fog and settled on everything, painting the area dull monochromatic shades of gray.

At the front, a large sign brought attention to the fact that every one of the hundreds of houses to be built on this site would be a Brandon-designed home.

Andrew felt a surge of excitement. "Let's go find the model homes." He stepped out of the car and walked toward the rows of houses. Minutes later, they found six, each with a different floor plan.

They crossed a long narrow board bridging the trench and at the entrance of the first house, a friendly salesman greeted them. "Hi! Fill this in and I'll be right with you." He handed them a form.

"Thanks but we're not looking to buy," explained Andrew. "We're with Brandon & Company. We just want to look around."

The man's attitude immediately changed to one of nervous enthusiasm. He put away the forms and almost bowed in his effort to please. "Sure. No problem. Why didn't somebody tell me they were sending you guys out here? All I have to offer you is a cup of coffee. Would you care to look at the brochure while I go turn on the percolator?"

"Sounds good." Andrew replied.

The man, introduced as Sidney Leopold, gave them the advertising material and hurried to the kitchen. "This is a great kitchen. It's fully equipped with all the latest modern appliances," he called out over his shoulder. He laughed. "I can't tell you how any of those gadgets work but it sure impresses the ladies, and in the end..." The sound of water running drowned out his voice for a moment. "... they are the ones who decide whether to buy or not."

Andrew opened the prospectus and scanned the first few pages. There were dozens of artists' drawings of beautiful homes on perfectly tended lawns with shiny new automobiles sitting in each driveway. They had impressive names, the Aristocrat, the Ambassador, the Executive, names that conveyed success and prestige.

Andrew nudged Alex. "Look at this."

Alex leaned over to see. On a loose printed page, was the price list.

Andrew checked them quickly. "I'm surprised at the prices they charge. They seem high. Considering the building cost per square foot, these houses are being sold for..." He performed the calculation in his mind. "I can't be right! Or am I? Almost eighty per cent profit? That's unheard of."

Sidney reappeared carrying two brimming cups of freshly percolated coffee and the conversation stopped.

"Here you are. Hope it didn't take too long."

"No, not at all." Andrew hurried them through the social chatter.

Sidney, acting as guide, gave them a complete tour of the model homes along with a running commentary. "Each house is decorated in a different style. That way, you have a better chance of pleasing everyone. Customers have no imagination. If you show them an empty house, they can't imagine what it can look furnished."

Alex listened eagerly as Sidney showed them through a home decorated in soft shades of blue and accented with touches of yellow. "It doesn't hurt that our model homes look a lot better professionally decorated than they would with the customers' own furnishings."

"I feel as though I'm getting a quick course in marketing."

Sidney laughed. "It's all part of the selling process."

After the tour, Andrew politely thanked the salesman for his time.

"My pleasure." Sidney shook hands with the two men. "Feel free to wander around," he added as he walked away toward a young couple that looked like potential customers.

As soon as the man was out of sight, Andrew motioned to Alex. "Come with me." He pulled out a small army knife and a screwdriver, and went back inside the last of the houses. There, with his ear to the wall, he knocked until he found what he wanted. Then he used his knife and scraped away a bit of the paint.

"What are you doing?" asked Alex, nervously standing guard.

"I want to find out what quality of materials was used here." He picked up a few chips of wood and looked at it closely, and then he stuck his finger inside the hole. "Not very impressive." He folded the knife and put in his pocket. "Follow me." He went outside and walked around, checking the foundation. "Just as I thought." He shook his head in disgust. "Let's go back inside."

Next, he looked at the wiring and the plumbing. His inspection was thorough. He stood inside closets and crawled behind staircases. In the end, he shook his head in disbelief. "I have to admit that as far as I can tell, the houses are built according to code. But I never saw anything like this."

"What are you talking about?"

"They are barely legal. They've used the cheapest possible materials everywhere. The workmanship is barely acceptable. I wouldn't be surprised if those houses started to fall apart within the first year."

"I noticed that the floor plans are really pathetic. I've already thought of half a dozen ways to increase the living area without adding to the cost of construction."

Andrew looked thoughtful for a moment. "That certainly gives us a thing or two to think about, doesn't it?"

"Sure does." Alex had no idea what Andrew was talking about.

On the way back toward the parking lot, they walked by the construction site again. Andrew was almost hopping with excitement. The smell of the freshly cut wood in the dusty air and the sight of the men pounding away at the skeleton of the houses awakened in him a strong feeling of purpose. "This is what I want to do," he said suddenly.

"What are you talking about?" asked Alex.

"This is what I want to do. I want to be a builder! You saw the shoddy construction of those houses. There is no need for that. No matter what kind of budget Brandon has, he should build his houses with pride. He should build them to last.

The way he throws these together, the problems will start as soon as the buyers move in. When I build them, my houses will be beautiful and strong."

Alex had never seen Andrew so enthusiastic. "If that is what you really want to do, there's no reason why you can't," he said with conviction as they reached the now dust-covered Corvette. Andrew did not even notice. They climbed in and headed back toward the city in silence. Each, dreaming his own dreams. *Someday...*

* * * * *

Over the next few weeks, Alex realized what a godsend the visit had been. Suddenly, he knew at a glance what was right on a plan and what needed changing. He went back to work with urgency.

Meanwhile, Andrew had fallen into the habit of eating lunch at Alex's drafting table and watching him work. Although intrigued by Alex's ideas, he never participated in Alex's project, but every now and then, would ask a question or offer suggestions.

Often, Alex tried to persuade Andrew to join him in his project. "Don't just sit there. Why don't you help me?"

Invariably the answer was the same. "I know architecture is not for me anymore."

"So when are you going to do something about it?"

Andrew shrugged. "When I'm ready I'll let you know."

Within a few months, Alex had what he knew were a dozen house plans far better than any created by William Brandon & Company. At last, he felt ready to show Bill Brandon.

* * * * *

"Come in." In the year since Alex had joined the firm, Bill Brandon had gained more weight and lost more hair. He greeted Alex enthusiastically and invited him to sit. "So you have something to show me. Always interested in looking at my junior architects' work."

Alex put the stack of plans on the desk and carefully unrolled them. Brandon watched with mild curiosity. "That's an impressive amount of work." He puffed on his eternal cigar and leaned forward to study the plans. For the next few minutes, Alex waited anxiously while Bill Brandon silently puffed his way through the stack of plans. Finally, the big man pushed it away and leaned back. "These are all yours?" He sounded impressed.

"Yes sir. I've been working on them during my spare time."

"Not bad." Brandon flipped through the stack again and pulled one out at random. "Actually they're pretty good. Some of them show originality. Mind if I keep these for a few days."

"Not at all sir."

"Very good. I'll get back to you."

* * * * *

Andrew was busy putting the final changes to a bathroom design when Alex walked over. Andrew looked up from his work. "You look like the cat that swallowed the canary," he said.

"I just did it. I showed Brandon my plans."

Andrew whistled softly. "Great! How did he like them?"

"He said they were good. In fact, what he said was they showed originality. It's just a question of time before I'm transferred upstairs."

Andrew seemed genuinely happy for him. "I hope you get the promotion. Unfortunately I probably won't be here to see it happen."

"What is that supposed to mean? Come on, tell me."

Andrew lowered his voice. "I'm leaving this place."

"What are you going to do?"

"I'm toying with a few ideas," Andrew said, but no matter how Alex pushed, he would say no more.

Alex laughed. When Andrew was in one of his secretive moods, nothing would make him talk. "I've got a few ideas of my own and one of them is called Anne Turner," said Alex. He winked and walked away.

"Hah! Good luck." Andrew watched his friend strut over to his drafting table. "Anne Turner has more sense than to go out with a bum like you. If I asked her out, now, that would be a different story."

Alex turned back. "May the better man win," he called out jokingly.

* * * * *

In the four years since Alex had begun to work for Durring & Durring, the decrepit warehouse had only worsened. Alex looked around at the shabby, run down area with affection. Now that it was time to leave, he felt strangely sad.

Barney was equally sad. "I'm really sorry to see you go kid. This place won't seem the same without you. I'm no good at saying goodbye, but I think you've got what it takes to make it."

Alex felt a lump form in his throat. Ever since his arrival at Durring & Durring, he and Barney had enjoyed a special relationship, one that had been as beneficial to Barney as it had been to Alex. Barney had come to accept the death of his son and Alex had enjoyed the fatherly attention of the old man.

"Thanks Barney. From you, those words mean a lot to me." He felt as awkward receiving the compliment as Barney felt giving it.

"I mean it. Someday, when you're a big shot,

I'll come over and you can show me around your buildings." Barney gave him a mild punch on the shoulder.

"You can count on it, Barney. Better yet, you can come and work with me. How's that?"

"You'll have to get rich fast. I'm not a young man anymore."

"Deal." Alex slapped Barney on the back and Barney did likewise. It was the most affection the two men could allow themselves to show.

Alex turned and walked away. A part of his life had just ended. After one year at Brandon & Associates, he at last felt secure in his position. It now made sense to put all his energy into his long-term goal.

With his last Durring & Durring paycheck in his pocket, he hopped the bus and quietly rode home. In his mind, the same thought played repeatedly. *Someday...* Lately he felt that someday was getting closer.

* * * * *

Alex was at home, lying in bed, staring at the ceiling. Since his first day in the city, he had never bothered finding another apartment. *This is good enough for me*, he told himself whenever the idea crossed his mind. *Besides, this is the cheapest I'll find in Manhattan, and I would rather save the money.*

Now that Alex no longer worked nights, the dinginess of his surroundings, the cracks in the plaster, the dust on the floor and the faded furnishings depressed him. It reminded him of the apartment in Brooklyn and of Marlena. *I'll be damned if I turn out like her*, he thought. He pulled himself off the bed and threw himself into a frenzy of cleaning. He changed the burnt ceiling bulb, took out the garbage and swept the floors.

He sat on the bed, overcome with anxiety. He had nothing to do. It was a strange sensation, one that left him feeling nervous, jumpy. He wanted... No, he needed something to keep him busy. I could go out. However, after years of double shifts, his social life was nonexistent. Apart from the occasional dating he did in response to his physical needs, he had never had a regular girlfriend. Apart from the relationships he had with his coworkers, he had no friends. *Now,* he thought, *is the time to make some changes in my life*. His mind wandered again to Anne Turner, as it frequently did in the last few months. He had often thought of asking the attractive secretary out, and had even joked about it with Andrew, but for some reason he kept putting it off. On the few occasions at work when he had shared a few words with her, he had been surprised at the pleasure he felt in her company. *I think I could handle a couple of dates with her.* Alex resolved to do something about it soon.

He picked up 'Modern Design & Architecture' and settled in comfortably for an evening of reading. He quickly found an article that grabbed his attention.

Every year the magazine, in cooperation with a major city, sponsored an international design competition. This year the contest involved the proposed construction of a large commercial building in Paris. It was just the kind of project to stimulate Alex's imagination. From the aerial photographs of the proposed area, he could see that the project would cover one entire city block, where a row of medieval buildings now stood.

Here is something I can do, he thought, still searching for ways to occupy his newly found free time. He pushed away all thoughts of Anne Turner and read the regulations thoroughly. The contest deadline was three weeks away. If he worked like crazy, he might have a chance to complete the rough sketches and preliminary plans. *I don't have to do this. I can just take it easy for a while, go out, have fun, and get to know Anne Turner. Isn't that what any normal person would want to do? Whoever said I was normal?* he thought as he made up his mind.

He jumped off the bed and crossed the room to his bookshelf. For the rest of the night he looked up every example of a large commercial center he could find. There were a few particularly interesting ultra-modern glass and steel designs as well as some beautiful examples of older restored buildings.

Too bad I can't combine the two styles. He stopped for a moment, when the thought hit him. *Why not?* Like a man possessed, he worked the rest of the night on his wild idea.

A few days before the contest deadline, Alex added the last touches to what he thought was an original, cost effective and esthetically pleasing proposal. The plans were impeccably drawn; the ink sketches of the proposed project beautifully executed. It was work he felt proud to call his own.

He filled out the information sheet and at the last moment added the name of William Brandon Architecture & Design alongside his own. Nobody had ever heard of Alex Ivanov. Having the name of a reputable firm on the entry form would only add weight to his presentation.

He rolled up his plans, slid them into a cardboard tube and dropped them off at the post office. *If nothing comes of this, William Brandon will never hear of it. If I win, he can only be pleased about the publicity generated for his company.* Alex headed for the office.

Anne Turner looked up as Alex walked in. "Good morning Alex."

"Good morning." He approached her desk and gave her his most friendly smile. "Anne, I'm hoping you can help with a problem I'm having. I would very much like to ask you out to dinner for Saturday night, but I'm worried you might turn me down. What do you think I should do?"

She laughed. "I guess you'll just have to take your chances," she replied with a twinkle in her eyes.

* * * * *

Andrew hunched over and painstakingly burnishing each small Letraset symbol onto the nearly completed plan. Carefully he lifted the tissue paper to check the results. Half of the lettering came away with it. "Damn! I hate doing this." He bent down over his work again and started over.

Alex walked up behind him. "I see you inherited the interesting work again."

Andrew sighed. "Right! Real interesting."

"I've got some news that'll cheer you up. I've got a date with Anne Turner."

Andrew's eyebrows shot up. "How did you manage that? Everybody else in the office got the cold shoulder."

"Must be my irresistible charm."

"I don't believe you. Ten bucks, you're bluffing."

"Do I get double if I score a home run?"

"You wouldn't..." Andrew's jaw dropped.

Alex laughed smugly. "You bet I will." He picked up his briefcase and headed for the door. "See you in the morning." He walked out whistling happily, his mind full of plans for Anne Turner. Now that he had finally gathered the courage to ask her out, he could not understand why he had waited so long.

* * * * *

CHAPTER 13

Pierre Fortune carefully polished the chrome on his Rolls Royce with the *chamois* and stood back to admire the shine. *"Magnifique!"* He put away the cloth in the trunk of the car. From a plastic bag, he pulled out an alcohol-soaked wash cloth and wiped his hands until they were meticulously clean. Satisfied, that he was germ free, he climbed into the soft leather interior and turned the key in the ignition. As the motor gently purred to life, he glanced back at *Le Gallet*, the famous art gallery he had founded seventeen years before, and glowered at Cigogne's painting still in the window.

During his career as an artist's agent and gallery owner, he had enjoyed many fat years, as was testified by his ample waistline. There had been some difficult times at the beginning, when no one had ever heard of Pierre Fortune, but that was a long time ago. Now, his reputation was solid and his record impressive. Why Cigogne, the most famous of his protégés, his roommate and lover over the last seven years, should decide to leave him and join another gallery was beyond Fortune. "And after everything I've done for him," grumbled Fortune, conveniently forgetting that he charged Cigogne double the standard commission, even after Cigogne had long become an established name. *If he wants to leave me, let him. He'll soon find out that he needs me more than I need him. I could make a famous artist out of a monkey if I had to.* He popped open a box of breath mints and popped one into his mouth.

The Rolls Royce rounded the Arc de Triomphe and headed towards Montmartre. Today, Fortune was about to do something he had not done in years. He was on a talent hunt. It was a great idea. He could imagine the headlines in the art magazines now. 'Fortune's new discovery.' In actual fact, he had no need to go out of his way. In an average week, anywhere from one to a dozen hopefuls came to his door uninvited. But there was something romantic about the idea of a talent hunt. It was the kind of story the public loved.

He remembered how Cigogne had first come to him, a disheveled young man of amazing sensuality but limited ability. The first thing Fortune had done was direct the boy to the shower. Then Fortune had made long and slow love to the young man, teaching him all the secret ways to please him. Cigogne had learned his lessons well. In return, Fortune had made Cigogne famous. He had encouraged the eager young man to paint oversized, surrealist figures with black outlines. With a well coordinated campaign of advertising, public appearances and a few exclusive showings, Cigogne's reputation was soon established. Now his paintings sold for an average 100,000 Francs each. Until two weeks ago, forty percent of that went directly into Fortune's pocket. *Damn that Cigogne! If I was able to make him famous, I can do it again.*

In Montmartre, he parked his car along a quiet street. He stepped out to make sure he was neither too close to the car in front or in back and only then locked the doors carefully and headed for the square. It had been years since any talent had been discovered in the tourist infested area, but one just never knew.

At the square, he quickly made himself anonymous by joining a group of tourists. He hated to be recognized. The mangy artists would want to talk to him, shake his hand. They would get their filthy germs all over him. He shuddered and pulled back a step to keep from bumping into the fat lady in front of him. He followed the crowd around the square, glancing briefly at the tableaux on display.

"*Par ici messieurs, Mesdames.* Have your portrait painted."

Fortune heard the voice and turned to look. Ten feet away, a young man in a poet's shirt and black *bérêt* was waving his arms, trying to attract the group's attention. Out of idle curiosity, he wandered closer. As expected, there were a dozen or so very mediocre paintings displayed along the fence. *What am I wasting my time here for?* He turned away in disgust. Suddenly a flash of bright, vivid color caught his eye. He walked over for a closer look. He pulled out a handkerchief from his pocket and with it, he picked up the oil. To his vast surprise the painting, a modern rendition of a window with an old lace curtain and dandelions in a cracked vase, was stunning. The colors were like jewels dazzling in the sunlight. Fortune felt his pulse race. This was good, very good. He sneaked a peak at the artist. The scruffy young man was working furiously on a pastel of some flaccid tourist in a bright Hawaiian shirt. There was no trace of a rare talent in those strokes, and nothing appealing about the boy either. Fortune sighed. He looked down at the painting in his hands. It was signed simply and in tiny block letters, 'Dartois'. He looked at the signature on the other paintings along the same stretch of fence. They were signed 'Julien', in large flourishing letters. *Definitely not the same artist.*

Suddenly, the young man noticed him. His eyes narrowed, and then lit up. "Hey! You're Pierre Fortune aren't you?" He dropped his pastel and hurried over.

Fortune took a few steps back and put up the 'Dartois' oil as a shield. "Who did this?" he asked nervously.

"Not me. That's not mine." Julien rummaged around and picking up one of his own painting, tried to push it onto Fortune. "This is mine. Here, take a look at this."

"Listen to me!" ordered Fortune, still backing away. He was desperate to get away before the disheveled young man touched him. "Do you know this Dartois?"

"Sure I know Dartois. But, I haven't seen her in a while."

Her? Dartois is a girl? "Do you know where

Dartois lives?" he asked suddenly less enthusiastic.

Julien shrugged his shoulders and scowled. "I don't know. She's usually here every day but I haven't seen her in weeks."

* * * * *

In his office, the young doctor sat with Brigitte and explained the procedure. "What we're going to do is give David a few simple IQ tests. The hospital is conducting a study on young epileptics to find out what effect, if any, the disease has had on their intelligence." Seeing Brigitte's look of concern, he added quickly, "If anything, victims of childhood epilepsy seem to have a higher than average IQ. There really is nothing to worry about. You can watch everything through there." He indicated the small window across the room.

Brigitte nodded. "Will it take long?"

"No more than an hour or so." He waited for a moment and when Brigitte nodded again, he took David by the hand. "Are you ready young man?"

David jumped off the chair. He was a beautiful three-year old. His hair was reddish gold; his green eyes were fringed with long thick lashes; his cheeks were round and covered with a multitude of freckles; and his smile was quick and friendly. "*À tout à l'heure Maman.*" He waved happily to Brigitte and followed the doctor into the next room. As soon as the door was closed, Brigitte hurried to the window.

The next room held nothing but a child-size table and chairs, a few shelves with toys and picture books, and a large clock on the wall. Brigitte watched nervously as the doctor helped David into one of the small chairs and set a box of wooden blocks before him. David looked at them with curiosity for a moment then began to pull them out of the box. Soon, he was putting different shapes of blocks into a slotted board. Meanwhile the doctor watched and took notes. After a few minutes, he took away the blocks and gave David a stack of large, bright pictures. Brigitte couldn't hear what was being said, but she could tell that David was answering questions about the pictures. The doctor would hold up a picture and David would look at it and say a few words. Suddenly, David laughed and pointed at something in one of the pictures. The doctor chuckled, and nodded encouragingly.

Brigitte breathed a sigh of relief. There was nothing ominous about any of this. She went back to the couch and sat down.

Brigitte was dozing when David bounded into the room. "Maman, look at what he gave me," David exclaimed. He held up a coloring book.

Brigitte struggled awake and smiled lovingly at her son. "That was very nice of the doctor. Did you say thank you?"

David nodded vigorously. "Yes, and he said I was a nice boy."

"He certainly is," said the doctor. "Very nice and very energetic." Brigitte laughed.

"Well, one thing you don't need to worry about is David's intelligence. He is a very bright little boy. As a matter of fact, in the two years I have been conducting these tests, I have never seen such a high score." He shook his head in wonderment as he spoke. "His conversational skills are at the level of a six year old child. His language comprehension and reading..."

Brigitte shook her head in disbelief. "David can read? I thought he only memorized the words to each illustration."

The doctor laughed. "He can read. He is at the level of high first grade or low second grade. His mental arithmetic skills are just as advanced, as are his analytical thinking abilities. All in all, David doesn't seem to have any weaknesses."

"Really?" said Brigitte, feeling a bit overwhelmed with all this information. "I-I didn't realize. I mean, I knew he was bright..." She stopped for a moment, remembering how David had always seemed to memorize rhymes and children's songs so easily. She remembered how he had astounded her by counting to one hundred when he was just a little over two years old. There was also the time she had taken him to see a film. Months later, he still remembered every word of dialogue and every song from the movie. "Is there anything special I should do for him?"

"That's a very good question. Unfortunately, there are too few children like him for the government to develop special programs. Therefore, until he is five years old he will not be eligible to start school. In any event, I'm not sure accelerated classes would be the answer. Emotionally, David is still only a little boy and he needs to experience his childhood. There will be plenty of time for serious things like school later," he said as he tousled David's hair.

Brigitte breathed a sigh of relief. She couldn't imagine sending her baby off to school.

"How is he doing on his medication?" asked the doctor.

Brigitte bit her lip. "He hasn't had an episode

since the first one, two months ago. I watch him all the time."

"I can imagine how frightening that experience must have been. The best thing now, is to go on with your lives as normally as possible. You must not fall into the habit of waiting for another episode to happen. David needs to lead a normal life."

* * * * *

The next day, over coffee, Brigitte told Réjeanne about her decision. "I'm going back to the square tomorrow."

"I'm so glad," replied Réjeanne with obvious relief. "I just don't think it's healthy for you to keep following him around the way you have. It's not good for David," she added quickly. "I think this deserves a celebration. Let's make something special for dinner. How about inviting *monsieur...*"

"No!"

Réjeanne sighed. "It was just a thought."

"I'll go out and get a small roast and a bottle of

wine," offered Brigitte. "Mon chéri, do you want to come with me to the grocer?"

The boy's eyes lit up instantly. "Can I have *un nougat?*"

Brigitte laughed. "How can I say no to such a face? Only if you promise not to eat it until after dinner."

* * * * *

During the shopping excursion, David he was irritable and Brigitte rushed through her errands to get him home fast. On the way back from the boulangerie David lagged behind.

"Hurry up sweetheart. Auntie Réjeanne is waiting for us with dinner." Brigitte switched the heavy bag of groceries to her other arm and took hold of David's hand.

David squirmed and cried sullenly. "Ouch! You're hurting me." He pulled away suddenly and rushed away.

"David, come here." She tried to grab him again when suddenly David's eyes rolled up in his head. "Oh no..." She dropped the bag of groceries and reached for him. Apples rolled around the sidewalk. David let out a soft moan. His head snapped back and he fell to ground, his small body gripped by a series of convulsions.

"Oh, my God! Help! Somebody help me." While Brigitte frantically tried to perform the simple moves the doctor had taught her, the crowd slowly grew. Dozens of curious onlookers hovered by whispering amongst themselves. "Somebody help me, please," cried Brigitte again. Nobody moved. David's little body jerked about on the hard sidewalk. Then, just as suddenly as they had begun, the seizures stopped.

Still shaking from fright, Brigitte picked up her small son and cradled him in her arms. "Are you all right my darling?" David looked up at her, a confused expression on his sweet face.

From the crowd a single voice called out above the whispers. "The child is possessed." There was a hush during which Brigitte thought her heart might stop. Then murmurs of approval went up around her. An old woman moved through the crowd and stopped in front of Brigitte. She spoke again, her face contorted with hate. "Get that boy away from here. There is evil in him."

David struggled in her arms and Brigitte looked down at him. He was staring at the old woman, his eyes full of fear. "*Maman*, what is that woman saying about me?"

"Nothing, *mon chéri*, nothing at all. She's just a crazy old woman." She helped him up and together they hurried away, leaving the apples and groceries behind. How can anyone be so hateful to an innocent child? wondered Brigitte, sadly. People are so ignorant. Don't they know that epilepsy is just a disease?

* * * * *

CHAPTER 14

The small apartment building was simple but elegant. In the mirrored lobby, Anne Turner picked up her mail and hesitated for a moment between taking the easy way up in the old brass caged elevator or sweating it up the marble staircase. *The exercise will do me good*, she decided, and briskly walked up to the sixth floor. A minute later, she unlocked the thick mahogany door, hurried in and turned the double bolt on her security lock.

Home at last. On her way to the kitchen, she quickly shuffled through the envelopes. *Bills, bills, and more bills. The salary I get at William Brandon & Company is a joke. I can't wait to get my hands on some real money*, she thought, frustrated. Just as she was about to throw this new pile on the counter, one of the envelopes caught her eye. *Wait a minute, that's Sally's handwriting.* It had been ages since she had last heard from her sister. She tore open the envelope eagerly.

> ***Dear Anne,***
>
> ***Well, it finally happened. Jim left me. I don't know why I'm surprised. It's just that with the baby coming in February...***

She read the letter quickly and with growing anger. For the thousandth time, she asked herself the same question. *What in heavens is wrong with that girl?*

Sometimes it seemed to Anne that her sister was just plain dumb. All of her life Sally had made one blunder after another, and always in the name of love. Her worse mistake by far, had been marrying Jim. Now, just as Anne had predicted, Sally was in yet another predicament, and this time it would not be so easy for her to get out of it.

I would rather die, than end up like her. Sally was twenty-six, uneducated and unemployed. She, her husband and their two children had been surviving on the meager salary he earned as a truck driver. Now she was pregnant again and Jim had walked out on her.

I will never let that happen to me. Quickly, she crumpled up the letter and threw it into the garbage. She opened the refrigerator, pulled out a few cartons of leftover Chinese food and shoved them into the oven. She slammed the oven door shut and turned on the heat. *Never! I would rather die than let anything like that happen to me.*

At twenty-two, Anne knew exactly what she wanted. More than anything else in the world, she wanted money, lots of it. It was not impossible. All she had to do was marry the right man. She thought of sexy Alex Ivanov who had just asked her for a date and laughed. Now there is a prime example of a long shot.

From watching a few of her friends', and now her sister's experiences, she knew that picking a husband was the equivalent of choosing the next winner at the Triple Crown. One just never knew. She had long ago concluded that it was much safer to go for an older man, one with a ready-made fortune.

The idea had first begun as a vague daydream a few years before. Slowly, over time, as she thought more and more about it, the scheme took shape. Obviously, the first step was to find the perfect catch. She read countless social and business magazines. Through ingenuity and determination, she made friends with all the right people — or at least with a few powerful men.

She went to all the right places, and while playing the role of the contented wealthy man's mistress, she kept her eyes open.

In the end, it was Scott Wilson, her latest lover, very well connected, rich, and married, who inadvertently caused her to notice Bill Brandon. She remembered the scene.

They were having lunch at 21 Club and Scott was in one of his frequent foul moods.

"I don't see why you had to buy an original. I can't believe you did that, going to Sotheby's and just charging an antique bed to my account. The department stores are full of perfectly good copies. Why in heavens do you always have to get the most expensive of everything?"

Listen, you foul-breathed old man, why do you think I sleep with you if it's not for your money? Anne wanted to answer. Instead, she pouted prettily. "But darling, this is our bed you're talking about." She smiled suggestively. "I wouldn't expect the best lover in the world to sleep on anything but the real thing."

The way she said it, Scott was not sure whether the best lover in the world was himself, or Anne. He chose to believe she meant him and his mood lifted slightly.

"Still, you shouldn't go and charge such a large amount to my account without consulting me first," he added sullenly.

What do you think I am, stupid? You would have said no. Then where would I have been? "Maybe you're right sweetheart. I guess I just got carried away."

At that moment, a couple walked by and sat at the next table. Scott, who always behaved as if he were royalty, never acknowledged anyone before they greeted him. This time, Anne was astonished to see him crane his neck in an attempt to catch the man's attention.

"Who is that?" she asked.

"That," he whispered, "is William Brandon. Have you ever heard of him?"

She shook her head.

"He is probably one of the richest men in the country. I am not surprised you never heard of him. Few have. He keeps an almost invisible profile."

"How do you know about him?"

"I sold him some land a few years ago. When I checked his credit references, I found out he owns half the state. The way his company has been growing, I would not be surprised if he owned half the country by now. And I had never even heard of him," he concluded, amazed that anyone so rich could have escaped his attention.

Anne's eyes wandered over to William Brandon. He was tall and well dressed, but the expensive Brooks Brothers' suit did not disguise the man's doughy body. His hair was gray and receding. His features were strong and she realized he must once have been a handsome man. *Interesting!*

She glanced at the woman with him. Time had been kinder to her. Somewhere in her mid-forties, she was a few pounds overweight but still looked fashionable in a stylish suit. *Schiaparelli,* Anne noted expertly. Her eyes dropped automatically to the woman's left hand. *The wife*, she concluded. Then the woman moved her hand slightly and Anne got a full frontal view of the diamond. It was the largest she had ever seen. *Good god! At least six carats, maybe more.* Suddenly Bill Brandon looked very attractive to her, Very attractive indeed!

Once Anne had found her target, everything began to move at a dizzying speed. With one quick anonymous telephone call, she arranged for Scott's wife to 'accidentally' find out about her. As expected, the next evening for dinner, Scott arrived at their usual restaurant half an hour late, looking harried.

"Are you feeling all right? You look terrible." Anne's question was spontaneous. Scott looked ill.

"I have to talk to you about something." His voice quivered.

Oh please! Spare me the tears. "What's wrong?" she asked with just the right amount of concern.

"It's Rosemary. She's found out about us."

"Don't make it sound like it's the end of the world. It's not as though you weren't planning to tell her eventually."

"Sweetheart, you just don't understand. The children are still so young."

"For god sake, Scott, the children are seventeen and twenty-three. Just how old are they supposed to be before you plan to leave Rosemary?" She managed to make her voice sound choked. *That's it, create a scene. It will drive him crazy.*

"Anne, please don't make a spectacle of yourself. I can't stand that kind of behavior and you know it."

Anne looked down at her untouched plate of poached salmon in Hollandaise. *Think of something sad. Quick!* A memory came flooding back, unbidden and unexpected. She was sixteen years old and her mother was telling her that she could not get a new dress for her graduation. Surprisingly, her eyes filled with tears. *Good! Think some more.* Details she had long forgotten emerged. Herself, yelling that it was not fair, that she would be the only girl in the entire class without a white graduation dress. Her mother tried to explain to her that since her father had lost his job, they could not afford many of the things they used to take for granted.

Now her tears flowed freely.

"Please Anne. You know I love you. This is just the wrong time."

You have that right. Your time just ran out. "How am I going to live without you? I love you Scott." Fat tears rolled down her cheeks. "What about my apartment? I can't afford it by myself."

"How much do you need?" Almost with relief, Scott pulled out his checkbook. "Will a thousand dollars be enough?" Anne broke into uncontrolled weeping. Scott was almost beside himself. "Will you please stop? People are looking. Listen; just tell me how much you need? Two thousand?"

By the time the waiter came over with the bill, Anne had managed to get the amount up to ten thousand dollars, *a fortune*, and Scott was in a hurry to leave.

Later, he dropped her off at her apartment with some reassuring words. "Don't worry baby, as soon as things cool down at home, I'll call you back."

Don't bother sweetheart. I won't need you anymore. "I don't know if I can wait too long," she replied, her eyes still pink and swollen from crying. He moved closer to kiss her and she began to sob loudly. He hesitated for a moment, then climbed back into his Lotus and drove off.

"Good riddance!" Anne spat out the words. As soon as his car was out of sight, she ran upstairs to her apartment. She was so excited, she wanted to sing and dance.

Inside, she counted the zeros on the check then carefully hid it. *This deserves a celebration.* Half an hour later, after a festive dinner of hard boiled eggs, caviar and one of Scott's bottles of Perrier Jouet, she poured herself a second glass of champagne and sat down to do some serious thinking.

Now the question is; how do I get William Brandon? By her third glass of champagne, the details of the plan were beginning to take shape. The more she thought about it, the more she believed it would work.

In a fever of excitement, she picked up the telephone and dialed. A familiar voice answered.

"Jason Stoddart," she said, her voice low and caressing. "It's been a long time."

The voice at the other end answered congenially. "Well! Colin! What a surprise." Then in a furious whisper, it continued. "What the hell are you calling me here for? You should know better than that."

"I just want to ask you for an itty-bitty-little favor. You can do that, can't you? For old time's sake?"

There was silence at the other end, and then the voice picked up pleasantly. "Of course I'd be delighted to hear about any business ideas you might have Colin. What have you got in mind?"

Two weeks later, armed with an impressive list of credentials and references, one from each of the many companies belonging to good old Jason Stoddart, Anne Turner walked into William Brandon & Associates.

"Hi, I'm here to apply for the secretarial position.

"How did you know about the position? I just gave my notice yesterday and the job won't even be advertised for another few days," said the secretary, an attractive brunette in a conservative suit, much like the one Anne was wearing. "I haven't even contacted the personnel agencies yet.

"You're leaving to work for Mr. Jason Stoddart, aren't you? I applied for that job too. I them called this morning to find out if I had the position and they told me it was already filled. It occurred to me that whoever was hired was probably leaving another interesting position. Mr. Stoddart was kind enough to tell me where you worked. I took the chance of coming right over. Who should I talk to?"

Anne sat in the reception area and waited. It was nearly an hour and a half before she was ushered into Mr. Brandon's office. The wait was well worth it. Brandon took one look at her and his eyes lit up.

"Susan told me how you found out about this job. That took a lot of initiative on your part. I like that."

Too bad I can't tell you the real story. You would be really impressed. "Thank you Mr. Brandon. I believe luck is not something that just happens. It's something you create."

"Have a seat Miss...?"

"Turner. Anne Turner." Anne sat, and crossed her long slender legs. Bill Brandon could not peel his eyes away from them.

"Can you type?"

"Eighty-five words per minute." She focused her large blue eyes on him and smiled. From that moment on, Bill Brandon did not stand a chance.

During the next twelve months, there were days when Anne doubted she had the patience to follow her plan to completion. She sometimes remembered that her life had been much easier when she had rich lovers financing her every whim. Even combined with the interest from the ten thousand dollars in her savings account, her income was only a fraction of what she was used to spending. At those times, all Anne had to do was close her eyes and picture all those Brandon houses going up everywhere in the country and the thousands of dollars each one of them brought in. Just thinking about all that money gave her goose bumps. Bill Brandon, she reminded herself, had exactly what it took to make her one very happy woman.

The only problem was that in the year since she had begun working for him, her employer seemed to have no more than a professional interest in her. *I'll just have to lend fate a hand*, she decided. By mid-summer, Anne Turner decided the time was ripe.

The weather report predicted one of the hottest days in recorded history. As usual, Anne chose an irreproachably proper outfit, a navy skirt and classic matching jacket, worn over a high collared, long sleeved blouse. Although the style of the blouse was chaste, the fabric was sheer and allowed a hint of the lacy brassiere.

At lunchtime, taking advantage of a moment when everyone was out, Anne went down to the furnace room. Two minutes later, there was a loud clanking sound and the air-conditioner stopped. The silence seemed to reverberate though the building. Anne hurried back to her desk.

By mid-afternoon, the temperature indoors had shot up to nearly 90°. Throughout the office, jackets had long been discarded and everybody was down to their shirtsleeves. When Bill Brandon called her into his office for dictation, Anne powdered her face until she looked pale as death itself, then she went in.

"Take this down for me. It's a letter to... Are you feeling well Miss Turner? You seem a bit faint."

Anne looked up at her overweight and unappealing boss, and smiled weakly. "I'm fine sir. It's just so hot in here. I should not have worn this long-sleeved blouse today. Please go ahead."

"If you're sure you're all right." He continued. "Dear Sir..."

Bill Brandon spoke slowly, keeping a concerned eye on the lovely Anne Turner. Since she began working for him, he often caught himself fantasizing about his delicious-looking secretary. The fact that her clothes were always so demure only added mystery to the enchanting creature. With a strong effort, he chased away the impure thoughts that danced through his mind.

Bill Brandon had been married for nearly twenty-five years. During those years, he had built his business into an empire. This, he prided himself, was largely due to his determination. As far as Brandon was concerned, the same commitment he brought to growing his company he also brought to his marriage. Not once since their wedding vows, had he ever seriously considered leaving his wife. Having an affair, now that was different. *An occasional fling doesn't count*, Bill Brandon told himself. *What a wife doesn't know won't hurt her.*

He noticed Anne's lacy brassiere showing through the shear fabric of her shirt and he felt himself blush. He pulled at his shirt collar, which, until moments ago had not seemed so tight. He cleared his throat and continued. "Where was I? Oh, yes. For the past fourteen years, the Chase Manhattan Bank has..."

Anne Turner suddenly gave a small moan and her eyes fluttered. She slid slowly off her chair and onto the floor. Her blond hair settled artfully around her exquisite face.

"Miss Turner! Anne!" Bill Brandon was in a panic. He leaned over the young woman and felt for her pulse. What was it she said? Something about feeling hot? He quickly unbuttoned her blouse and his eyes wandered to the full breasts straining against the lacy fabric of her underwear. At that moment, Anne stirred and the bra, which she had conveniently weakened at the seam, fell apart disclosing the most appetizing pair of pink nipples he had ever seen. Anne's eyes fluttered open and her arms wrapped themselves around him.

Almost before he knew what was happening, the middle-aged man found himself on his mahogany partner's desk, making wild and passionate love to the irresistible Anne Turner who, by some enchantment, had fully recovered.

Over the next few months, Anne tightened the net around her prey. Slowly, almost imperceptibly, she made herself indispensable to her employer. She took care of all the details of his life.

"Don't worry about birth control, Bill. That's my responsibility. I'll use a diaphragm."

"But you don't have to worry. I..."

"I insist. You have so many things to worry about."

"If it makes you feel better."

"It does. You look tired Bill. Let me give you a back rub."

"Ahhh! What would I do without you?" replied William Brandon as Anne massaged his non-existent trapezoids.

She smiled her appreciation. "Isn't tomorrow your wedding anniversary, Bill?"

"Damn! I forgot about it. Mildred will kill me."

"Don't worry about it. You have so much to do, why don't you let me run out during lunch and pick up something for her."

"You are amazing. Do you know that?"

She blew him a kiss and walked out of his office.

I cannot believe how lucky I am. His gaze followed her with adoration. *And she doesn't even want anything for herself.* He pushed away the mild feelings of guilt that stirred in the back of his mind.

At lunchtime, Anne rushed over to Saks fur department. "Do you have a platinum mink in a size twenty?"

The salesgirl left and reappeared moments later with the perfect coat. It was the most unflattering thing Anne had ever seen. She could just imagine how it would look on Mildred Brandon.

"Perfect. I'll take it." She pulled out her employer's card and authorization letter. "Could you please have it delivered to the following address?"

Mildred Brandon sat on the silk tapestry chair and tapped her foot impatiently on the marble floor. William Brandon faced his wife's anger with puzzlement.

"It looks like a perfectly nice coat to me. I don't understand why you're so upset."

She stood and stormed over to the discarded coat. "Look at the size of this." She lifted it by the shawl collar before letting it fall back down to the floor. "For goodness sake, do you think I'm fat? I know I should lose a few pounds but..." She bit her lip and muffled a sob. "And a platinum mink! Those are for old women. Is that how you see me, as an old woman?"

Bill Brandon looked at his wife in surprise. It had been ages since he had really looked at her. *She is an old woman.* His mind wandered to Anne and her young perfect body. The guilt resurfaced. "Of course not Mildred, you know I love you." However, his eyes were devoid of any such emotion.

"So did you have a nice weekend?" asked Anne on the following Monday as she stirred the sugar in Bill Brandon's coffee.

"Yes, yes. Not bad." There was hesitation in his voice. He sipped his coffee and sighed.

"Not bad?" She repeated, making it sound like a question. She knew her man well. It would only take a bit of prodding to get the juicy details.

"Mildred hated the coat." He looked apologetic.

"Oh Bill, I'm so sorry. You look upset and I feel it's my fault somehow. Is there anything I can do?"

"Don't worry about it. You're not to blame." His eyes roamed over her body and he felt the familiar reaction in his loins. "But if you really want to make me feel better..."

Before he could finish speaking, Anne Turner's hands were already tugging eagerly at his fly. A moment later, as his beautiful young secretary knelt before him, Bill Brandon forgot all about his wife.

The next time Anne made love to her employer, she smudged a bit of her lipstick on his shirt collar. A few weeks later, she discreetly sprayed a bit of her perfume onto his jacket before he went home. As expected, it did not take long for Mildred Brandon to react.

"I want to know who she is. Don't bother telling me I'm imagining things. I've been your wife for twenty-five years and I know when you're lying to me."

William Brandon sat on the edge of the bed, shamefaced.

"Say something," she yelled. "Anything."

"I don't know what to say." He shook his head sadly. "I don't know how it happened. It just happened."

"Are you telling me you're in love with somebody else?" Now that he had as much as admitted it, she was shocked.

"I don't know. I just don't know," he said.

Mildred hid her face behind her hands and began to cry.

Dinnertime at the Brandon's was usually a pleasant family occasion. That night the atmosphere was strained. The children, Paul sixteen, Martin twelve and Janet six, sensed that something was wrong.

At the end of the meal, over her peach cobbler, Janet looked at her father with big solemn eyes. "I heard you and mom fighting. Does that mean you're going to get divorced?"

In his booming voice, Bill emphatically denied it. Meanwhile Mildred smiled bravely over the edge of her coffee cup. "My goodness, what a silly thought." As soon as the children looked away, she discreetly wiped away a tear with her lace handkerchief.

Guilt was eating away at him. When he went home, Mildred, her suffering written all over her face, followed him around with her sad eyes; the same questions ever present in the silence that hung in the air. *Who is she? Did you see her today? Do you love her?*

It became easier just to avoid her. He spent more time at the office and accepted with gratitude the warmth and understanding Anne offered

"I don't know what it is about you Anne. I think you're a very special woman."

"How special?"

"I've grown very fond of you."

Anne felt her heart skip a beat. Soon, all his money would be within her grasp. "I've become very fond of you too Bill," she said and smiled. *Keep it light and easy. Don't push, or you'll end up pushing him away.*

The more Brandon tried to decide what he should do, the more confused he became. Anne made him feel young and alive, as he had not felt in years. On the other hand, there was Mildred and the twenty-five years they had spent together, not to mention the children.

Maybe I should distance myself a bit from Anne. Seeing her all the time only made it impossible to gain perspective.

"I understand," said Anne calmly when he told her. She allowed herself to look sad, but no more. "Take all the time you need. I'll be here if you need me." Inside, she wanted to scream. *If you think you can just dump me sweetheart, you've got another thing coming.* She deliberated about it until she found the answer. *Time I gave Billy boy a run for his money.* She knew just how she would do it.

The next time she noticed Alexander Ivanov walk by her office, she casually waved at him. It had long been obvious to her, that the man liked her. Bill was about to get a good, old-fashioned dose of jealousy. With luck, she might get some decent sex out of it. *God only knows ? correction ? Mildred Brandon knows, what a terrible lover Bill is. I could really use a good fuck, and Alexander Ivanov sure looks like one.*

"Is something going on between you and that guy?" Bill asked her one day, after noticing him leave her office with a particularly beaming expression on his handsome face.

Anne looked at him wide eyed with surprise. "Of course not. You know there is nobody else in my life but you."

"Why is he hanging around your office so much?"

Anne laughed. "I think he likes me. You must understand Bill, nobody knows about you and me. As far as Alex is concerned, I am a single girl."

"Do you like him?" he asked, hating himself for it.

Anne thought quickly. Her answer would be very important. She had to find a way to make him jealous while seeming to reassure him. "If things were different, if I was not so much in love with you, I think he might be the kind of man I might like. But I love you, remember?"

"I love you too," said Brandon. He had never felt worse in his life.

* * * * *

Alex stepped out of the shower humming, completely off key, the words from Elvis Presley's "Heartbreak Hotel". He quickly toweled himself dry, pulled out a comb and a tube of Brylcreem and smoothed his hair in place while gyrating to the music in his mind. He was in a great mood. *Tonight is the night.* He glanced at his watch. *Six thirty. No need to rush.* Anne wasn't expecting him until eight.

* * * * *

CHAPTER 15

Pierre Fortune's office was a tribute to a new form of art called 'POP'. His desk was a thick sheet of glass resting on what looked like two giant Campbell's soup cans. His chair was a stack of Brillo pad boxes; and on the walls were large paintings of hamburgers, hot dogs and French fries. Fortune sat stiffly on his 'Brillo' chair and turned on the bright desk lamp. *Now let's take another look at this.* He put on his small gold rimed glassed and looked closely at the 'Dartois' painting. *Hmm, the brush strokes are a bit rough, but the color, the composition and the balance are good. Whoever this Dartois is, she's a natural. With a bit of guidance, I could really do something with her. Too bad she's a woman.*

In the last month, he had been to the Montmartre square half a dozen times in search of the elusive Dartois. After every one of those visits, he had sworn never to return. No one, not even this talented unknown, was worth submitting himself to the horrors of the square. The place was infested with *ersatz* artists. They followed him around, pleading with him to look at their ugly paintings. *All those hands touching me. It's disgusting!* Just thinking about it made Fortune's stomach feel queasy. He quickly reached for the can of room deodorant and sprayed it about. The fresh smell of pine filled the air and Fortune felt better.

Fortune looked down at the painting again. *Damn it's good.* But the thought of those awful, mangy, dirty, filthy people, breathing on him, touching him. *No! I can't go back there. If I go there again they'll swarm all over me like flies.* He shuddered. Besides, working with a woman would not be much fun as working with a sexy new young man.

Having made up his mind, Fortune pushed himself away from his desk and strode over to the file cabinet in the corner. *What about that fellow, what was his name? Jérome something or other?* The man had ability, not genius perhaps, but enough ability for Fortune to work with. *Yes, yes! That's a good idea. Besides*, thought Fortune remembering the young man's cute behind. *Who knows? After a good scrubbing and a decent haircut...*

* * * * *

The sun peeked in through the lace curtains and danced on Brigitte's lashes. She stretched wearily and groaned. *Time to get up*, she thought regretfully, and instead, buried herself deeper under her covers. Luckily the night had been dreamless, but her sleep had still seemed too short. From downstairs she could hear Réjeanne moving about. In a few minutes, she would be coming upstairs. Brigitte moaned again. *How can I face her? I owe her so much money.* For months now, Réjeanne had paid for all of Brigitte's and David's living expenses. The sum amounted to a small fortune, and Brigitte was painfully aware that Réjeanne could not afford to be so generous.

Brigitte desperately needed to return to work. It will take me months to pay Réjeanne back. She sighed. What was it Réjeanne always said? 'No point in worrying, something always comes up.' Well, this time 'something' would not be enough. *What I need, thought Brigitte, is a miracle.*

* * * * *

Brigitte approached the square and saw Julien before he saw her. "Julien," she cried out, happy to see her friend after such a long time. It felt so good to be back. Nothing had changed in the months of her absence and yet...

Julien looked up and smiled, and then the smile became a scowl, and a smile again. He swallowed hard, remembering the two hundred francs Fortune had paid him for Brigitte's painting. The money had long ago been spent. He wondered if there was any chance of Brigitte finding out from anyone else. Probably not. Fortune hasn't been here in weeks.

"Why didn't you save me my spot?" asked Brigitte, teasing. In the area where Brigitte usually set up her easel, stood a young man in fedora next to a sandwich board full of colorful sketches.

At last Julien threw his arms around her and kissed her on both cheeks, left, right then left again. "Brigitte, how are you? You've been away so long; I didn't think you were ever coming back. What happened?"

"David was..." She stopped. She hated to mention the word epilepsy. People simply did not understand. *For David's own good, I'd better tell no one about his condition*, she decided. "David was sick," she said, as she thought quickly. "He has a heart problem." It was an excuse that would be more easily accepted.

Brigitte found a spot on the other side of the grassy knoll and set up her easel. It was good to be back, even though, she admitted to herself, Julien's behavior had seemed strange. It was almost as though he wasn't happy to see her. She brushed that thought away and concentrated on more positive things. She hoped for a good day of sales, so she could start repaying Réjeanne.

Soon she was lost in her art. She mixed some vermilion and ochre on her palette and added a few drops of thinner. With a quick and experienced motion, she brushed a few small strokes on her canvas. Flowers sprung to life. Suddenly a shadow moved across her canvas.

"Brigitte?" She looked up to find Julien standing there. "I have something to tell you," he said, nervously twisting his *béret* in his hands. He slapped the *béret* on his head and shoved a hand in his pocket. He pulled it out holding a few crumpled francs and handed them awkwardly to her. "This is yours. I haven't got all of it right now. I'll give you the rest when I can. While you were gone, I sold one of your paintings to Pierre Fortune."

"Pierre Fortune t-the...?" Brigitte stuttered as she recognized the name.

"You'd forgotten it by the fence. Fortune saw it, and liked it," explained Julien, shamefaced.

"H-he liked it?" she repeated, numb from the shock.

Julien nodded. "He even came back a couple of times to try and find you."

But Brigitte was not listening anymore. Tears were brimming behind her lashes. *Thank you God. This is the miracle I've been waiting for.* "Pierre Fortune liked my painting." She threw her paints back half hazardly into her carrying case and folded up her easel.

"Brigitte! Your money!" Julien called after her as she walked away.

"Keep it," she answered over her shoulder as she rushed away, her red hair swinging with the rhythm of her long strides. "And wish me luck."

* * * * *

CHAPTER 16

The antique, gold-leafed four-poster bed was draped in heavy silks and brocades. Above it, the ceiling was mirrored, as was the wall behind it. Across the room, Anne sat at her dressing table and studied her reflection in the ornate gilt-framed mirror. She picked up her eyebrow pencil and adroitly drew short, feathery lines in two precise arches. Then, with a brush, she carefully applied 'Melon Pink', the latest fashion color lipstick. She pulled back and surveyed the results. *Good!* It was important that she look gorgeous. If not for her beauty, she could never have come this far.

Anne Turner put down the pencil. She looked at her reflection in the mirror and arched her brow. *Perfect.* From her cosmetics bag, she pulled out a perfume atomizer and sprayed the inside of her wrists and her cleavage with Chanel # 5. Then as an afterthought, she sprayed the inside of her palm, reached down into her panties and rubbed the scent on her hair. Now she was ready.

At eight o'clock sharp, the bell from the lobby rang. Alex Ivanov had arrived. A few moments later Anne ran down the stairs and stepped out. She was a vision of beauty. Her dress was a black off-the-shoulder creation with sheer sleeves. Her blonde hair fell in a perfect flip just above her bare shoulders. She looked up and smiled. Alex was dazzled.

"I made reservations for us at Margarita's. I hope you like it."

"I'm sure I will," she said huskily and Alex read a hundred meanings into those few words.

'Margarita's' was a small Italian restaurant that specialized in homemade pasta served al dente and opera sung live. Small, gingham covered tables brightened the otherwise stark room.

The service was friendly but somewhat unusual. Talented wait staff doubled as performers as they went about their regular duties. Sometimes in the middle of service, they would stop and dramatically become whichever character was theirs for the evening.

As he poured the wine, the portly steward sang in a luxuriously deep baritone. In the corner, a piano player provided the background music. Tonight's feature was La Traviata.

Alex watched Anne during the meal. She ate with hearty enthusiasm, a quality he liked to see in a woman. In his experience, a woman's appetite at the table was a clue to her appetite in bed. He hoped to find out if the old adage proved right in Anne Turner's case.

"So tell me," she said and somehow managed to make it sound suggestive. "Who exactly is Alex Ivanov?"

He chuckled. "Are you sure you want to hear my entire life story?"

She leaned forward and whispered. "I love a good bedtime story. Maybe we should keep it for later."

Alex nearly dropped his fork. This girl was hot. He grinned. "I like to do other things in bed than tell stories." He launched into his prepared monologue. He told the story of a bright kid from a hard working widowed mother who sacrificed everything to send him to college. When told properly it could almost move a girl to tears. Then he went on to talk about his fierce ambition in such a way that a girl felt drawn into his dreams until she thought they were her own. Somehow, no matter how hard he tried, Anne Turner was not playing into his hands the way all the others had. Rather than disappoint him, it only made him want her more.

"Just a bit ambitious, aren't we?" Anne looked at him mockingly. Alex loved it. Here was girl who was not fawning all over him. It felt refreshingly different.

"Are you seeing anyone else at the moment?" Alex found himself holding his breath.

"I take it you mean seeing, as in dating?"

"You know very well what I mean." He looked at her and her eyes held his for a moment. Alex felt a rush of desire run through his body.

"I don't see anybody else here but you and me."

* * * * *

Alex paid the driver, helped Anne out of the cab and walked her to the door. She turned to face him. She brought her mouth inches from his and teased him with her eyes. "Alex, I want to thank you for a truly wonderful evening."

"I had a wonderful evening too. Maybe we can do it again sometime." He waited until he could not anymore. "Aren't you going to invite me in?"

She laughed a low deep laugh and handed him the key to her apartment.

Inside the apartment, she showed him through the rooms. "Here is the living room." She opened the French doors. "And here is the dining room." She moved on and he followed her.

"Very nice," said Alex, impressed.

"Thanks. The bedroom and bathroom are over there. She waved vaguely down the hall. "And this is the kitchen. Would you like a glass of champagne?"

Alex watched as she took a bottle from the refrigerator and expertly popped open the cork. She handed him a glass.

"To us," he said and took a sip. He put his glass on the table and pulled her toward him. She offered no resistance. "I've been looking forward to this all evening," he said.

She backed away from him and smiled

knowingly. "Only all evening?" With practiced ease, she unzipped her dress and stepped out of it. "Now, why don't you show me exactly what you were looking forward to?"

* * * * *

Afterward, Alex lay contented, looking up at the mirror on the ceiling. Next to him, on the bed, Anne was on her stomach, her well shaped back and round buttocks reflecting from the mirror on the ceiling. "Nice view," he said, and turned to plant a kiss on her bare shoulder.

She stirred. "Are you still here?" she asked irritably.

"What is that supposed to mean?"

"Do I have to spell it out for you?"

"You want me to leave?" He was shocked.

She tugged at the sheet tangled around her legs and pulled it up to cover herself. "We both got what we wanted. I think it's better if you go home now."

"No problem lady." He jumped out of bed and pulled on his clothes in record time. At the door, he turned to throw his parting shot. "By the way, I only asked you out on a bet."

She opened her eyes. "What are you talking about?"

He laughed. "I won't be able to collect unless I tell them what happened. Sleep well." With that, he calmly walked out of her apartment.

An hour later Anne Turner was still wide-awake. Maybe her idea of using Alex Ivanov to make Bill jealous had not been so wise after all.

* * * * *

Embarrassed! That was all he felt, or so he tried to convince himself. Alex was trying to concentrate on his work, but he could not put Anne Turner out of his mind. There had only been one date for Christ's sake! Then why did he feel like he had been punched in the stomach every time he thought of her.

He looked at his watch again. Eight forty five. Andrew would be here any minute. The last thing Alex wanted was to admit that Anne Turner had kicked him out of her bed in the middle of the night. Andrew would never let him hear the end of it. It would be easier to pretend nothing at all had happened.

Just as he expected, as soon as Andrew walked in he rushed over for the latest news. "So how did it go?"

Alex shrugged. "We talked about business all evening. As far as dates go, I'd give this one a B for boring."

Andrew stood there for a moment, a thousand thoughts going through his mind. "You mean that's it? You're not going to tell me anything else? What about after dinner?"

"After dinner she went back to her place and I went back to mine."

Andrew nodded. "Oh, I get it. She dumped you didn't she?"

Alex shrugged. "I guess you could say it was a mutual decision. Now, enough about that. We have work to do."

* * * * *

Five weeks had passed since Alex had shown Brandon his house plans. Still he had received no word of any kind. He picked up his courage and walked into Anne Turner's office.

Anne Turner was busy typing and did not look up for a moment. When she did, her expression was carefully blank.

"I'd like to book an appointment with Mr. Brandon," said Alex, avoiding her eyes.

"I'm sorry, Mr. Brandon is busy." She turned away and began to type again.

He gritted his teeth. "Anne, I only want an appointment with Brandon. It doesn't have to be today or even tomorrow. Next week will be fine. How about opening his calendar and finding me fifteen minutes with him?"

"I told you he's busy. Now, I'm trying to work here. Do you mind?"

"What the hell is your problem? I am only asking you to find a few minutes in his appointment book. Making Brandon's appointments is part of your job, isn't it?"

Anne turned away from her typewriter and without Alex noticing, she switched on the intercom to Brandon's office. "Mr. Ivanov," she said crisply. "Please understand. I think you are a nice man but I am not interested in going out with you. I wish you would just leave me alone. I would like to get back to my work."

"You know something, lady? I don't know what your problem is, and I don't care. One thing is clear. You are one hell of a bitch." He strode out, unaware of Bill Brandon in his office, listening to every word. As soon as Alex closed the door, Brandon stepped in.

"How long has he been giving trouble?"

Anne was trembling. "I'm so sorry. I didn't want to tell you. You have so much on your mind."

Brandon interrupted her. "How long?"

She sighed. "Since he asked me for a date a few weeks ago and I turned him down. He went wild. I thought he might hit me. He started shouting, saying he was going to fix me that he would tell everyone exactly what kind of girl I was, whatever that's supposed to mean." Tears threatened to spill.

The big man put his arms around her. "Why didn't you tell me sooner?"

"The last thing you need is more problems, but now I'm frightened. I just don't know what he'll do next."

"Book him an appointment with me," said Brandon. "I want to see him a.s.a.p."

* * * * *

In the cafeteria, where gossip flowed freely, the air buzzed with excitement. The financials for the past fiscal year, just published, showed the highest profits since the birth of the firm twenty-five years ago. As every year, the company published their financial profile in a newsletter, along with news of contracts, developments and special architectural awards and circulated among the staff.

"This time, Brandon will have to give out a few promotions," said Joey, who after over three years with the firm, was still hoping for the ever-elusive promotion.

"I hear Brandon is preparing a new profit sharing policy," one of the new employees ventured.

"That's ridiculous," said one of the senior architects. "He's planning no such thing. Has anyone ever seen any kind of financial incentives here? The only incentive is the hope of keeping your job."

Andrew had been listening for the last few minutes. "You want to know what I think? I think there will be considerable internal reorganization. There are bound to be promotions and believe me, Brandon can afford it. This contract," he lifted the news letter, "is nothing compared to what's still to come."

"Hey, do you know something we don't know?" asked Joey.

"I've been doing a bit of research on my own and I expect there will be dozens of other projects like this one. Look at statistics. In the last ten years birth rates have climbed higher than ever and the demand for houses right along with it. Prices have never been this high and I believe they'll go even higher. We're going into a real estate boom the likes of which this country has never seen."

"Amen!" said Ben from across the room. "And next, Andrew will be giving us advice on which stock to buy this week."

Andrew shrugged. "I know what I'm talking about." He left the group to their discussion, walked over to Alex and handed him a cup of coffee. "I have a message for you. You have an appointment with Bill Brandon tomorrow afternoon."

"Really?"

"Don't look so surprised. You have been trying to see him for weeks. He's been playing harder to get than Anne Turner."

* * * * *

Alex walked into William Brandon's office, nearly bursting with nervous anticipation. Brandon sat, his hands folded neatly on the desk. "Alex, you showed me some plans a few weeks ago."

It had already been well over a month since then but Alex did not bother pointing that out to Brandon. "Yes sir. The plans I worked on in my spare time."

Brandon leaned back in his chair. "I've looked at those plans. They were very impressive, especially considering the fact that you really have no experience to talk of in residential architecture."

Alex nodded proudly. "Thank you sir." His hopes shot up.

"I asked a few of the seniors of the firm to take

a look at the plans and they all agreed. The plans are beautifully executed." Brandon crossed his arms and frowned. "There's only one problem. Not a single one of them was original."

For a moment, Alex thought he had misunderstood. "What?"

Brandon continued. "They were all copied from our inactive files. Every one of those plans was designed by somebody else."

Alex didn't know what to think. It had to be some kind of a sick joke. "This isn't funny Mr. Brandon."

Brandon stared back grimly. "You're damn right, it's not funny."

"But that's not possible. I drew them myself. Every one of them." Alex was shocked. His heart was pounding. His palms were sweating.

Brandon shook his head. "I'm sorry, but I have no choice but to let you go."

This could not be happening. "I'm being fired?"

"Consider yourself lucky I'm not bringing fraud charges against you."

* * * * *

They stood around Alex, in shocked silence as he filed a cardboard box with his belongings. Of all the workers, only Andrew dared to voice his anger. "I don't believe it. I'll go up there right now and tell him what I think of his accusations," said Andrew.

Alex ignored Andrew's outburst and bent down to look under his drafting table. He grabbed a wrench and began to loosen the bolts on the legs of the table. "If you want my advice, stay out of it. Do not get involved. You'll only get yourself fired too."

"I couldn't care less whether I get fired or not. I know how hard you worked on those plans. I don't understand it. It makes no sense. Did Brandon tell you who supposedly drew those plans?"

"No, he didn't. Something is going on, but I have no idea what the hell it is."

"There has to be an explanation for this, and I'll find it. Don't worry. You'll get your job back."

Alex put the wrench down for a moment and looked up at his friend. "Don't bother. I have wasted enough time here. I'll find another job." Half an hour later, with the drafting table folded under one arm and a box full of his other belongings under the other, he walked out of Brandon & Associates.

From the window of her pink office, Anne watched in triumph as Alex loaded his belongings into the trunk of Andrew's Corvette. It was just a small victory, but each victory kept Bill Brandon more securely in her grasp.

* * * * *

William Brandon was in his office, sorting through his mail. *I don't believe this*, he thought as he stared at the letter in front of him. It was a large, official looking form, beautifully printed on thick creamy paper. At the top, it had the well know logo of Modern Design and Architecture magazine. At the bottom, over the signature of the editor was an official looking seal. For the third time since Anne had brought it in to him, Brandon picked it up and read it.

> **'It is with great pleasure that we wish to inform you, that your submission has been selected as one of three finalists for this year's 'Modern Design and Architecture's International Competition.'**

He put down the letter. *I don't believe this. I have to call him back.* There was no way he could avoid it. The magazine was a widely circulated publication and they were sure to publish the names of the finalists for everyone to see. He rocked back and forth on the hind legs of his chair and drummed his fingers on the desk in frustration.

Lately, his whole life had been getting more and more complicated. Often, he found himself wishing he could just go back to the easy existence he had shared with Mildred. Life had been... predictable. Boring, certainly, but predictable. There was something to be said about a situation being stable and unchanging. It made for a certain level of comfort and sanity. *With Anne, I never know what to expect*, he thought and suddenly the vision of Anne's luscious body flashed through his mind. All momentary dreams of stability were instantly quashed.

Bill Brandon leaned forward and pushed the intercom button. "Miss Turner, could you please come in for some dictation?" It was their signal. He turned off the intercom, comforted with the knowledge that for the next ten minutes he would be in the throes of his favorite sport. He crushed his cigar in the silver ashtray and brushed back his thinning gray hair with a damp palm. By the time Anne walked in, he was already down to his boxer shorts. "Come here luscious. Time for a break," he said.

She laughed. "I could use a break just about now," she said, and in one easy movement, she pulled her dress off her shoulders and let it drop to the floor. She moved closer to him and ran her fingers through the silver hair of his chest, lower, and lower, and lower still, until she found his swollen member and he was moaning with pleasure.

"Oh God, Anne! You don't know what you're doing to me."

Don't bet on that, sweetheart. I know exactly what I'm doing, she thought as she kneeled before her unappealing lover.

* * * * *

Alex stormed into the mahogany paneled office. His blue eyes flashed with anger in his handsome face. "You wanted to see me?" The question was curt, almost insolent.

Brandon did not even look at him as he went

about his usual ceremony of unwrapping, sniffing, moistening and lighting his eternal cigar. At last he spoke. "Have a seat Alex."

Alex sat; his face a mask of controlled fury.

After what seemed like an eternity, Bill Brandon put his cigar in the ashtray and spoke. "I would not have called you unless it was for a very important matter," he explained grudgingly. "I have some good news for you." He handed over the sheet of paper. "Here, take a look at this."

Alex did not bother looking at it, throwing it back on Brandon's desk.

"I think you should take a good look at that letter before you dismiss it so easily."

Alex picked it up again and began to read. Slowly, the words on the page filtered through his anger. He looked up and smiled tightly. "So I'm one of the three finalists," he said, carefully suppressing any excitement from his voice. "Are you going to tell me I cheated my way into this too?"

"Don't push me Alex," said Brandon, exasperated. "I can very easily give this opportunity to somebody else." He paused and waited for the words to sink in.

"You can't..."

"Oh yes I can," he bluffed. "You very kindly sent in your application in the firm's name. I could choose to send anybody I like to represent my company." He smiled victoriously. "Now before you get yourself all worked up, I want you to listen to my offer. The magazine will pay your travel expenses to Paris and cover all your living expenses while you're there. Since you will be a representative of our firm, I am willing to pay you full salary during that time. Who knows, if you do well in Paris, you might even have a job here when you come back." He stopped and took a few short puffs of his cigar. "So, Ivanov, do you take it, or do I give it to one of my senior architects?" The look on Alex's face was all the answer Brandon needed. "I think that's a wise decision, Ivanov," added the man with satisfaction.

* * * * *

Anne was busy arranging the roses in the crystal vase in her living room. She read the card again.

I love you,
Bill.

She laughed with glee. Since Alex Ivanov had left the firm a few weeks before, Bill had been more and more possessive of her time. It was obvious the man was madly in love with her. It was only a matter of time before he admitted it to himself.

Now for my final act, she said to herself. She picked up the Manhattan telephone book and flipped through the pages until she found what she wanted.

* * * * *

The brass sign on the outside of the building read 'St. Mary's Medical Building'. Anne walked in, stepped into the elevator and pushed the 'up' button. From across the crowded elevator she noticed an old woman watching her. When Anne stared back, the woman gave her a friendly nod and turned away. *This is crazy. I'm getting paranoid. Nobody knows why I'm here.* For a moment she thought of stopping the elevator at the next floor and simply going back home. *No, I will not change my mind now*, she told herself. *I have to do this if I want Bill for myself. This is the only way I will ever get a wedding ring out of him.*

The elevator door slid open and she walked out.

The waiting area was crowded. Anne stood nervously for a moment, unsure of her next move. The name on the door said 'Doctor Simon Ledner, Obstetrician and Gynecologist'. She looked around and noted that most of the women waiting were visibly pregnant. I'm in the right place all right. She took a deep breath and marched into the office.

"Can I help you?" A receptionist in a white starched uniform looked up from her desk.

"Yes. I'd like to see Doctor Ledner."

"Do you have an appointment?" asked the receptionist as she flipped open an appointment book.

"No," Anne hesitated. "But this is important."

"I'm afraid you can't see the doctor unless you have an appointment."

Before Anne could say anything else, a very

pregnant woman waddled in and handed the receptionist a small glass jar filled with a clear yellow liquid. The receptionist carefully put it on the filing cabinet next to her desk. "Thank you Mrs. Roberts. It won't be long now. Have a seat and the doctor will be with you soon." She turned back to Anne. "Have you ever seen doctor Ledner before?"

"No, this is my first time."

"Well, I can't give you an appointment without a referral, you know." The telephone rang, forestalling any need for Anne to come up with an answer. "Doctor Ledner's office, how may I help you?" The receptionist listened for a moment, and then looked up mildly annoyed. "Hold on one minute," she said into the phone. She covered the mouthpiece with her hand. "Ask your doctor to give you a referral. Then you can see him." She went back to her call. "Yes, I can talk, but just for a minute." She swung her chair around turning her back to Anne.

Anne's pulse raced. This was the chance, which she had been hoping for. She grabbed the bottle of urine from the top of the filing cabinet and furtively slid it into her bag. "Thank you very much. I'll get my doctor to call." She said loudly and hurried out.

* * * * *

The old pharmacist looked down at Anne from behind his counter. "Can I help you with anything?"

"Yes," she pulled out the bottle from her bag. "I'd like a pregnancy test please."

He took the urine sample from her and pulled out a form. "Name?"

"Anne Turner," she replied in a clear voice. "And I'd like a written confirmation of the results please."

One week later, results in hand, she picked up the telephone and dialed the number of The Plaza, where Bill had been staying since leaving Mildred.

"Could I have Mr. William Brandon's suite please?" Soon she would be Misses Anne Brandon.

"Bill? It's me, Anne. I have to talk to you. Could I see you right away?" she asked. Her voice held just the right amount of anxiety.

* * * * *

The Palm Court of the Plaza hotel was discreetly out of view, separated from view of the lobby by a jungle of tall, feathery tropical trees. Behind the wall of foliage, tables were far enough apart to give concerned patron the illusion of privacy. Bill joined Anne at a table and ordered tea and watercress sandwiches.

Anne waited for their order to arrive, and then launched into her prepared speech. "I guess it's just one of those things. I mean, accidents do happen," she said, her voice only mildly apologetic. "It isn't as though I wasn't careful."

Bill Brandon looked stunned. "It's impossible. Your period must be late."

Anne shook her head. "No." She opened her purse and pulled out the indisputable proof. She tried to keep herself from looking triumphant as she handed him the piece of paper. Bill Brandon picked it up apprehensively. As he read, his expression went from one of disbelief, to one of fury.

Anne watched, nervously assessing his reactions. *I can't really expect him to be thrilled with this. He'll have to fly to Reno for a quick divorce. As soon as we are married, I'll fake a miscarriage.* "Bill, it isn't as though you don't like children. You love your own three children. I'm only twenty-four. I want to have children too. Our children."

"I don't believe this!"

"Believe it. There's no mistake about it."

"You bitch," Bill said, his voice a low menacing growl. He stood abruptly and the entire table wobbled dangerously. Anne's cup of tea slid out of her hands and shattered on the marble floor. Porcelain and Earl Grey flew everywhere. Brandon towered over Anne, his mouth twisted with anger. "To think I actually believed I was in love with you. You're nothing but a cheap slut," he sputtered and bits of saliva flew into Anne's face.

"Bill, please! Stop it. You're scarring me."

"You should be scarred, you whore. If I did not stop myself, I would gladly strangle you right now. For your information, I am sterile. I have been all my adult life. My children, all three of them, are adopted." He started to leave and changed his mind. He came near her again and added, his voice like ice, "I just hope Mildred finds it in her heart to forgive me. Otherwise, I'll make you pay."

Anne felt the blood drain out of her as she watched him walk away. No, it can't be. Dear God, don't let this be. How could she have made such a mistake? Not now. Not when she already had him. All she wanted to do was get him to marry her. That was all. She had to find a way to fix things. Maybe she could tell him the lab was wrong. Maybe she could tell him there was a mix-up. If only she had not handed him the written report. *Oh God, what do I do now?*

* * * * *

A hundred times, Anne picked up the phone and dialed. A hundred times, she hung up before it rang. It was better that she wait for him to call. Surely, he would. It was just a matter of time.

Two weeks after the fiasco at The Plaza, the telephone rang. She picked it up, her heart already in her throat.

"This is the Kidney Foundation…"

The disappointment was like a stab in her heart. "I am not interested. Why would I want to give your stupid charity my hard-earned money? Don't call me anymore," she screamed into the telephone and slammed down the receiver. It took half an hour for her heart rate to return to normal. *Bill will call. I know he will.* She went back to waiting.

Time passed slowly. Days, then weeks, finally

one whole month went by. Still Anne lay in bed, staring at her reflection from the mirror on the ceiling. Since the scene with Bill at the Plaza, she had been unable to find the energy to dress in the morning. She did not care about clothes anymore, or even makeup. She reached over to the bottle of Vodka on her bedside table and took a large swig. *Two years! Two long fucking years!* She had wasted way too much time trying to snare Bill Brandon, only to fail miserably.

I wonder if he told anyone. People are probably talking about me and laughing. Maybe she should move somewhere else, Florida maybe, or California. There would be other opportunities there, plenty of other opportunities. No point in crying over spilt milk. I have to get on with my life, she thought, still unsure of what exactly she would do. She forced herself to sit. As she did, a sudden wave of nausea hit her. *Oh, not again. I thought this damned flu would be over by now.* For three days now, she had been carrying this stomach flu. *If I did not know any better, I would think I really was... Oh my lord!* A horrible thought occurred to her. *No, it could not be!*

* * * * *

This time, Anne handed the druggist a bottle of her own urine. One week later when she went back for the results, the druggist smiled down at her. "Congratulations" he said. "You're going to have a baby."

Anne walked home in a daze. What she had always feared most was now happening. She was in no better a situation than her sister was. *I know what I have to do. I'll call Alex. He will help me. After all, I am carrying his baby.*

* * * * *

At LaGuardia airport, he boarded the plane and handed his ticket to the stewardess. She glanced at it quickly and handed it back with a pleasant smile.

"Welcome aboard Air France, sir. I hope you have a pleasant flight."

"Thanks," replied Alex Ivanov. "I'm sure I will."

* * * * *

CHAPTER 17

Inside Le Gallet the ceiling, the walls, everything was painted black. Even the floor was covered in a velvety black carpet. The result was a room that seemed to go on forever. Here and there, throughout, were large sculptures of twisted, gleaming metal, shining brightly under narrow beams of light. Enormous paintings were strategically placed under spotlights, the only splashes of color in an otherwise colorless environment. The effect was surrealist, with art pieces appearing to float in mid-air.

Brigitte walked into the gallery filled with hope. The door closed softly behind her and she became aware of the silence inside. She hugged her canvases tightly to her chest.

Suddenly, the stillness was interrupted by the sound of laughter. Across the cavernous room a group of people were gathered around a large, white canvas with a single, small red dot in the center. One man stood slightly apart from the others. Chubby and middle-aged, he wore an elegant gray suit and was pointing to the painting. *Fortune*, thought Brigitte, recognizing him from the many articles she had read of the famous gallery owner.

From across the room, he turned to look at her. Brigitte felt his eyes travel over her from head to foot before he casually turned back to the couple. The dismissal was obvious and Brigitte was suddenly aware of the shabbiness of her dress. Three and a half years ago when Marcel had bought it, it had been her favorite outfit. Now it was faded and outdated. *I'm being silly; the man wants to see my paintings. He won't care about my clothes.* She pulled back her shoulders, held her head tall and walked over to the far end of the room. She leaned her canvases against the wall and choosing the nearest painting, stood in front of it, trying in vain to stop her knees from shaking.

Fifteen minutes later when the people left and Fortune walked over, she was still standing in the same spot, an expression of avid concentration on her face.

"*Mademoiselle* Dartois, I presume?"

She took a deep breath. "Yes. I'm sorry I'm late, the *métro*..."

With a wave of his hand, Fortune interrupted her "Judging from the single painting of yours that I saw, you seem to have some talent."

Brigitte smiled nervously. "Thank you."

"How do you like this one?" He indicated the oil she had been staring at for the last fifteen minutes.

Brigitte risked another smile. "I like it. It's... very nice."

"I don't think 'nice' is quite the word I would use to describe it."

Brigitte turned to look at the painting again. Streaks of red, purple and yellow were intermingled indiscriminately as though someone had thrown the paint haphazardly onto the canvas. There didn't seem to have any planning to the piece. Indeed it seemed no more than a jumble of angry colors. "Well... I guess it doesn't leave anyone indifferent."

"Ah! And that my dear is the true mark of genius!" exclaimed Fortune. "Art must awaken emotions. That is the whole *raison d'être* of art. If a painting does not make you feel something, love, hate, anger, sadness, melancholy, anything, then it is not art. It is," he paused dramatically, "garbage! And now, we will find out if what you do is art. Are those yours?" he asked, looking in the direction of the stack of oils leaning against the wall. Brigitte nodded. "Let's take them into my office for a closer look."

With her heart hammering against her ribs, Brigitte followed him into the back room.

Fortune bent over the oil on his desk and peered at it through his gold rimmed glasses. The expression on his face was inscrutable. "Where in heavens did you learn to use a brush this way? And the subjects you choose! What in the world made you think of painting an old wall with pealing paper?"

Brigitte listened helplessly, while Fortune made one critical comment after another. She could feel tears hovering dangerously behind her lashes. Instead of the happy occasion she had expected, the meeting was turning out to be a disaster.

Fortune laughed. "And look at this, an old lace tablecloth on a clothes line."

Brigitte jumped up. "I don't have to listen to

this," she said, her voice trembling with emotion. "You are under no obligation to like my work, but I'll be damned if I'll stand here while you laugh." She pulled the painting from his hands and fumblingly picked up the others.

"My dear Miss Dartois, please don't throw a tantrum. I don't like tantrums. What in heavens gave you the impression that I don't like your paintings?"

"Y-you said..."

"I said art must awaken emotions. Your paintings do that. When I look at yours, I feel amusement, tenderness. The point is, I feel. I like your paintings very much miss Dartois."

Brigitte swallowed hard. "You like them?"

"I like them." Fortune handed her a tissue. "Here. Dry your eyes. I can't stand to see a woman cry."

* * * * *

Brigitte hurried home, full to bursting with news. With Fortune's advance, she repaid Réjeanne. "And I still have enough left over to invest in canvases and paints to prepare for my vernissage," she told Réjeanne excitedly. "Fortune likes my paintings. Do you know what that means, Réjeanne?" She lifted up her skirt, displaying her long lean legs and twirled around the room. She stopped and turned to David who stood watching, his green eyes filled with merriment. "Did you hear me *mon chéri*? Fortune likes my paintings." She scooped him into her arms and danced around the room with him.

Although he wasn't sure what his mother was so happy about, David laughed with glee. "Does that mean you won't have to leave me any more?" he asked when Brigitte finally put him down.

"Well, I'm still going to have to work hard." David's face fell. Brigitte quickly continued. "But I'll be able to spend much more time with you. I promise."

"Fortune is a really nice man, isn't he?" he asked, his childish face full of wonderment. "Is he like Santa Claus?"

"I guess you could say that?" answered Brigitte laughing. "And today is like Christmas."

After David had gone to bed, Brigitte sat with Réjeanne making countless plans. "First, we're going to take a holiday. I've always wanted to go to the Riviera."

"What do you mean 'we'?" asked Réjeanne.

"You're coming with David and me," answered Brigitte. "If you come with us, I can take my easel and do some painting."

"I think that's a great idea," answered Réjeanne, who was becoming more and more excited at the thought of traveling.

That night, Brigitte fell asleep on the old couch; her mind filled with visions of lazy days spent lying on a sun drenched beach. *In all my life I've never been on a real holiday. I think it's about time.*

The next day when she told Fortune of her plan, reality came crashing back.

"You have no time for a vacation now. You have a vernissage to prepare for," he told her firmly.

"But what about all the paintings I already have?"

"*Ma chère mademoiselle Dartois*, you could barely sell them in Montmartre. Do you really think I will allow you to show those in my gallery?"

"But you said you liked them."

"True, but I don't put everything I like in my gallery. Under my guidance, you will produce paintings better than any you've ever done, I promise you. Those are what you will show for your vernissage." Then Fortune gave her detailed plans of the work he expected from her.

Brigitte listened aghast. "But, that amount of work will take months to do."

"As I said, you don't have time for a vacation." And the subject was closed.

The next morning, when Brigitte showed up at Le Gallet, Fortune showed her into his large, sunny studio in the back. For the rest of the day, under the watchful eye of her new mentor, Brigitte began to learn technique.

That night, she arrived back at her apartment in Montmartre, bone tired. "You think I'm hard on myself? You should hear Fortune," she told Réjeanne. "He doesn't like a thing I do. Every time I pick a color, he tells me it's wrong. Every time I put my brush to the canvas he yells at me. According to that man, I can't do anything right. I don't understand why he wants to work with me."

"Are you sure you want to continue working with him?"

"Of course I do. I've never learned so much in my life. He's brilliant!" And it was true. Under Fortune's expert guidance, Brigitte's technique was improving rapidly. Her natural talent was being honed and polished until the results astounded even her. From early morning to late at night she stood in front of her easel and patiently added stroke after stroke of paint under Fortune's sharp eye, until the results satisfied him. Then, at last, he would allow her to put away her paints for the night.

Long after Brigitte had left his studio, Fortune would stay behind and study the work she had accomplished that day. Her paintings were like nothing he had ever seen. The woman had a style all her own. Her choice of subjects and her compositions were always surprising. She combined colors and textures, working with a speed and a force unexpected in such a young and inexperienced artist. She managed to break all the rules and still her works were brilliant. Her few weaknesses quickly disappeared. *She's wonderful. More talented than anyone I've ever worked with. But I'll be damned if I let her know it.*

In preparation for her vernissage Brigitte created a bold new collection. She ventured into portraits and they were bright and colorful and erotic. She painted people from the street, vendors and beggars and prostitutes. Her paintings had the harsh, raw edge of reality, seen through the eyes of a romantic. It was a thrilling combination. Even Fortune, who was never entirely satisfied with anything his *protégés* accomplished, was overwhelmed. "Mark my word," he whispered to a few people. "This girl is going to take the art world by storm." As he expected, his words were repeated until everyone waited in unabashed anticipation for the mythical Dartois collection to be revealed.

Early one morning when Brigitte was adding the finishing touches to a painting of a flower merchant on a street corner, Fortune came in and stood behind her. "How about April?" he asked.

Brigitte put down her brush. "What are you talking about?"

"I think you're ready for your *vernissage*. How about April? That gives me two months to plan the event. I have to prepare the guest list, contact the media, and select your best paintings..."

It was the moment Brigitte had been waiting for. Suddenly she was terrified. "I-I don't think I'm ready. Maybe we should wait until..."

"I've invested a small fortune in getting you

ready. Now it's time you earned me some of that money back. You're as ready as you'll ever be."

Nothing she said could dissuade him. In two short months Brigitte was to have her *vernissage*. Brigitte only hoped the art world was ready for her.

* * * * *

On the appointed night, Fortune rushed about like a nervous host, making sure all was perfect. He rented additional lighting for the event until the entire room was bathed in brightness. In one corner, a row of waiters in tails stood at the ready, next to endless ice buckets of champagne bottles. In another corner, a string quartet played softly, a soothing background to the murmurs of conversation. Across the room was a small podium with a microphone and a large photograph of the artist of the evening. The photo had been taken a week earlier. It showed a self-assured Brigitte in a deep *décolleté*. Prominently displayed on every wall, were Brigitte's paintings, bold, energetic oils that commanded attention. People were already standing in front of them in admiration. Fortune breathed a sigh of relief. *Yes, everything is ready.*

He hurried to his office where Brigitte waited nervously. "I'll come and tell you when it's time. Now wish me luck," he told her and ran out again.

"*Merde!*" she called out as the door closed behind him.

Through the glittering crowd, Fortune noted with satisfaction the presence of enough stars to guarantee the success of the evening. Louis Malle, Brigitte Bardot and her new husband Jacques Charrier, Romy Schneider and Nobel Prize winner Albert Camus, were there. In a corner, with his bejeweled wife, was Doctor Armand Hammer, chatting with the ever dowdy Hélène Richoux and her new young and handsome husband. A photographer hovered nearby, snapping pictures madly. Fortune was ecstatic.

Not only had the gallery never looked so dramatic, but *le tout Paris* was there. Even Simon Fleuret, Fortune's arch rival was there. "I must say, I couldn't keep away. Looking forward to meeting this Dartois. You certainly have been keeping her a secret," said Fleuret, his eyes furtively searching the crowd for his competitor's new *protégé*.

Fortune laughed. "If you're thinking of trying to steal Dartois from me, forget it. She's mine. I have an iron-clad contract with her. Besides, you have Cigogne." His voice lowered to a whisper. "Tell me, is there any truth to the stories I hear about Cigogne having a dry spell?" The look on Fleuret's face was all the answer he needed. Fortune walked away silently congratulating himself. *I wouldn't take Cigogne back even if he crawled here on his hands and knees, not even for a quick tumble in bed*, he told himself merrily.

An hour into the evening it was obvious that Dartois' works were enthusiastically received by all. Comments of 'brilliant', 'explosive new talent', 'original vision' flowed about the room as abundantly as the champagne.

Fortune was almost beside himself with excitement. *Dartois will make me a fortune. Who needs Cigogne?* He looked at his watch. It was nearly ten-thirty. It was time for Dartois to make her entrance.

In Fortune's office, Brigitte in her evening gown, paced nervously. "You will look beautiful in black," Fortune had told her as he gave her instructions for the evening, and right he was. With her hair swept up into a simple twist and her makeup lightly but impeccably applied, Brigitte looked more like a movie star than an artiste. Nevertheless, she was as nervous as an *ingénue*.

"How do I look?" she asked Fortune when he came in.

"Enchanting, my dear. Absolutely enchanting. Ready?"

"I'm ready." She smoothed down the folds of her black chiffon gown and smiled brightly.

"Okay, here goes." Fortune blew her a kiss and stepped out.

A moment later, Fortune's voice came on the microphone. *"Et maintenant, Mesdames et Messieurs.* The moment we have all been waiting." Brigitte heard her name called out. "I present to you, Dartois!"

She stepped out of the back room and for a moment was blinded by the spotlight. The applause was enthusiastic. For the next hour, she was swept into a whirl of introductions and handshakes.

"Mademoiselle, your paintings are wonderful," one affable gentleman told her.

"You are so talented," said another, his lips grazing her hand.

"Where have you studied? Rome? Athens?"

"You are brilliant, just brilliant." The

compliments abounded and Brigitte hardly had time to answer one question before the next.

"Bonjour *mademoiselle*, it is a great pleasure to meet you."

Brigitte smiled and shook the man's hand. Suddenly her heart skipped a beat. The woman standing next to him was Hélène Richoux. *He must be her new husband. I wonder if she knew about.... No, she couldn't.*

The man continued. "I am very impressed with your work."

Hélène tapped her husband on the shoulder. "I see the Thompsons over there." Her voice was like ice. Without waiting for his reply, she walked away.

Hélène Richoux's handsome young husband blushed. "I'm terribly sorry." He turned and chased after his wealthy wife.

Before Brigitte had a chance to think, another man stepped in front of her. "You are so young for such a great talent. Tell me, how did you..." Brigitte lost herself in the conversation.

Men flocked to her in troves. From a distance, Fortune watched as Brigitte was surrounded by admirers.

She's fantastic, he rejoiced.

We'll be rich, he thought happily.

Suddenly his mood changed. *This could be a disaster*, he realized as he noticed the angry stares from a group of wives. *How could I have been so stupid?* Immediately he called over one of the waiters and gave him a few brief instructions. The *garçon* nodded. Moments later half a dozen waiters hurried through the room, carrying magnums of champagne and began to pour fresh glasses for all the guests. Fortune signaled to Brigitte and she hurried over. "We have a problem on our hands," he told her.

"What?'

"I don't have time to explain now, but whatever I say, just keep smiling. Trust me."

He picked up the microphone. "Ladies and gentlemen. May I have your attention please?" The crowd slowly gathered. Brigitte stood smiling as instructed. "Tonight is a very special night for me. Not only have I had the pleasure of introducing to you an artist who will have a major influence on the art world." He paused for a moment and looked at Brigitte. "I also have the great pleasure of announcing my engagement. Ladies and gentlemen." He grabbed Brigitte's hand. "I present to you, my *fiancée*."

Brigitte stared back at him with a frozen smile on her face. "What the hell do you think you're doing?" she whispered through clenched teeth.

"I'll explain later. Just trust me," he whispered back.

* * * * *

Fortune escorted the last of his important guests to the door. "I'm so glad you were able to come. I'll call you next week to book a private appointment." Then he turned back to the now deserted gallery.

Brigitte stood in the middle of the empty room, an expression of fury on her face. "What kind of a stunt was that?"

"You saw the way those men were looking at you?"

"What does that have to do with anything?"

"Just think for a minute Brigitte! Every one of those men has an older wife, not nearly as attractive as you are. I saw the way those women looked at you. They wanted you dead."

Brigitte remembered the way Hélène Richoux

had turned away when they were introduced. Could she have known about Marcel? Should she say anything to Fortune about this?

Fortune continued. "To be truly successful, an artist needs to be socially prominent. Wives control the social life in this city. Don't be so *naïve*. As a single, attractive female, you will get nowhere. On the other hand, as my wife..."

"You can't really expect us to get married!"

Fortune laughed. "You flatter yourself. At the risk of offending you, my dear, I have no interest in becoming your husband, or for that matter, your lover."

"No offense taken Fortune, the feeling is entirely mutual," replied Brigitte laughing. "For how long do we need to play this charade?"

"For as long as we have to. Will this cause any problems in your personal life?"

Brigitte laughed. "In my personal life? None. None whatsoever." Again she laughed.

* * * * *

"You've got to be joking!" Réjeanne stood,

hands on hips, a shocked expression on her face. The shock slowly mellowed into a smile. "You're engaged to Fortune? I had no idea. I'm so very happy for you. How long has this been going on?"

Brigitte shrugged and smiled secretly. "You see, all that time you were worrying about my personal life? You were worrying for nothing."

In the doorway, David stood in his pajamas his eyes filled with wonder. "Does that mean I'm going to have a daddy?"

Later, after Brigitte had put David back to bed and explained to him that Fortune would always be a good friend but would never be his father, she felt terrible. David had seemed so very happy at the thought of having a daddy.

* * * * *

The next morning the first reviews of the vernissage appeared. 'Dartois, genius!' cried the headline of one article. 'New talent applauded', lauded another.

"This deserves a celebration," declared Fortune. That evening, he took Brigitte to Maxime's. Seated comfortably in the elegant restaurant, Fortune ordered a bottle of Château Margot. "Now that we are engaged—" He winked. "...—we will have to be seen together occasionally. I want you to find yourself a new apartment," he told her. "Get a housekeeper and buy yourself a new wardrobe." He pulled out his check book, scribbled fast, and handed the check to Brigitte.

She glanced at the sum and gasped. "Don't you think we should sell a few of my paintings first?"

"Selling is my job. You, my dear, are my *fiancée*. And as my *fiancée*, you must have the right clothes and the right apartment for your new social level. You are about to start entertaining. Don't worry about the money. The money will follow."

One week later, Brigitte found a six room apartment on the Avenue Foch. The first time David saw it, the four-year old ran from room to room until his mother managed to calm him. "You mustn't run around in here. There are people living downstairs." David continued to jump up and down. "Are we rich now? Can we buy a car?"

Brigitte laughed. "We're not rich sweetheart. But we don't have to worry about money anymore."

Soon Brigitte had the walls covered with her art. Then she carefully chose a few good pieces of furniture. The master bedroom had a small sitting area, which she transformed into a mini studio for herself. The second bedroom she filled with overstuffed toys and electric trains for David.

The third bedroom, Brigitte furnished in a classic but feminine style. When the last detail was in place, she put a beautifully gift-wrapped box in the middle of the bed. Then she invited Réjeanne for a visit.

Réjeanne walked around the apartment in awe. "Never in my life have I seen such a beautiful apartment!"

"You like it?" asked Brigitte smiling.

"Of course! Oh Brigitte, I'm so happy for you."

"Wait till you see this," said Brigitte as she opened the door to the third bedroom.

"Oh my!" exclaimed Réjeanne as she walked in. Her eyes immediately focused on the large gift-wrapped box. "What's that?" she asked, a smile creeping on her face.

"Why don't you open it and find out?"

Réjeanne tore through the wrapping and pulled out a mink stole. "Oh, my! Is this real fur?"

Brigitte laughed. "It is. And it's also a bribe. I'm hoping you'll agree to live with David and me."

"Me? But what about my house?" The pudgy woman's eyes took on a mischievous glint. "Can I keep the mink even if I say no?"

"Réjeanne, I've given this a lot of thought. You'll be living here rent free and I'll pay you to keep house and mind David. In the meantime you'll have one more apartment pulling in rental income. Please say yes. There's nobody else I would trust to take care of David."

Réjeanne wasn't sure why she was hesitating. Her financial situation continued to be a worry for her. Her mortgage was high and even with the income from the second apartment she still had to dip into her income every month to make ends meet. She was fast approaching her fifty-fifth birthday and often worried about outliving her small inheritance. Brigitte's offer was the solution to her problems. "I don't know what to say."

"Réjeanne, if you live with David and me, you would be family, both David's and mine. Why don't we give it a try?"

Réjeanne nodded slowly. "Yes. I'd love to come and live with you and David."

Brigitte threw her arms around the older

woman. "That's great Réjeanne. I'm so very happy."

"So when do I move in?" asked Réjeanne, suddenly excited with the prospect.

"As soon as you can."

Ten days later, Réjeanne moved in and incredibly, Brigitte's life was suddenly wonderful. For the first time since David's birth, money was no longer a problem. Réjeanne was a wonderful homemaker and took great pride in her housekeeping and her cooking. Even the arrangement with Fortune was perfect. The two enjoyed each other's company, and Brigitte found, to her immense surprise that she enjoyed the respectability of her new position as Fortune's fiancée. Everywhere she went, people treated her with regard. It was the kind of courtesy she was unused to but in which she now reveled. *There really is something to be said for being treated with respect. I will never again go back to being a nobody.*

But happiest of all about the engagement, was Réjeanne. "I knew it was just a question of time, but I must admit, I had imagined you with someone... well... different. At least you're not alone anymore. You're going to have a husband. You must be so happy."

Brigitte laughed. "I'm very happy. Fortune is perfect for me."

Over the next few months, Fortune concentrated on promoting Brigitte's name with an enthusiasm he had not felt since discovering Cigogne. Newspapers regularly published articles extolling the talent of his new *protégé*. Yet, Brigitte's paintings were not selling as fast as Fortune had expected. *It's time to involve her socially*, he decided. He thought for a moment. Thérèse Martel, *that's whom I should call. She loved the Dartois collection at the vernissage. I'm sure I can get her to give a small party for Brigitte.*

He picked up the telephone and dialed. "Thérèse, *ma chérie*! I want you to do me a small favor. I would be eternally grateful if you would give a small diner party for Brigitte and me. Nothing large! Only fifty or so people. And of course, I will show you my gratitude by letting you pick any of the Dartois painting you like at a very good price. Would you mind?"

There was a pause before the social queen replied. "Fortune, *mon amour*. This is so very embarrassing. You know how much I care about you, don't you my dear? What I have to tell you is for your own good and in the strictest of

Scorpio Rising 275

confidence. Do you remember Hélène Richoux's first husband, Marcel Latreille? Well my darling, did you know that..." She proceeded to tell Fortune the entire story.

The next morning, Fortune made one of his rare appearances in the studio where Brigitte was busily painting. "Brigitte, I want to see you in my office right now!"

A few minutes later Brigitte breezed in, filled with excitement. "Fortune, wait till you see the oil I'm working on." She saw the anger on Fortune's face and stopped. "What's wrong?"

Fortune walked around the desk until he stood inches from her. "Why didn't you tell me about yourself and Hélène Richoux' first husband?" he asked, his voice icy.

Brigitte struggled to stay calm. "Because there's nothing to tell."

"I wouldn't say that having a man's bastard child is nothing," Fortune shouted, his fury suddenly exploding. "You've made me look like a fool. I've spent thousands of francs trying to promote the mistress of a man who was married to one of this city's most important social figure. Do you realize that Hélène Richoux is probably the most powerful woman in France? You are finished in this town. All that money I've spent on you is gone, vanished, money thrown down the drain. I'm never going to see any of it again." Brigitte wanted to cry. She stood rooted to her spot while Fortune went on. "How could you use me that way? Why didn't you tell me about Latreille and yourself?"

When at last he stopped, Brigitte spoke softly. There was no arguing to her voice, only defeat. "Before you listen to gossip, I suggest you get your facts straight. For your information, nothing happened between Marcel Latreille and me. He did no more than help a young girl in trouble. Marcel Latreille is not David's father." She turned and closed the door behind her.

* * * * *

"I never did like him," said Réjeanne, conveniently forgetting how the very previous day she had called Fortune the nicest man she had ever met. She stirred her *café au lait*. "I can't believe he broke off with you. Just like that. No explanation. No nothing. Don't worry *ma chérie*. You'll meet somebody else."

Brigitte hesitated. She had not told Réjeanne the entire story. "Meeting someone else is the last thing I'm worried about."

"Of course you can't think of seeing other men right now, my poor *chérie*. Your heart has just been broken, but in time you will. Time has a way of mending broken hearts."

Before Brigitte could think of anything to say, the doorbell rang and Réjeanne hurried over. "Oh, *monsieur* Fortune," she said loudly, for Brigitte to hear. "We were just talking about you. I don't think Brigitte wants to see you right now."

From the kitchen, Brigitte called out. "It's all right Réjeanne. I can see him," she said and came out. To her surprise, she saw that Fortune was carrying a bouquet of yellow roses.

"I'm afraid I owe you an apology," he said. "I shouldn't have judged you without hearing your side. If you don't mind, I think I'd like to hear the whole story about you and Marcel Latreille."

Réjeanne looked from Fortune to Brigitte. "Marcel Latreille? Who is Marcel Latreille? Will someone please tell me what's going on?"

* * * * *

Long into the night, Brigitte, Réjeanne and Fortune sat at the kitchen table, drinking cup after cup of coffee and talking. It was the first time Brigitte had ever divulged the full story about Marcel Latreille to anyone. She avoided any mention of David's real father, choosing instead to allude vaguely to a youthful mistake.

Réjeanne shook her head in disbelief. "You poor child. You truly went through hell."

Brigitte looked nervously at Fortune. "So you see, nothing really happened between Marcel and me. I left suddenly because I came to realize that he was hoping for something more than a platonic relationship." she said. "There is no question that I was foolish to think that a grown man would help a girl, the way he helped me, out of nothing but the kindness of his heart but I was a frightened child. Fortune, please don't abandon me now. Look at all that money you've invested, and all the work you've put into promoting me. I think quitting now would be a mistake. The critics applauded my vernissage."

Fortune shrugged. "If you're black-balled by Hélène Richoux, it won't matter what the critics say. In this town you will be a pariah."

Desperately, Brigitte tried another angle. "Maybe this time you won't be creating an overnight success. Maybe it will take a few years before I'm accepted as a serious artist. In all honesty, I never expected it to be any other way. In the meantime, you could diversify."

"What do you mean diversify?"

"I don't think it's a good idea for you to concentrate on only one major artist. Maybe you should find other talented artists and carry a variety of styles. That way you'll be covering all your angles. When one artist leaves, you will always have a backup. If one takes longer than another to become profitable, another will be covering your overhead. Your business will only be stronger for it."

Fortune swallowed the last of his coffee. "Any more left in the pot?" he asked.

Réjeanne jumped up and poured him another cup.

For a long time, Brigitte and Réjeanne waited while Fortune thought quietly. "This is what we'll do," he said at last. "You will start giving dinner parties. They will be small, very elegant and very exclusive. Never more than eight people at a time, but eight selected people. I'll organize everything. In no time everyone will be dying to get an invitation from you." He sat back and smiled, happy with his new plan.

"Oh, I think that's a wonderful idea," exclaimed Réjeanne. "Didn't I tell you Brigitte? Fortune loves you. He would never let you down."

The next day Fortune drafted the guest list for the first dinner party. Cornelia and Leopold Thompson from New York were in town, Lord Merriweather, the art collector and his wife; and Olivier Terrebonne, the famous Ferrari race-car driver and the international beauty Lausanne, Olivier's girlfriend. It was the perfect mix of old money and new fame. It would make for interesting dinner conversation.

Then he prepared the menu. *Langoustines à la fine champagne*, followed by *Faisan au nid*. Next would be the *Salade de pleurote* and desert would be a spectacular *Soufflé au cognac flambé*.

"Oh my goodness, I've never cooked anything like that," exclaimed Réjeanne when Fortune listed the menu. "Wouldn't you like me to make *coq au vin*? I make it very nicely."

"Indeed not! I was planning to hire a chef to prepare the meal and a professional waiter to serve."

Brigitte mentally calculated the costs of such an evening. "Do we really have to go to such expense?"

"Absolutely. It's the only way. And of course, we need flowers."

After he left, Réjeanne shook her head. "I still think my *coq au vin* would have been a good idea," she said. "As if some chef and a fancy menu can make you a famous artist."

"Fortune only wants what's best for my career."

"Sometimes I wonder about him. Are you sure he's the right man for you *chérie?*"

"Réjeanne, you've always wanted me to find a man. Now that I have one, don't start criticizing him."

Long after Brigitte had gone to bed, she lay awake worrying. Fortune was taking everything so seriously. He planned everything, where she lived, what she wore, how he wanted her to live. The thought of anyone exercising so much control on her, was uncomfortable. Would she have any time left for herself and David? It was only hours later, that she finally pushed those worrisome thoughts aside and fell into a fitful sleep.

On the morning of the party, Brigitte was in a state of barely controlled panic. The florists arrived with flower arrangements the size of funeral wreaths. *I hope this is not a bad omen*, she thought.

"Where am I supposed to put those?" asked Réjeanne.

"I don't know! Anywhere," Brigitte answered as she struggled with the table extension.

Five minutes later the chef arrived. Réjeanne showed him to the kitchen.

"Do you really expect me to prepare a meal in this broom closet?" asked the portly man, as he stood in the large, fully equipped kitchen.

"No, you can go and prepare it in the courtyard if you prefer," snipped Réjeanne. She went back to the dining room where Brigitte was setting the table. "Did you hear what he said?'

"Not now Réjeanne. David just knocked down the centerpiece."

On the floor, dozens of broken flowers lay scattered in a puddle of water and broken glass. A few feet away, David stood looking innocent. He shrugged his shoulders. "I didn't mean to. I only wanted to smell them from up close."

What next? Brigitte asked herself as she went for the mop.

The first hint of what would happen next came at seven thirty when Lord Merriweather called. "I'm so terribly sorry. I'm sure you'll understand. I just spoke to Madame Richoux. She is considering selling her Rembrandt. I have been trying to get my hands on that painting for years. She's willing to negotiate tonight. Tomorrow, she's off to Zurich. You understand don't you?"

"Of course I understand Lord Merriweather. I would do the same myself," answered Fortune, who had taken the call.

Minutes later the phone rang again. Brigitte handed the receiver to Fortune. "It's Cornelia Thompson," she whispered.

"Fortune, *mon chéri,* please forgive me. I'm still in New York," said Cornelia, her voice sounding suspiciously clear for an international call.

"I guess it will be diner for four," Fortune told Brigitte as he hung up the telephone.

At eight thirty, Olivier Terrebonne and his girlfriend arrived. Brigitte greeted them at the door and Fortune handed them a glass of Perrier Jouet. Five minutes later the chef stormed out of the kitchen. "*Monsieur, madame*, I am sorry but I cannot cook in these conditions. The counter is too small. The stove is not gas." He pulled his chef's hat from his head and threw it to the ground. "The *faisans*, they are ruined!"

* * * * *

The next day, in his office, when Fortune opened the newspaper, the first thing he saw in the society column of the paper, was a large article about the wonderful party given the night before by Hélène Richoux at Bellevue, her country home. The accompanying photo was of a frumpy looking madame Richoux wearing a prince's fortune of priceless emeralds and rubies, almost unnoticeable amid the glitter of her sequin dress. Standing next to her and her young husband in the photograph were two of her party guests, the Thompsons from New York. Fortune crumpled up the paper and threw it away in disgust.

"This is just not going to work!" he muttered to himself.

* * * * *

No matter how hard Fortune pushed to establish Brigitte socially, Hélène Richoux exerted a continuous and equal effort to prevent it. After a few months of unrewarded efforts, Fortune called Brigitte into his office. "I've decided to take your advice. It makes no sense for me to represent only one artist. I think you already know Jérome."

The shock was quickly replaced by fear. Would Fortune's next move be to dump her? She smiled. "Welcome Jérome. You must be very talented. Fortune has impeccable taste." She then excused herself with a gracious smile. "I have to get back to work. I'm halfway through another piece. I'm really excited about it." She hurried back to work, wondering if this would be the last time she would be allowed in Fortune's studio.

Over the next year, Fortune continued following Brigitte's advice and signed on other promising artists. For every new 'discovery' of his, Fortune would throw himself into promoting his new 'genius' with the same enthusiasm he had shown Brigitte in the first few months of their association. Every time, Brigitte was convinced that Fortune was about to wash his hands of her. But slowly, with every new artist Fortune adopted, Le Gallet's reputation rose even higher and as Fortune's 'première', Brigitte's credibility increased along with the gallery's. Over time, a few influential people began to buy her work. And gradually, Brigitte developed a solid and enviable reputation as one of Paris' leading artists.

One evening, as Brigitte was about to leave after a long day's work, Fortune called her into his office. He sat on one of his 'Brillo pad' chairs and invited her to use the other. "I think it's time we talked," he said. "I see you're still wearing your engagement ring."

Brigitte looked down at the third finger of her left hand. She had become so used to it in the last two years, it felt like a part of her. "Yes, of course. It's part of our deal. Isn't it?" she added nervously.

Fortune looked fiercely serious. "You won't have to wear it anymore."

"W-what?"

Fortune smiled. "Don't look so worried. We don't have to pretend anymore. Your reputation is solid now."

"B-but what happened to make you..."

"Le Monde is sending over their top journalist to interview you tomorrow. This is the perfect opportunity for us to announce that we are no longer engaged. You can simply say that we both care a great deal about each other, but that we have come to the conclusion that we will be happier as friends." He paused for a moment and smiled. "We couldn't continue the charade forever, now could we?"

"I suppose you're right," she said, then asked in disbelief. "Le Monde? Really? Why would they want to interview me?"

"They're running a series on influential women. One of their subjects is a politician, another is a business woman and you are the artist. The interview will be on you as Brigitte Dartois the person, rather than the artist. That's why I thought this might be the perfect opportunity to end our little charade." Fortune smiled. "So, should I confirm the appointment?"

Brigitte smiled. "Of course. But can I still keep the ring?" she asked with a teasing glint in her eyes.

* * * * *

CHAPTER 18

Every city has a personality all its own. When Alex stepped off the Air France Boeing 707, Paris was under the sway of Charles de Gaulle, who only three years before had been voted president of France by a landslide. It was home to the cinema of Brigitte Bardot, who in the movie 'And Man Created Woman', forever changed the standards of female beauty. It was home to the incomparable voices of Edith Piaf and Maurice Chevalier, who more than any others, romanticized Paris as the city of love. It was home to the designers who dressed rich and famous women from every country, thus making Paris the fashion capital of the world. More importantly, it was a city full of elegance and beauty, a city graced with an almost magical atmosphere. Paris was the city of love, the city of light, and for Alex, it was the city of inspiration.

Although his *per diem* allowed for a generous hotel budget, Alex registered at La Petite Tuillerie, a small family-run auberge minutes from the offices of Modern Architecture & Design. The *auberge* had eight tiny rooms, and provided minimum services. The only meal served was breakfast, consisting of coffee and *brioches*. Even then, the price for the room sounded ridiculously high to the ever-frugal Alex.

Alex stood in the doorway and mentally assessed the size of the room, debating whether the space was worth so many of the large colorful bills. There was a narrow bed with no more than two feet on either side, one small dresser, a mirror and a window through which Alex could see the street inches away. The room made, even his apartment in New York, seem large. *If that were possible.*

"*Alors, je n'ai pas toute la journée, monsieur. Vous la prenez, ou vous la prenez pas.* Make up your mind," said the landlady, gesticulating as she spoke.

Alex pulled a wad of francs from his pocket and counted out enough for three days in advance. *It's still only a fraction of what I could be paying at any hotel. I'll bank the rest.*

"*Merci.*" She bowed as she backed out of the room her smile as sudden as it was wide on her homely face. "*Merci beaucoup, monsieur. Breakfast is served every morning at seven. Café et brioches. After eight, no more room service.*"

That night, as Alex was reading his tourist information book, the lights went off suddenly at midnight. Alex climbed out of bed, fiddled with the switch and they turned back on. Three minutes later, they turned off again. For the next half hour, he obstinately kept turning them on, only for them to turn back off again, moments later. Finally, he gave up and put away his book.

The next morning, he had barely stepped into the shower when the water turned off. *What is going on?* He dressed quickly and went to look for the owner.

"In France, electricity is very expensive," explained Madame Durand. "It's the same everywhere. Hot water and electricity in most small hotels are on a timer."

"I have work to do at night." He explained the project he was working on and the amount of night hours he would need to work in order to finish the plans.

Madame Durand thought for a moment, and then snapped her fingers. She rushed away and reappeared minutes later with a dusty old oil lamp, which she promptly wiped with a corner of her apron. "*Voici monsieur.* With this you can work all night."

All the comforts of home. A small room, a cold shower in the morning, an oil lamp to work by at night and a bed I will never get around to sleeping in. He laughed. There was no denying it, he was happiest when the work was hard and his bank account was full. Now, the money he would save on the hotel plus his entire salary would go straight into his account and his capital would grow even faster. *Someday soon, very soon...*

* * * * *

The first meeting with M.D.A. was three days away. Until then, Alex walked the streets of Paris. Never had he felt such a sense of the exotic as he did trying to familiarize himself with the French capital.

He strolled along the *Champs Elisée* breathing in the crisp fall air. He window-shopped and people-watched. He climbed the Eiffel Tower and peered down at the Lilliputian city below. He visited the *Louvre* and walked through the gardens of the *Tuileries*. He stood at the foot of the *Arc de Triomphe* suffused with the wonder of actually being there. Everywhere he went, his senses were assaulted with fascinating sights and smells and sounds.

"Aie! Mon mec, vous voulez des fleurs pour une jolie demoiselle?" a flower merchant called out to him.

At a street corner, a small waif of a girl sang in a woman's voice, full of adult passion. *"N'oublis jamais le jour où on s'est connu..."*

"Par ici monsieur. Venez, entrez," a small bar owner beckoned.

He shook his head, completely baffled by the torrent of sounds. A few feet further, his stomach rumbling, he was seduced into a small *boulangerie* by the enticing aroma of freshly baked *petit pains au chocolat*. Later, he sat by the banks of the Seine and fed the remaining crumbs to the pigeons.

Over the last few days of sightseeing, he had gradually felt a better understanding and respect for the distinct flavor of Paris. Only then, did he feel ready to go to the left bank, to the proposed site of the new project. He brushed off the crumbs from his trousers and went in search of a *Métro*.

On a city block smaller than any he had ever seen in New York, was the handful of medieval buildings scheduled to be torn down. *Unless the plan I suggest is accepted.* He pulled out a measuring tape, a pad of paper and began to take notes. He walked around the structures and recorded the details.

The stones were old and black with age. Caved-in roofs. Cracked foundations. What windows remained had long lost their panes and most of their framework. The doorways were astonishingly small and low. Still, even after years of neglect, the structures had an undeniable charm and beauty that time had failed to erode.

How can anyone think of destroying these buildings? Alex wondered, outraged. *They are history.* He measured, calculated and recorded the figures he needed. Satisfied, he put away his notebook and headed back to the small hotel.

As he walked into *La Petite Tuillerie*, he felt almost at home. He waved a greeting to Madame Durand behind the front desk and she rewarded him with one of her rare smiles. In his room, he settled down to a night's work by lamplight.

On the appointed morning, his stomach churning with *croissants et brioches*, his portfolio thick with last minute sketches, and his soul bursting with nervous anticipation, Alex walked into the large, prestigious offices of Modern Design and Architecture, on the avenue George V.

The reception was a modern area with floor-to-ceiling columns, diffused lighting and a turquoise Formica desk upon which sat an elaborate floral arrangement. Against the wall was a row of modern steel and leather chairs. A collection of M.D.A. magazines were neatly piled on a coffee table. The receptionist, a young woman with rhinestone glasses, looked up when Alex walked in.

"Alex O'Brian. I have an appointment with Frédérique Marchant."

"Un instant, s'il vous plait monsieur."

Alex sat and waited. He pulled out his Berlitz translator and flipped it open. Moments later, a tall thin young man stepped out of an office.

"Je peux vous aider?"

"Bonn-joor, jay oon randy-voose..." Alex stopped, confused and looked down in his book.

The man burst into laughter. "That has to be the worse French I've ever heard," he exclaimed.

"And I'm sure you've heard some pretty bad

French in your life, right?" added Alex, embarrassed. "I guess I won't need this." He indicated his translation book.

"Please! Do yourself a favor and throw it in the garbage. Now, who is it you want to see?"

"I have an appointment with Frédérique Marchant."

"And you are?"

"Alexander Ivanov, Alex for short."

"Nice to meet you Alex, I am Frédérique Marchant. Come, I'll introduce you to the others." He led him into a conference room where three other men were gathered around a small round table. "Have a seat Alex."

Alex went around the table and sat between two of the men. Frédérique, a tall thin man with surprisingly beautiful features, remained standing and waited for every one's attention. He cleared his throat and began the meeting. "I would like to introduce you to my assistant on this project, Jean-Pierre Fauchon."

The plain little man with the receding hairline looked up from a thick stack of papers, nodded, looked around the room and let his eyes rest on Alex for a moment. Expressionless, they went back to his papers.

Frédérique continued. "Jean-Pierre is in charge of the contest and any questions or special requests are to be addressed to him.

"I would like to congratulate Alex Ivanov of New York, Darren Bishop of Birmingham and Guillermo Bernardi of Palermo for being this year's finalists in our annual Architecture and Design international contest. And a special mention to monsieur Bernardi for his perseverance. This is his third time as a finalist in the contest "The two other finalists looked at him. Bernardi stared back determinedly.

Frédérique continued. "Winning is not everything. Being chosen as a finalist is in itself a great honor. Most of the past finalists have moved on to international careers as Guillermo can attest. Since his first time as a finalist seven years ago, he has become one of the busiest architects on the continent."

Guillermo smiled. "I'm hoping the third time around will be lucky for me." Although the words were congenial, Alex detected resentment in the Italian's voice.

Frédérique took over again. "The criteria for this competition are elementary; superior architectural design must have esthetic beauty without looking out of place in its surrounding.

Practical aspects such as cost and efficiency are also important. Each one of you has presented ideas that combine those ingredients. You were invited here to complete your plans with the full cooperation of this office and the city of Paris' planning committee. You will be able to study firsthand the environs of the proposed project. You will meet with the members of the planning committee and finally each of you will have the opportunity to make your own presentation. Today's meeting is our opportunity for to welcome you and to acquaint you with a few of the city's concerns about this project. You have two months to prepare for the official presentation to the city.

"A press conference has been scheduled to take place at the building site, tomorrow morning at ten o'clock Thank you and good luck. Now, Jean-Pierre has some information I am sure you will find important."

Jean-Pierre took the floor. He shuffled his papers for a minute, cleared his throat and launched into a long and detailed brief of the Paris building code. Alex pulled out a pencil and paper.

After the meeting, coffee was served and the finalists had the opportunity to chat and look at each other's designs. From the doorway, where he stood watching, Frédérique studied them. The finalists were an oddly mismatched group.

Guillermo Bernardi, a middle-aged overweight man with over thirty years experience in the profession, enjoyed a noted reputation as one of Italy's leading architects, greatly enhanced by his being twice selected as one of the M.D.A. finalists. Bernardi was studying Darren Bishop's plans. "Very nice," he said, in a superior tone. "But I prefer modern structures similar in style to 'De Corbusier's'. I don't like all this tra-la-la." He punctuated his remark with a slap to the blueprint. "Concrete! Now that's what I like to use. Not expensive to work with. Solid. If I cannot give grace to a building without using expensive materials, then I have failed."

Darren Bishop was as thin as Guillermo Bernardi was large. Although barely in his thirties, Bishop's hair was completely white. That and his habit of dressing in an almost old-fashioned way gave him a distinct air of aloof nobility. Towering over Guillermo, he replied calmly. "Really? Concrete? I detest it." He gently but firmly pulled his plans from Guillermo's hands and put it back down on the table.

Alex Ivanov, standing nearby, was handsome with dark, movie star good looks, dark hair brushed back, showing off his chiseled features to perfection. Although he was the youngest, he looked intelligent and self-assured. Alex listened avidly as the other two contestants espoused the merits of each other's diametrically opposed opinions. They had obviously dismissed him as a minor competitor. Neither had shown any interest in looking at his sketches. He inched closer and studied their plans discreetly.

From the doorway, Frédérique Marchant watched, amused. After a moment, he strolled over to Alex. "I know you have less experience, but don't be intimidated. I have rarely seen a proposal of such inspiration as the one you submitted. I have no idea if the building committee will agree with me, but if they do, you have just as good a chance of winning as they do." Frédérique gave him a pat on the back and wandered off. From across the room, Jean-Pierre watched Frédérique's hand rest on Alex's back for a second longer than necessary before he walked away.

At the doorway, Frédérique Marchant turned and cleared his throat again. "Lunch will be here shortly. I wish I could join you but I have work to do. Bon appétit, everybody," he said, and left.

Jean Pierre hurried out of the room after Frédérique and caught up with him in his office. "*Alors?*"

"Alors, I think we have three exceptionally talented architects," Frédérique answered casually. "Call Paul Leduc at Paris Match. See if he'll give us a story."

Jean-Pierre hesitated. "What do you think of the American?"

Frédérique looked up from his appointment calendar. "Jealous, are we?" He patted Jean-Pierre on the behind and picked up a large folder from his desk. "Don't be ridiculous. Call me tonight. Maybe we can get together." It was Jean-Pierre's signal to leave.

* * * * *

The next morning Alex hurried through his morning shower-and-shave and rushed all the way to the left bank only to find Frédérique and Jean-Pierre waiting with a photographer. Guillermo and Darren arrived moments later. Neither of them appeared any happier to be there than he did. The three finalists stood in front of the medieval building and posed for the camera.

What the heck am I doing here? Alex wondered. He felt acutely uncomfortable standing before a camera. *I should be working instead of wasting my time here.*

The reporter asked Frédérique a few question, then left, leaving the photographer to finish with the pictures.

"*Vraiment*, don't look so gloomy. This is important." Frédérique called out impatiently to the finalists. "I'm sure you know about the power of the media. I want to make sure that whenever somebody mentions this project, your names are associated with it. Do you understand? Now be good boys, and smile."

Alex cringed. There was some underlying tone in Frédérique's comments that were blatantly patronizing. He gritted his teeth, pulled back his shoulders and fixed a wide smile on his face.

"That's much better Alex. You look beautiful." To the photographer, he spoke politely. "Go ahead. Just make sure they look good." He turned to Jean-Pierre who until then had not uttered one word. "I don't understand why Paris Match would not send their photographer," Frédérique whispered furiously. "This is an important architectural development for the city. Did you tell them that?"

"Yes, but..."

"Did you tell them that we received over twenty-thousand applications from all over the world?"

"Yes, yes but..."

"...and they still would not give us any coverage? That's preposterous. When I get back to the office, remind me to call them myself." Frédérique's eyes swept over the group and paused on Guillermo. "Guillermo, my dear man, why don't you try standing sideways," called out Frédérique. Guillermo looked stricken. "Oh, don't look at me like that. It is only for your own good. Sideways you will look twenty kilos thinner." His eyes moved on to Darren Bishop. "Darren, whatever possessed you to wear such a tie? Oh, and Alex, that's a great suit you're wearing. Great style." Frédérique was going out of his way to make Alex's competitors uncomfortable.

He's enjoying this, Alex realized, surprised. As Alex was busily watching Frédérique, he did not notice Jean-Pierre eyes on him. He also missed the look of pure hatred in Jean Pierre's eyes.

I have to find a way to keep Frédérique far from him, thought Jean Pierre.

The photographer took a few more pictures and decided that the session was over. Alex picked up his portfolio, which he had once again brought needlessly and looked at his watch. It was already noon. Half the day had gone by and he still had hours of work to do. *At this rate, I'll never finish in time.*

* * * * *

The worst part of being an architect was the constant hunching over papers. Sometimes Alex felt like his back was about to break. Still he sketched on, hour after hour, day after day, always bending over the rickety table. The old chair Madame Durand had given him was hard and uncomfortable. *If not for the money I'm saving, I'd be at the George V too.* He sat up, stretched his back and pulled his arms over his head in an effort to relax his tense muscles.

He was in a miserable mood. None of his sketches satisfied him. He rubbed his eyes and for the hundredth time, he looked down at the sheet of paper before him.

His idea was simple enough. He wanted to keep the existing small buildings and incorporate their exterior into new walls of a similar style along the entire city block. He planned to design large and elegant entrances to allow easy access to the main structure. On the inside, the small, restored medieval houses would be small individual boutiques. The entire inside complex was to be a park-like area complete with waterfall, a wishing well, park benches and growing trees. To further the impression of natural surroundings while allowing plenty of daylight, the roof would be of green-house-type glass. The idea was simple, but with his limited experience in large construction, every technical detail became an obstacle.

There was a knock at the door, dispersing his morose thoughts.

Madame Durand appeared, wiping her hands on her apron. "*Téléphone pour vous*," she said and promptly disappeared.

Alex hurried to the front desk and picked up the receiver. "*Bonjour Alex?* It's Jean-Pierre. Frédérique wants you to meet us at Maxim's tonight at eight-thirty for dinner. He's arranging for a photographer to be there, so don't be late. Then we go on to the Moulin Rouge for the late show and a few more publicity pictures."

"I'll be there." Alex put down the telephone, and wondered if Guillermo and Darren were any further ahead with their plans than he was.

* * * * *

Maxime's was a restaurant like none Alex had ever seen. The place was packed with a multitude of small tables and large overstuffed chairs. Each place was set with so much silver and crystal the entire room seemed to sparkle.

Frédérique patted the seat next to his. "Sit here Alex."

Alex felt out of place in such elegant surroundings. "Thanks. Nice place."

"I thought you might like it." Frédérique smiled and his beautiful face glowed. He handed Alex a heavily embossed menu. "Go ahead. Order whatever you want."

During the meal, waiters hovered nearby, catering to their customers every need. *I could learn to like this*, thought Alex, reveling in the luxurious surroundings.

From across the table Jean Pierre watched his every move surreptitiously. "So how do you like Paris?" he asked pleasantly.

"I love it. I love the city, the food, everything," replied Alex.

"How about French women?" prodded Jean Pierre.

Alex shrugged. "Sure. I just haven't had time to meet them."

Jean-Pierre's smile widened. "Did you hear that Frédérique? Alex would like to meet some French women." Frédérique was engrossed in a conversation with Guillermo and did not answer. Minutes later when the group left the famous restaurant and headed for their next stop, Frédérique seemed disturbed. Jean-Pierre, on the other hand, wore a victorious little smile.

* * * * *

The Moulin Rouge, one of Paris' most famous nightspots, was a large, smoky, cavernous room filled to overflowing with small tables. Every night, on a lavishly decorated stage, beautiful women danced and sang in scanty feather and sequin costumes. The floorshow was one of the city's most famous attractions.

This was a special occasion. Not only had Paris Match agreed to send a photographer, but they had also promised Frédérique a feature story about M.D.A.'s contribution to a focal real estate development for the city.

At this famous nightclub, Frédérique had used his influence to reserve a table in the front row. "Bring us a bottle of Don Perignon," he ordered.

"I feel like celebrating tonight."

At that moment, the lights dimmed and the music began. A spotlight focused on the center of the curtain as it lifted on a row of elegant semi-nude dancers. Slowly the mirrored platform began to revolve as the dancers' choreography became more intricate. The effect was mesmerizing. The entire stage became a giant kaleidoscope. Hundreds of naked legs moving in perfect unison, reflected on the mirrored ceiling.

Alex sat in the front row, totally captivated.

"So you like the women of Paris Alex?" asked Frédérique, leaning over to speak above the music.

"I never saw women like this in New York," replied Alex, in awe.

"Some say a man hasn't lived until he's had a French woman."

Something in Frédérique's voice made Alex turn around. "I guess that means I haven't lived. But then I only just got here."

"Now there is a French woman who is worth meeting," commented Frédérique.

Alex turned to look at the singer who was just making her entrance. "She certainly is!" He followed the woman's movements as she glided to the center of the stage. There she stopped with her arms stretched out in an all-embracing gesture. The audience went wild. Her hair was platinum blond and styled in Marilyn Monroe-esque curls. Her long beaded flesh-toned gown gave the illusion of nude shimmering skin. A side slit extended all the way up from her ankle to her waist, exposing a long, shapely leg. Even in such a revealing outfit, there was nothing cheap about her. Her whole bearing was regal. She gracefully blew a kiss to her audience and raised her hands to quell the applause.

"Did you say something Frédérique?" asked Alex.

Frédérique shouted above the applause. "I said would you like to meet her?"

"You know her?" Alex was impressed.

"I know everybody in this town," answered Frédérique, casually.

On the stage, the woman took the microphone. "*Bonjour.* Good evening. My name is Gigi L'Amour," she whispered seductively to the audience. "Tonight I will sing you a very special song."

She languidly strolled along the stage, rolling

her hips, graceful and fluid, her voice low and suggestive. Suddenly the music changed from a slow romantic song to a rock-and-roll number. Immediately Gigi's body turned into a tornado of energy. During a fast twirl, she whipped off her skirt and threw it into the audience. Underneath she wore a mesh outfit that left almost nothing to the imagination. Then, just as unexpectedly, the suit was gone and she was playing the audience with only a tiny gold triangle covering her pubic hair and matching pasties on the nipples of her small but perfect breasts. The whistling and stamping drowned out her voice. Then the chorus of scantily clad dancers coalesced around her and the stage became a flurry of bright colors and dazzling jewels. When the circle of dancers opened again, Gigi had disappeared. The audience went wild.

Chants of *"On veut Gigi! On veut Gigi! On veut Gigi!"* were taken up until the blonde bombshell reappeared for an encore, this time more decently covered up in a shimmering but still transparent gown.

"So what do you think of Gigi?" asked Frédérique.

Alex shook his head, still overwhelmed. "She's beautiful."

At that moment, Paul Leduc arrived with a case of camera equipment.

"Before you set up," said Frédérique. "I think it might be a good idea to add some local color to the photos. Why don't we ask some of the girls to come and pose with the finalists?"

"*D'accord*," agreed the photographer. "We could use it for the social column as well."

Moments later, Gigi and three of the chorus girls joined the table.

"Gigi, could you be a dear and stand here?" asked Frédérique. He whispered a few words in her ear and steered her between the finalists.

"*Oh là là! Quels beaux hommes!*" She wrapped one arm around Alex and gave him a seductive smile. Alex's blood rose ten points. Following the photo shoot, Gigi lingered at the table. "Alex, you don't mind if I sit next to you do you?"

Alex was almost speechless. "Y-yes, I mean no, please do."

During the rest of the evening, Gigi had eyes only for Alex. She completely ignored Darren and Guillermo. When she spoke, it was to Alex. When she smiled, it was to Alex. To Alex's great surprise, he suddenly felt her hand on his thigh. Gradually it moved up and up until it cupped his testicles. Alex could hardly breathe. When Frédérique suggested they call it a night, Gigi agreed enthusiastically. She pulled her hand away and leaned over to Alex. "Meet me outside in twenty minutes. Okay?"

Outside the *Moulin Rouge*, the men bid each other goodnight and dispersed. Alex paced, scanning the giant posters advertising upcoming performances, and waited impatiently until Gigi appeared. "My place or yours?" she asked.

"Yours," he replied, remembering the thin walls and the three-minute timer on the water and electricity in his *auberge*.

In the taxi, Gigi's hands were all over Alex. "I love your body Alex. You are such a beautiful young American."

Alex looked at Gigi appreciatively. "You're not bad yourself," he started to say, but was muffled by Gigi's mouth covering his.

Gigi's apartment was a shrine to sensuality. The bed, a gigantic round creation taking up half the space of the large room, had a panel of buttons on the side. Alex glanced at the buttons with curiosity.

"Make yourself a drink, *mon amour*. I won't be long." Gigi disappeared behind a mirrored door.

Moments later, she reappeared in a shear silk robe. She drifted over to Alex and almost before he knew what was happening, she was extracting him from his trousers. At the sight of his proud erection, Gigi gasped with pleasure. "You are going to make me very happy, *mon amour.*"

Alex chuckled. "It will be my pleasure," he replied. He guided Gigi to the bed and eagerly slipped off her robe. A second later, he leaped from the bed. "God damn it! Why the fuck didn't you tell me?"

Gigi lay contrite on the disheveled bed. "But, *mon amour*, everybody knows Gigi is short for Gilbert."

Fifteen minutes later Alex was back at *La Petite Tuilerie* and scrubbing furiously in the shower. Although nothing had actually transpired between himself and Gilbert, a.k.a. Gigi, he felt dirty, soiled. *Damn that Frédérique*, he fumed. *He set me up*. Alex vowed not to give the man the satisfaction of showing his anger. *From now on, when I want to meet a girl, I'll do it on my own.*

* * * * *

For the remainder of his stay in Paris, Alex pushed all thoughts of women and sex out of his mind and concentrated on the competition. He had so much work to do. Every morning he got up at the crack of dawn, gulped down a hurried breakfast of *croissants and brioches* and worked on his plans. He labored furiously all day, every day, often into the early hours of the morning, resting only when he his hand cramped. Riddled with self-doubt, he revised his plans over and over, fixed in belief they were mediocre at best. Weeks went by and still he was convinced he on the wrong track. His ideas, so original at the beginning, now seemed bland. As the deadline approached, he began to panic. One week before the final date, he called M.D.A. and asked for a meeting with Frédérique.

Frédérique was in his office, editing an article for the next issue of M.D.A., when Alex walked in. He listened patiently while Alex admitted his doubts. "You want my advice?" asked Frédérique afterwards. "Put away your work for a few days. You need to look at it with a fresh eye."

Alex was near despair. "I wish I could. The only problem is that I still have so much work to do. I can't afford to put it aside for a few days."

Frédérique was sympathetic but firm. "I wish I could help, but I can't give you an extension. Unless you bring all the plans in by the deadline you will be automatically disqualified."

Alex's hopes of getting a few days' grace immediately evaporated. "I understand," he said doubtful. Still he hesitated. "I don't suppose you could take a look at my designs and give me your opinion?"

Frédérique slowly shook his head. "That would be unethical under the circumstances."

Alex nodded. "I guess I'd better get back to work."

He hurried back to his auberge and pulled out his plans. The next morning, he was working at his usual frantic pace when a knock rattled the door. "There is a telephone call for you," Madame Durand announced.

He hurried to the front desk and picked up the receiver.

"Alex, it's Jean-Pierre. Frédérique has asked for you to come in with your plans this afternoon. He wants me to go over them with you and make sure everything is O.K. If there are any changes to be made, they should be made now, while there is still time."

Bless Frédérique. He's coming through after all. "Absolutely!"

"I'm sure you must realize by now that you've been getting a lot of special treatment." Alex had noticed no such thing, but he was more than happy to believe it. "Frédérique thinks your ideas are brilliant," continued Jean Pierre. He lowered his voice. "Now, just between you and me, I have a feeling you're being groomed to win. Don't blow it! Come in this afternoon at three o'clock and I'll see if I can get your deadline delayed."

"Alex was elated. This was more than he dared hope for.

"I don't see why not," Jean-Pierre answered reassuringly.

* * * * *

When Alex walked into M.D.A.'s offices, the short, balding man was already in the lobby waiting for him. Jean-Pierre quickly ushered Alex into his office and closed the door.

"I have good news for you," he said. "I got you an extra three days to finish your presentation."

"Great," exclaimed Alex, in disbelief.

Jean-Pierre smiled. "Just do me one favor. Don't tell anyone about this. I wouldn't want Darren and Guillermo to find out. Now let's take a look at those plans."

Back at his hotel, Alex calculated the number of hours he would need to complete the required changes. *It will take every minute of those extra days just to make the corrections.* He moaned and settled down to another night of work. However, for the first time in weeks, he was optimistic.

Meanwhile, at M.D.A.'s headquarters, Guillermo walked into Jean-Pierre's office. "Here's the money," said Guillermo as he threw the thick brown envelope on the desk. "You're absolutely sure Ivanov won't be finished on time?'

"Absolutely," replied Jean-Pierre reassuringly, as he picked up the envelope and pulled out a wad of francs.

Guillermo still hesitated. "What about Bishop?'

"Don't worry about him. I've got a plan."

Guillermo nodded. "I'm counting on you," he said.

Jean-Pierre laughed. "You have nothing to worry about."

After the fat Italian had left, Jean Pierre leaned back in his chair and reflected on the irony of the situation. From the moment he had first laid eyes on the American, Jean Pierre had decided to do anything in his power to make sure he would not win. He had spent many sleepless nights wrestling with the problem, and now he was getting paid to accomplish his own goal.

He spread the large colorful bills on the top of his desk and counted them. Twenty-thousand francs. Not a fortune, but certainly enough to buy Frédérique a very special gift. The little man smiled in anticipation. For nearly two months now, the mere possibility of Ivanov winning and spending the next two years working at M.D.A. had driven him wild with jealousy. Jean Pierre despised everything about the handsome American. His youth, his vitality, his drive, but mainly, he hated the way Frédérique's eyes followed Alex around continuously. *There is no way I can allow that man to win.*

The next day, Jean Pierre summoned Darren Bishop. He greeted the Englishman in the reception area and invited him into his office. "Would you mind leaving your plans in the hall? I have so much junk on my desk, I wouldn't want to risk damaging them," he offered solicitously.

I want to go over the winner's itinerary for the next few weeks." He smiled and shrugged easily. "You never know, you just might be the one."

Darren's eyes lit up. *He knows something*, he thought, just as he had been meant to believe.

"Sure. I'll take out my agenda." He eagerly followed Jean Pierre into his office.

Fifteen minutes later when Darren Bishop left Jean-Pierre's office he was so excited his feet hardly touched the ground. He picked up his roll of plans, thanked Jean-Pierre and left. It was only later, back at the *George V* that he noticed half of his sketches were missing from the cardboard cylinder. Frantic, he called Jean-Pierre at M.D.A. "One of my perspectives is missing!" he yelled into the telephone.

"Calm yourself. What are you talking about?" came Jean Pierre's innocent reply.

Darren was beside himself. "One of my sketches is gone. They were all there when I went to see you. Someone must have taken it while we were in your office."

Jean Pierre's voice was cold. "If this is just some plan you've cooked up to get an extension, I must warn you that it won't work."

As he put down the receiver, Darren Bishop was in a state of shock. For the next hour, he went crazy trying to think of where else his plan might be. *Did I leave it behind? Did I throw it out by mistake?* At this late date he knew that however it had happened, this meant he was out of time and out of the contest!

* * * * *

Alex pushed away from the table and stretched his aching back. *That's one more sketch finished.* If he kept this pace, he might finish by the original deadline, but his vision was blurred and his head was spinning from too many long hours and too many late nights. *What I need is a break.* Not only did he well deserve it after all the work he had put in, but a break would re-energize him. He looked at the clock. *Two-thirty.* He could take off a few hours and come back refreshed and ready to buckle down to another night's work. He grabbed his jacket and walked out of *la Petite Tuilerie.*

* * * * *

La rue du Faubourg St Honoré, one of the trendiest in Paris, was where most of the important art galleries were situated. A few doors up, and across the road from Cedric's, where fashionable ladies bought pink-ribbon shoes and other such mad and boldly decorated footwear, and two steps from A Fragonard, where the chic *Parisienne* went to buy lush little dresses of deceptively simple and subtle designs, were the best galleries in the city. *L'Ecole de Paris, Le Chapelin, Ror Valmar, Knoedler* and *Le Gallet*. The five galleries offered works by the most sought after names in art. Here, there was something for every taste. There were modern and impressionist, cubism, realist, and old masters along with the latest *au courant* names.

Alex strolled through the many galleries; studying the different styles of paintings. Some he admired, others he hated. *I don't believe people actually consider this art*, he thought, as he stood before a window display of a giant tableau of electrically brilliant colors. The gallery was *Le Gallet*, the most modern of the group. On impulse, he wandered in.

The inside was pitch black. Beams of light projected from the ceiling and highlighted a dozen or so boldly modern paintings. Alex looked around in amusement. Each painting was uglier than the last. *They call this art?* Out of curiosity, he walked up to one of the paintings and looked at the price tag. He shook his head and chuckled. "That's crazy," he muttered under his breath. "What kind of fool would pay that much for this junk?"

* * * * *

Chapter 19

A few weeks later, when the article appeared in Le Monde, Brigitte waited in unabashed anticipation for Réjeanne's reaction. When Réjeanne came home that afternoon, she dropped the heavy bag of groceries on the kitchen counter and groaned with relief. "I'm not a young woman anymore," she mumbled to herself.

"Why don't you have them delivered, like I always tell you?" asked Brigitte from the doorway.

Réjeanne jumped. "Brigitte, you scared me. What are you doing here so early?" she asked suspiciously. "Are you feeling all right?"

"I'm feeling fine," replied Brigitte as she picked up the heavy bags and carried them to the counter. "I just wanted to be here when you read the paper." She walked over to the table, pulled a chair for Réjeanne and handed her the newspaper.

"I have to put away the groceries and fix dinner. I don't have time to—"

"I'll do that," interrupted Brigitte with a smile. You sit and read," she ordered.

Réjeanne glumly picked up the paper. "I don't see why..." She stopped suddenly as she recognized the picture of Brigitte. "It's you," she exclaimed. There, on the first inside page, was a large photograph of her standing next to one of her paintings and wearing a beaming smile.

"This is so exciting," exclaimed Réjeanne. She read quickly, nodding and smiling. Réjeanne read with fascination about Brigitte's life and her career, until she came to the part about Brigitte and Fortune's broken engagement. Without a word, Réjeanne folded up the paper and stormed over to the counter. She took out some potatoes from the cupboard and began to peel them. Suddenly, she was crying.

"Réjeanne, why are you so upset?" asked Brigitte, surprised.

Réjeanne continued pealing the potatoes,

stopping every few seconds to wipe her eyes. She pushed away her bowl of potatoes abruptly and turned back to Brigitte, her eyes glaring. "I just don't understand you," she shouted. "I don't understand you at all. When I accepted to live with you and work for you, you told me I was a part of this family, that I would never be treated like an employee. But the truth is I don't know you at all. All I know is what anybody who bought this issue of Le Monde knows. Now I find out that you and Fortune called off your engagement by reading it in the newspaper."

Brigitte was stunned. "I had no idea you felt that way."

"You are so secretive, I feel like I'm living with a stranger."

"I'm so sorry. About Fortune and I—"

"That is just one example," continued Réjeanne passionately. "There are hundreds of other things you never talk to me about, like David's father. You never even told me about him." She stopped, suddenly exhausted. "The truth is," she continued more calmly. "You and David are my only family, and I feel left out and lonely." She dried her tears with her apron. "I'm sorry. I'm just a silly old woman. You can just tell me to mind my own business, if you like."

Brigitte walked over to Réjeanne and put her arms around her. "You're right. And I'm sorry. I haven't been a very good friend have I?"

Réjeanne shook her head and began to weep again. "That's not what I said."

"No, but it's the truth. I'm secretive and I keep everyone at arm's length. I don't do it on purpose. I just can't help it," she said regretfully.

"Is that why you and Fortune broke up?"

Brigitte shook her head. "Fortune and I never had any intentions of marrying."

"W-what? I don't believe it." Réjeanne looked at Brigitte and saw that it was true. Her anger returned vehemently. "Well that is the perfect example. You played this charade for two years. What else have you been lying to me about?"

"It wasn't a lie..."

"Wasn't it?" asked Réjeanne bitterly, then she turned and stormed out of the kitchen.

For a long time, Brigitte sat at the kitchen table, thinking. Everything Réjeanne had said was the truth. All of her adult life, she had never allowed anyone to get close to her. *Except for Marcel*, she thought bitterly. *And he was older and married, therefore not really available. What is wrong with me? Other women my age look forward to falling in love. Why can't I?*

* * * * *

The article in Le Monde launched Brigitte into the public eye. The next morning, when she walked along the Champs Elisées, people recognized her and nodded or greeted her with '*bonjour*'. She walked into Le Gallet and enjoyed the immediate stir of interest from customers. *After five years, I'm an overnight success.*

Brigitte walked briskly through the gallery, and knocked on Fortune's door.

"Come in." Fortune looked up from the art magazine he was reading. "Brigitte," he exclaimed and quickly put away his magazine. "I'm glad you're here. I've just sold another of your paintings."

"Which one?" asked Brigitte, feeling the usual mix of sadness and excitement at the thought of loosing another of her works.

He smiled expansively. "*Les pigeons du marché*," he said, naming Brigitte's largest and most elaborate oil. "And I got the full amount we asked for. This customer came back to look at it repeatedly for weeks. I think the article in Le Monde clinched it. "

"Great! I've just finished 'Passion' and I needed a large space to display it." said Brigitte, more interested in displaying her latest painting than in the amount of money the sale had just netted.

"I'll have it picked up from the studio and put on display immediately." Fortune picked up the telephone and barked a few orders. "Done," he said afterwards. "Passion will be here within an hour."

Later, Brigitte watched excitedly as her painting was hung on the main wall of the gallery. The spot was immediately facing the entrance so the first thing a customer saw upon entering, was the enormous, brightly colored oil.

"How's that?" asked the installer as he put away his tools. Émile was a pleasant old man, and had been Fortune's handyman for as long as the gallery had existed.

"Perfect," answered Brigitte. "Absolutely perfect."

"I'm no expert, but I think this one is the best one I've seen of yours," said the old man deferentially as he put his tools away.

"Thanks. I think so too. And if we're lucky, it won't be staying up there for very long. Hopefully you'll be taking it down again soon."

The old man chuckled. "I'm sure it will sell fast." He picked up his tool chest and nodded. "Have a nice day *Mademoiselle*."

"Have a nice day Émile."

The old man left, and Brigitte stood admiring her work. The gallery was almost deserted now, as it was almost every day after lunch. For that reason, mid-day was always Brigitte's favorite time at Le Gallet. For an hour or so, she could wander around leisurely, without having to deal with customers who often felt compelled to give her their opinion, or worse, unsolicited advice about her work.

She walked across the room and looked at 'Passion' from a distance. It truly was a striking work. Of all the paintings she had executed, this was by far her best. The oil was a giant rendition of wild flowers, and the petals were opened wide, displaying the flora's reproductive parts in a way that could only be described as erotic, hence the name, 'Passion'. *It's wonderful*, Brigitte thought to herself. At that moment, the door opened and a man walked in and slowly ambled over to her newly displayed painting. From her position a few feet away, Brigitte watched with interest. This was her first chance to witness the reaction to her new work.

The man stood staring at it for a moment, and then shook his head. "What a joke!" he said, chuckling.

Brigitte was stunned. *He hates it!* A sudden surge of anger propelled her to question him. She walked over and joined him. "You do not like the painting monsieur?" she asked, carefully hiding her irritation behind a friendly smile. The man turned and looked at her.

Alex Ivanov had the bluest eyes Brigitte had ever seen.

* * * * *

CHAPTER 20

"You do not like the painting monsieur?" The voice was gentle, almost a whisper and pleasantly accented.

He turned and found himself facing a striking young woman. Her hair was copper red and pulled off her face in a loose chignon. She was dressed in a pair of tight black Capri pants and a long-sleeved black turtleneck. She had deep green eyes, which seemed to see right into him. Her entire bearing seemed to say, 'And who the hell do you think you are?' At the same time, he realized that she was probably the most beautiful woman he had ever seen, and he was surprised to find that he wanted very much for her to like him.

He hesitated. "It's just not my style," he replied nervously. "I don't like all this modern stuff."

She smiled, amused. "Modern art is not for everyone." Her green eyes wandered away.

"I-I can certainly understand why," he said, eager to continue the conversation.

She looked at him again and laughed. "All right, tell me why?"

He cleared his throat. "Who would want to buy that? Rich, tasteless people whose need to acquire, outweighs their intelligence. I know junk when I see it. This is junk." She was interested, he could tell. Why else would she be smiling at him that way? He took a deep breath and plunged ahead. "My name is Alex Ivanov and I don't know anyone in Paris. Would you like to have dinner with me tonight? I could tell you about New York, and you could tell me about Paris."

She looked at him for a moment, still smiling, almost teasing. "I don't think so. You see, I'm the artist whose work you think is junk." She turned and walked away. A moment later she was out the door and lost in the crowd on *la rue du Faubourg*.

Alex felt as though he had just been hit in the

guts. He turned back to the painting. The brass plate underneath said simply Passion by Dartois.

* * * * *

When Alex returned to his room, he worked furiously all night. There was suddenly an urgent reason to finish ahead of schedule. With only a few days left in Paris, he desperately wanted to find time to see this Dartois woman again. Instead of interfering with his concentration, thoughts of the beautiful artist gave him a burst of energy. The way she had looked at him with her large green eyes, the way her mouth curled up when she smiled; there was something about her aloofness that enchanted him.

One by one, he finished the sketches, and added them to the completed pile until at last there was nothing more to add. Two days later, he delivered his finished plans to the offices of M.D.A.

Just as Alex was about to leave, Jean-Pierre walked into the modern reception area. "Alex, what are you doing here? Shouldn't you be working on your plans?" he asked, his voice full of concern.

"They're finished." He gestured toward the roll of sketches on the receptionist's desk. "I managed to bring them in for the original deadline." He sounded exhausted but exhilarated.

"That's great," answered Jean Pierre, but his voice sounded anything but pleased.

* * * * *

Later, freshly showered and changed, Alex rushed over to *Le Gallet*. "I hope you can help me," he said to the short, heavy-set man who greeted him. "I would like to leave this for *mademoiselle* Dartois." He handed the man a long narrow box and the small envelope in which he had included the card with his name and telephone number. Without waiting for an answer, he turned and left.

Never in his life had he bought red roses for a woman. *Surely all women like them*. He imagined her face when she opened the box. She would be curious, but delighted. Then when she read the card, she would smile. She would probably not rush to the phone, but wait for an hour or so. The main thing was that he would hear from her by the end of the day.

Late afternoon stretched into evening and every time he heard footsteps in the hall Alex was sure were Madame Durand's coming to tell him there was a call for him. As the hours went by, it finally occurred to Alex that she might not call. By eleven, he knew she wouldn't. *Why would a woman like her want to go out with me? I should have known better.* When he climbed into bed, still feeling foolish, exhaustion got the better of him and he fell into a deep sleep.

When the knock came at the door the next morning, he woke with a start. "Monsieur Ivanov, there's a call for you," came Madame Durand's voice.

Alex pulled on his clothes in a rush and ran out to the reception desk. "Hello. Oh, hello Jean-Pierre." He listened for a moment. "What do you mean; one of the spec sheets is missing? They were all there when I delivered the plans yesterday. I'll check in my room. I'll call you right back."

He tore the room upside down but the missing sheets were nowhere to be found. *Thank God, I still have the two days extension*, he told himself as he dialed M.D.A.'s number.

"I'm afraid you'll have to turn it in today," Jean-Pierre's voice came over the telephone.

"But you what about the extension you allowed me?" asked Alex still only mildly concerned.

"I don't know where you got that impression, but the deadline was never changed. Unless you can bring in those sheets by the end of the day, I'm afraid we'll have no choice but to disqualify you."

Alex put the telephone back in its cradle. He squeezed his eyes tightly shut. *That fucking bastard! Why?* He rushed to the M.D.A. offices, and burst into Frédérique's office.

"I'm sorry Alex," said Frédérique apologetically. "The committee is meeting this afternoon. If your work is incomplete, I have no choice but to disqualify you. Both you and Darren have failed to complete your plans on time. The rules are very specific in cases like this. Perhaps it was too much to expect such an inexperienced architect to be able to deliver such a massive amount of work in such short time."

Alex returned to his auberge feeling like death. For the next two days, he stayed in his room, lying on his bed and staring at the ceiling. He felt like a complete and utter failure.

* * * * *

Alex's suitcase was packed and lined up against the wall. His Air France flight back to New York was confirmed and only hours away. As he prepared to leave Paris, Frédérique's words were still on his mind, 'such an inexperienced architect...' He could not remember ever feeling this bad. After being so optimistic, he was going back to New York a loser. How could he face William Brandon, and Anne Turner for that matter? *Who cares about Anne Tuner? I don't care if never see her again.* Suddenly he remembered the woman in the gallery. After delivering the box of roses, he had fully expected her to call. Maybe that had been a mistake. Maybe he should have called her. He looked at his watch again. There were still a few hours until his flight. If he hurried, there might just be enough time. He grabbed his jacket and ran out.

Alex walked into the gallery and felt an immediate sense of relief. She was there, talking to a wealthy looking older man. A few moments later, the man wandered off and she noticed Alex standing a few feet away. "You again," she said. "I thought you didn't like the paintings in here."

This is crazy, he thought as he felt his heart hammering wildly in his chest. "Some tastes are acquired," he said. "Maybe you could teach me."

"*Ah vraiment!*" She began to turn away when

the chubby, middle-aged man to whom Alex had handed the box of roses a few days earlier, called to her from across the room.

"Un appel pour toi. C'est au sujet de David."

Even from a distance, Alex saw her blanch. "What about David?" she asked nervously and ran over to the telephone. She spoke quickly in French. Alex did not recognize any of the words, but she sounded panicked.

"Can I do anything to help?" he asked when she slammed the receiver back into the cradle.

"No, no you can't do anything. Just get out of my way. Fortune!" she called out to the heavy man. "Take me to the hospital! It's David!"

"I can't close just the gallery. Take a taxi," he answered apologetically. "It will be much faster anyhow."

"Come! I'll get you a cab," ordered Alex. He grabbed her by the wrist and ran out. A moment later, he was helping her into a taxi. He barely had time to slide in.

"L'hôpital Sainte Hélène, et vite," she ordered, almost sobbing.

The car shot through the city and minutes later, it pulled up in front of the emergency entrance of the hospital. Before the cab had fully stopped, she jumped and ran up the steps.

"Wait!" But she was already out of earshot. Alex handed the driver a fistful of francs. "Keep the change!"

"*Merci beaucoup!*" called the driver after him as Alex chased up the steps and into the hospital after her.

Inside, was a long white corridor with nurses and orderlies hurrying about. Where had she gone? He ran up the hallway until he came to an intersecting corridor. There were dozens of people going in all directions but not a trace of her. "Damn!" he exclaimed. He looked at his watch. "Damn!" he exclaimed again. "Now I'll never make my flight." He walked back out, feeling even more like a fool. He hailed another cab and hopped in. "*Le Gallet*," he ordered and sat back in the seat. *I'm at least going to find out where the hell she lives.*

* * * * *

As she ran along the corridors, the only thing on her mind was David. *Oh God! Please make him be all right*. She rushed into the nearest elevator and pushed the button to the neurological department on the fourth floor. Moments later, when the elevator doors slid open, the first person Brigitte saw, was Réjeanne sitting quietly in the waiting area.

"How is he?" asked Brigitte frantically, as she rushed over.

"Brigitte." Réjeanne stood to greet her and Brigitte saw the worry on the old woman's face. "This was the worst I've ever seen him," said Réjeanne, her eyes filling with tears.

Fear flooded over Brigitte. "Please Réjeanne. Tell me, how is he?"

At that moment, the doctor arrived. "*Madame* Dartois?" he asked.

"Yes," replied Brigitte, her heart beating wildly in her chest as she tried to read the doctor's expression. Oh please God, I'll do anything.

"Your son is fine," said the doctor, smiling reassuringly. "He'll be stiff and sore for a few days," he continued gently. "But by tomorrow morning, you'll be able to take him home with you."

Brigitte felt weak with relief. "Why did this happen? I thought his medication..."

"Dosages sometimes need readjustment. Unfortunately in David's case, his medication is no longer effective. I've changed his prescription for a newer drug." Seeing the worried expression Brigitte's face, he continued. "Don't worry. I'm sure he will be fine."

Brigitte dissolved into tears of relief. Réjeanne ruffled through her purse, pulled out a handkerchief and handed it to Brigitte. "Why don't I go home and bake David a chocolate cake. When he comes home tomorrow, we can have a celebration."

Brigitte wiped her eyes. "Thank you Réjeanne."

The old woman gave Brigitte a quick hug. "Don't stay too late. You need your sleep too."

As soon as Réjeanne had left, Brigitte turned to the doctor. More than anything right now, she needed to see David."Where is he?" she asked.

"He's still under observation, but he'll be out soon. I'll arrange for you to go in."

A few minutes later, Brigitte walked into David's room. For a long time, she stood and watched him sleep. Then she leaned over and kissed him softly on each eyelid. "I love you David," she whispered.

Hours later, he was sitting on the steps of her building when the taxi pulled up and she stepped out. She closed the car door and walked up to him.

"What are you doing here?" she asked.

Alex looked up at her. Her hair was a mess. She had dark circles under her eyes, but she still looked beautiful. "I was worried about you," he said. "I just wanted to make sure you were all right."

She hesitated for a moment. "I'm sorry. I'm being terribly rude. Would you like to come in for a cup of coffee?"

The relief was almost overwhelming. "Thank you. I'd like that." He followed her into the building and into the elevator. "Is David going to be all right?" he asked, his voice full of concern.

"Yes," she answered, and suddenly the compassion in his voice was too much. The emotions she had so tightly held back, overflowed. "I'm so sorry. I don't know why—" And all at once, tears were running down her cheeks.

"It's okay." He pulled her into his arms and until the elevator bounced to a stop that's how they stayed; Alex with his arms wrapped around her, surprised at how good he felt. "Go ahead, cry. You've had a rough day. By the way, what's your name?"

The irony of the situation struck both of them at the same time. Here she was, crying in the arms of a man who did not even know her name. Her sobs turned into giggles, then into laughter.

"Brigitte Dartois," she said and offered her hand as the elevator door slid open.

"Nice to meet you Brigitte Dartois," Alex replied, unaware that this was one of the most important moments of his life.

* * * * *

CHAPTER 21

It was almost midnight when the taxi pulled up in front of Brigitte's building. For a moment, she looked at the man waiting out front. "What are you doing here?" she asked in shock as she recognized the American.

Alex hesitated. "I was worried. I just wanted to make sure you were all right."

Brigitte saw the genuine concern in his eyes and felt herself warm toward him. "I'm sorry. I didn't mean to sound rude. Would you like to come in for a cup of coffee?"

"Thank you. I'd like that."

She led the way into the building and Alex followed her into the elevator. "Is David going to be all right?" he asked, and for the second time that day, Brigitte dissolved into tears.

Exactly how it happened, Brigitte would never be really sure. One moment in the elevator she was crying in his arms and the next, they were both laughing madly. "Would you like to come in, or are you planning to stay out here?" she asked still laughing as she opened the door to her apartment.

Alex looked almost embarrassed as he walked in. He stood in the hall while Brigitte took his coat and gave it to Réjeanne.

"Come into the living room and have a seat. I'll go make us some coffee and I'll be right back."

While Brigitte disappeared down the hall, Alex looked around, awed by the tasteful surroundings. In one corner of the living room stood a baby-grand piano, above which was what he recognized as one of her paintings. The style was unmistakable. He walked over for a closer look.

"I thought you didn't like my paintings," said Brigitte from behind.

He turned around. She was standing in the doorway with an amused smile on her face. "Didn't I tell you that some tastes are acquired?"

Brigitte joined him by the piano and looked up at her painting, an oil of a vivid, larger than life, bunch of lilacs. "That was one of my earlier paintings. I was just beginning to discover my own style." She sighed. "I still get goose bumps when I remember the joy I felt painting it."

"It's certainly..." Alex stammered for the right word and settled on "...something."

Brigitte laughed. "That must be the most *maladroit* compliment I've ever had."

"Give me time. I'm sure I'll grow to love it."

"Here's the coffee," said Brigitte as Réjeanne appeared from the kitchen, carrying a tray. "Why are there only two cups, Réjeanne? Aren't you joining us?" asked Brigitte.

Réjeanne set the tray on the coffee table. She spoke quietly. "No, if you don't mind, I'm really tired. I'd rather go to bed. Good night. It was nice meeting you Mr. Ivanov."

"Thank you Réjeanne. I'll see you in the morning."

Alex watched while Brigitte poured the coffee. Everything about this woman was lovely. Her beauty went beyond her large green eyes and sensuous mouth; it was more than just the richness of her red hair and the perfection of her figure. There was a gentle strength about Brigitte that Alex had never known in a woman before. *She is different from any girl I've ever met*, he thought. It was difficult for him to believe that he was sitting in her apartment, making small talk with the most beautiful woman he had ever seen, when what he wanted to do was take her in his arms and make wild, passionate love to her. He shook himself out of his daydream. "When is David coming back from the hospital?"

"Tomorrow. He's being kept under observation for the night.

"You love him very much don't you?" It killed him to ask the question, but he needed to know.

"Very much. He's the only family I have," answered Brigitte softly and Alex felt his heart sink.

He looked at his watch. "Do you have to leave?" asked Brigitte, surprised at how disappointed she felt.

Alex grinned sheepishly. "Not any more. I had a flight to New York earlier today and I completely forgot about it."

"But that's terrible. What are you going to do?"

He shrugged, and then asked her the question that was really on his mind. "How long have you and David been married?" he asked, feeling like a fool.

"Married?" Brigitte burst into laughter. "I'm not married. David is my son," she said and for some strange reason, the look of relief on Alex's face made her feel happy. "David is seven years old and he has a heart condition," she continued, giving the same explanation she always gave. After years of using the excuse, she almost believed it herself.

"Will he be all right?"

She nodded. "His condition is carefully monitored and controlled with medication," she said and changed the subject. "Tell me about yourself."

For the first time in his life, Alex had no desire to tell anything but the truth about himself. He began slowly, talking about his childhood and the cold water flat he and his mother had shared. He talked about the endless string of men, Marlena had brought home. He looked into Brigitte's eyes and saw genuine sympathy and interest. He kept talking. He told her about his dream of someday living in Manhattan and creating beautiful buildings, about how hard he had worked putting himself through university while holding down an evening job. He also told her of the joy he had felt working for Brandon and Associates and his bitter disappointment being disqualified from the M.D.A. competitions. "And now," he concluded grimly. "I don't know what I want to do."

Brigitte nodded. "I'm sure that's normal. You've just had a bitter disappointment. From what you told me of yourself, I'm sure you'll be back to your old, ambitious self in no time." As Alex talked about his life, a calm, peaceful feeling descended upon Brigitte. She felt close to this man, almost as though she had known him for years. Like her, this man had hopes and dreams. It was almost as though Alex's joys were hers, his disappointments, hers. In a way they were. Both of them had lived bitter childhoods. They both had the same burning ambition to succeed. When Brigitte looked at Alex, she felt the walls she had built around her, begin to crumble.

Long after the coffee had turned cold, Alex and Brigitte were still talking. Finally, Alex looked at his watch regretfully. "It's late. I really have to go." Brigitte held her breath. "Maybe I can call you tomorrow?" he asked.

She smiled. "Maybe you can."

Brigitte walked him to the door and when he took her in his arms and kissed her, she felt a new, surprisingly pleasant sensation, a sort of warmth all over. She closed the door behind him and hurried to bed.

* * * * *

The man's hands were on her breasts, grabbing, squeezing. Brigitte moaned in pain as she tried to squirm out of his hold.

"You like this don't you?" he asked sadistically.

"No!" she insisted. "I don't want you. Get away from me."

Her desperation amused him. He laughed. His booming voice echoed in Brigitte's ears. "Don't lie to me. I saw the way you looked at me. You want me. Come on," he goaded her. "Juste une petite caresse."

Those were Lucien's words, Lucien's voice. Brigitte looked into the man's eyes. No! It can't be. To her horror, Alex's eyes stared back at her, a malicious grin on his handsome face. "Nooo!" screamed Brigitte.

A moment later, she sat up in bed, damp and shaking from the nightmare. *God*, she cried. *Will this torture never be over?* she asked herself bitterly.

* * * * *

The next morning, when Brigitte took David home from the hospital, Alex was in the apartment waiting for them. His smile lit up the room. "I hope you don't mind. Réjeanne was kind enough to invite me in for a cup of coffee," he said, embarrassed.

"Of course," she answered, but there was only cool politeness in her voice. "Alex, I'd like you to meet my son. David, this is Alex. He is an architect from New York."

"Hello David," said Alex, wondering if he was imagining the coolness in Brigitte's voice.

David looked at him, his intelligent eyes wide with interest. "You're American? I bet you can't speak French."

"You're wrong," answered Alex. "*Bon-joor, comment alleze vooze?*" he continued in mock seriousness.

David hesitated. "That's not French, is it *Maman*?" he asked uncertainly.

"Only to an American," answered Brigitte, chuckling.

Alex pulled out a gift-wrapped package from behind his back and handed it to the freckled boy. "I brought you something."

"Thank you," he said politely and waited for his mother's signal before taking the package and opening it carefully. "*Maman*, look at what Alex gave me." Inside was a complete set of geometry tools. He held up a slide ruler.

"If you like, I can show you how to use them," offered Alex.

"Could you show me right now?"

Alex laughed. "Sure."

Brigitte watched as David led Alex to his bedroom. "David, you've got half an hour then you have to rest," she called after them as they disappeared down the hall.

Brigitte sat in the living room, filled with a sudden sense of panic. From the bedroom down the hall, she could hear David asking question after question, and Alex's voice, patiently answering. *I wish...* she thought and immediately wondered what it was she wished. I don't know, she realized with a shock. *I don't know what I wish.*

Later, Alex joined her in the living room. "Your son is quite a boy. He's bright. I showed him how to use the slide ruler and three minutes later, he already understood how to use it."

She spoke softly. "Alex I have to talk to you."

"I like him." Alex moved closer and kissed her. "But not nearly as much as I like his mother," he added.

Brigitte felt her heart skip a beat, and immediately reprimanded herself. *What is happening to me? I can't let some smooth talking American affect me.* She pulled away. "Alex, this is ridiculous."

"What?" he asked, puzzled.

"This." She gestured helplessly at him and her. "Last night I was vulnerable. I apologize for giving you the wrong idea. I think you're a nice man, but I would prefer if we didn't see each other again."

"Are you serious?" He searched her face for an answer and found only determination. "I don't understand."

"Believe me, it's much better this way."

Before Alex knew what was happening, Brigitte had walked him to the door and was waiting for him to leave. He searched wildly for some excuse to see her again. "David really likes me," he said. "If you don't mind, I'd like to come by one in a while to see David and say hello."

Brigitte hesitated. David did seem lonely sometimes. "All right," she said, and Alex knew he had just been handed another chance.

David was sitting in bed, reading the

instructions on the geometry kit. "This is really great mom," he said, his green eyes wide with excitement. He opened his arms for a hug and allowed himself to be tucked in. As Brigitte turned to leave, David's sweet voice followed her. "Do you like him better than Fortune?" he asked.

"My goodness, that's an odd a question. What makes you ask such a thing?"

He shrugged. "I like him a lot more than I like Fortune, and I think Alex likes you."

"Why in the world would you say that?" asked Brigitte, surprised.

"Mom! I might be just a kid, but I have eyes. The way he looks at you, I can tell, he likes you a lot."

Brigitte's heart did a happy little dance, but all she said was. "I think it's time for you to go to sleep." She tucked her perceptive son into bed and closed the door.

Over the next few weeks, Alex launched an all out campaign to win David's affections. Every day after school, Alex picked up the boy and together they would go for a walk, visit a museum or play in the park. To his surprise, he enjoyed David's company. The boy was a bright and happy child and he followed Alex around everywhere adoringly. *I wish his mother would look at me like that*, thought Alex. Every evening, after David was put to bed, Alex invited himself for a cup of coffee with Brigitte. Those moments became more and more important to Alex and even though she refused to acknowledge the fact, they were also becoming precious to Brigitte.

Later, Alex walked back to La Petite Tuilerie and climbed into his own bed, aching with desire for this strangely unreachable woman. He tossed and turned for hours, berating himself for hanging on to the hope of winning Brigitte's affections.

"My goodness, those two are almost inseparable lately," commented Réjeanne after David had gone to bed on evening. "In case you haven't noticed, that man is sweet on you Brigitte."

"Well if he is, he is wasting his time because I'm not interested." Even as she said it, Brigitte wondered if it was true. Lately looked forward to Alex's visits, and surprisingly she enjoyed every moment she spent with him. She saw the doubt in Réjeanne's eyes and shrugged. "Really! I am not interested."

Réjeanne's eyebrows shot up, but she bit her lip. One thing the old woman knew was that nobody could force Brigitte to admit anything unless she wanted to.

One morning, when Brigitte marched into Le Gallet, Fortune called her into his office. "I have some good news for you," he told her. "Le Figaro wants to do an article on you."

"They do? That's wonderful. When?" Brigitte was jubilant. "Does it have anything to do with the article in Le Monde a few weeks ago?"

Fortune beamed. "You're becoming a celebrity my dear. Everyone wants to interview you. Speaking of which, some old man came by yesterday. Big, blond guy; he refused to give his name, but he wanted to know all about you. How old was your son, where you lived, even what color your hair was. He said you reminded him of his daughter."

Brigitte felt the blood drain from her face. She struggled to keep her voice steady. "My father died when I was thirteen." She hesitated, adding. "Did you give him my address?"

"Of course not. Now, about your Figaro article..." And he went on to instruct Brigitte on her appearance and on what she should say during the interview. Brigitte could hardly listen. *Please God, let it not be Lucien.*

That night when Brigitte got home, Réjeanne greeted her with the news that Alex Ivanov was visiting again. He was in David's room, teaching him to read architectural plans. "Oh! And I almost forgot," continued Réjeanne. "Some old man came by. He asked me a dozen questions about you, but he wouldn't give me his name when he left. There was something peculiar about him. I didn't like him at all."

Brigitte felt her stomach lurch. "Was he a big blond man, about sixty years old?"

Réjeanne nodded. "Why yes, he was. He walked in here as though he owned the place and made comments about how much money everything must have cost. I tried to get him to leave, but then David came in. It was odd. The man took one look at him and for a moment I thought he might faint."

"He saw David?"

"He was only here for a minute and David just happened to come in from school. Réjeanne noticed that Brigitte was shaking. "Brigitte, is this some other mysterious man from your past or am I not supposed to ask?"

There was an uncomfortable silence for a moment while Brigitte tried to find something to say. The stillness was broken by a knock at the door.

"I'll get it," said Réjeanne coldly.

"Wait!" cried Brigitte, but it was too late. Standing in the doorway was Lucien, her stepfather, the man who still haunted her sleep.

Réjeanne took one look at Brigitte's face and immediately realized something was terribly wrong. "Get out! Get out," she shouted at the old man as she tried to push him out.

He shoved her aside easily and walked toward Brigitte "What's the matter Brigitte? Don't you recognize your own *papa*?" he asked.

Brigitte stood paralyzed with shock. "You're not my father. Get out of here," she said, her voice trembling with emotion.

The old man chuckled. "Aw, Brigitte, you're breaking my heart. Where's your gratitude for everything I did for you? Looks to me like you've done well for yourself. You're living in this fancy place, and with a maid. Seems to me you could show some gratitude to your father and help him out a bit in their old age."

From the back bedroom, Brigitte heard David laughing and prayed to God Lucien would leave before her son walked in. "How dare you come here?" Her voice was like ice. "You are nothing but a filthy bastard. Get out of here and don't ever come back."

Her words seemed to delight Lucien. "You're calling me a bastard? Me? I think you've got that wrong *ma fille*. It's your son who is the bastard, not me. And I have a feeling I might have a pretty good claim to that little boy. As a matter of fact I have a feeling I might have as much right to him as you do."

Brigitte opened her mouth, but no sound came out. Then, almost as in slow motion, she collapsed to the floor. Réjeanne screamed. From down the hall, Alex and David came running.

Alex took one look at the scene before him and grabbed Lucien by the collar. "What the hell did you do to her?" he shouted.

"Hey! Don't push me. I didn't do a thing. I was just leaving." Lucien walked out, and from the doorway, called out again. "But you can tell her that I'll be back. That's my boy she's got there and unless she and I can come to some agreement, she can expect a custody fight."

Brigitte sat on the edge of living room sofa as Réjeanne handed her a cup of tea. Alex stood by helplessly.

"Where's David?" she asked.

"I sent him to bed early. I don't think David should hear about this," replied Réjeanne soothingly.

Alex sat next to her and patted her hand. "I wouldn't worry about what this man said. I know the type. The last thing he wants is your son. What he's really after is money. Besides, he has no claim to David."

Brigitte hesitated. "What if he does?" she asked, her voice strained.

Alex shook his head in bewilderment. "Brigitte. If you want my help, I think you'd better tell me what's going on."

Brigitte closed her eyes and began to cry.

Alex was visibly shaken. "Brigitte, this is serious. Is he David's father?"

Réjeanne interrupted. "Of course not. He said he was Brigitte's father, not David's."

Alex looked from one to the other and finally settled on Brigitte. "I think you'd better tell us what the situation is," he said quietly.

Slowly, painfully, Brigitte explained. Alex and Réjeanne listened in stunned silence, torn between horror toward Lucien, and sympathy for her.

"I was so young, and I was afraid," she said. "He kept telling me that if I told anyone, he would kill me. I believed him." She stopped and began to cry again. "I feel so ashamed."

"You have no reason to be ashamed," exclaimed Réjeanne. "I wish you had told me this a long time ago. Now I understand. That explains everything. I'm sorry Brigitte."

Alex shook his head. He was shocked at what he had just heard and only felt more deeply for Brigitte. "That man belongs in jail" he said. "The problem is he is not your biological father. I'm not sure incest charges could be brought against him."

"I don't want to bring charges against him," exclaimed Brigitte, aghast. "It would be a disaster. It would kill both my reputation and my career."

"That is exactly what he's counting on. He wants you to pay him for his silence. And if you give him money once, you will never be rid of him."

"What should I do?" she asked helplessly.

"I'll think of something," he said. "There's got to be a way out, and I'll find it."

Brigitte looked at Alex's earnest face and felt a load lift from her shoulders. She was not alone. Alex would help.

* * * * *

Over the next few days, Brigitte lived in nervous anticipation of Lucien's next move. She knew Alex was trying to find a solution, but still worried constantly. Every day as she left for work, she gave Réjeanne a barrage of instructions. "Don't open the door to anyone. Don't let David out of your sight. If anybody calls don't give any information."

"You don't have to worry. I won't let that horrible man get anywhere near David," Réjeanne reassured her.

At times Brigitte was sure Lucien was close by. She could feel him, watching and waiting. Yet when she looked behind, there was nobody there. At night, the nightmares made sleeping impossible. Her appetite dropped and she lost weight. At work her inspiration was gone and with everyone, she was irritable and impatient.

"Have you thought of leaving the country?" asked Alex one evening.

"Don't be ridiculous," she snapped back. "I can't abandon my career. Where would I go? What would I do?"

"You should consider it. Lucien has no money. He would never find you if you moved to New York."

"What in heaven would I do in New York? My life is here. My friends, my work, everything is here. I can't possibly start all over again in a foreign country."

Alex felt like a fool. He should never have mentioned his idea. In truth he desperately wanted to find a way of enticing Brigitte from Paris to New York. He had already spent the last month pursuing her, to no avail. He was no longer on salary from Brandon & Associates, and M.D.A. had stopped paying for his expenses weeks ago. He could not afford to stay in Paris indefinitely. His only hope, now, lay in Brigitte's fear of Lucien. "Sorry. It was just a thought."

"You are right about one thing though," agreed Brigitte. Alex's hopes flared. "I'll have to be less visible. Every time another article is written about me it will only encourage Lucien to continue his harassment."

Any last vestige of hope Alex might have had, died. He would never win her.

The next day, without any explanation to Fortune, Brigitte canceled the Le Figaro interview. Fortune was livid. He sat behind his desk and glared at her. "After all the effort I've put into building your career, this is how you thank me?"

Brigitte tried to appease him. "It isn't as though it will hurt sales. My reputation is already established. People will still buy my paintings. Fortune, I'm sorry but—"

"You're sorry? If you were sorry, you would cooperate with me, not work against me. Do you have any idea how much effort went into getting you this interview? Do you have any idea how valuable an article of that kind can be? Anybody would kill for a chance like that and all you have to say is, "I'm sorry". Well, I'm sorry too." He stormed out of his office.

The following day, when Brigitte went back to the gallery, the first thing she noticed was that 'Passion' had been taken off the wall. She looked around in shock. Not one single painting of hers was anywhere to be seen. They were all gone. Every last one of them.

In their place was an assortment of oils by other artists. The message was clear. If she refused to cooperate, Fortune would no longer represent her. She walked out of Le Gallet.

Réjeanne put away the last of the clean dishes and wiped her hands on her apron. "What are you going to do?" she asked.

Brigitte shrugged. "I have no idea. No idea at all." She looked at her friend in despair.

Réjeanne patted her on the arm. "Things will work out. They always do. Oh, I nearly forgot. This just came." She picked up an envelope from the counter and handed it to her.

Brigitte picked up the sullied envelope. "What is it?" she wondered. She tore it open and pulled out a sheet of smudged note paper. As she read, she began to shake. "It's from Lucien," she said. "It is a letter from his lawyer, demanding visitation rights with David."

"Let me see that." Réjeanne pulled the letter from Brigitte's hand. As she read, the color drained from her face. "He says he has a copy of David's birth certificate." She looked up in horror. "Is that possible?"

Brigitte rubbed her temples. "I don't know," she said. "I want to speak to Alex. He'll know what to do."

Two hours later, when David came in, brimming with excitement over his school day, Brigitte listened patiently. Then, with his mouth full of cookies, he asked casually. "How come Alex isn't here?"

"Was he supposed to stop by?" asked Brigitte hopefully.

"No, I don't think so. But he usually stops by before diner. How come he's not here tonight?"

"Why don't you call and invite him over?" offered Brigitte.

David's eyes lit up. "Really? You wouldn't mind?"

Brigitte laughed. "I wouldn't mind at all."

"I'll call him right now. Where's his phone number?" Brigitte looked at David helplessly. "I guess we'll have to wait for him to call here," said David.

* * * * *

The next morning was a beautiful winter day. A fine snow was beginning to fall, lightly covering the streets. Alex looked out the window of his tiny room and thought of how much he would miss Paris.

Brigitte liked him. She did not love him. He had wasted weeks, hoping she might feel about him, the way he did about her. It had all been a waste of time. What he needed now, was to get back to his own life. With a sudden burst of determination, he marched to the front desk and picked up the telephone.

"Air France, bonjour?" answered the voice at the other end of the line.

"When is your next available flight to New York?" he asked.

"We have a flight tomorrow afternoon," the friendly voice informed him.

"That would be perfect." Alex took down the flight information and decided to start packing. He hurried back to his room and set to work.

* * * * *

Brigitte returned from walking David to school. She walked into the kitchen where Réjeanne was busily cleaning out the refrigerator.

"I wish Alex would call," said Brigitte glumly.

Réjeanne stuck her head out from the refrigerator. "I would not expect to hear from him anymore."

Brigitte was stunned. "Why do you say that?"

Réjeanne pulled off her rubber gloves and poured herself a cup of coffee. "That man is in love with you. And you gave him no encouragement." There was no reprimand in her voice. It was simply a comment.

Brigitte's heart sank.

The older woman shrugged. "I wouldn't be surprised if he was on his way back to New York right now."

Brigitte gasped. The thought of never seeing Alex again suddenly filled her with sadness. "I have to find him," she said. "He worked at M.D.A. for weeks. They'll know where he was staying," she said, as the thought suddenly occurred to her. She picked up the telephone and called information. Moments later, she had the number for La Petite Tuilerie. She waited nervously while the proprietress went off in search of her boarder. At last she heard Alex's voice on the line. "Alex! I'm so glad I reached you," she exclaimed, her voice trembling with emotion. "Why didn't you come by last night?"

There was a silence for a moment before he answered. "Why would you care, Brigitte?" he asked.

Brigitte heard the bitterness in his voice and knew Réjeanne had been right. A million emotions swirled through her mind. She had never felt so confused in her life. Then suddenly she knew. "Because I love you," she whispered.

Those were all the words Alex needed to hear. For the second time, he canceled his flight and unpacked his bags.

When he arrived at Brigitte's apartment and she opened the door, Alex took her in his arms, overcome with emotion. "You know what this means don't you?" he asked her when he was finally able to speak.

"What?" she answered breathlessly.

"We have to get married," he said and the words were as much of a shock to him as they were to Brigitte.

"If we must, we must" she replied. Before she could say anything more, Alex's mouth was covering hers and her body melted into his. In the kitchen doorway, Réjeanne stepped back and closed the door discreetly. *It's about time.*

* * * * *

On a bright, sunny December day, Alex and Brigitte were married at the *hotel de ville*. The bride looked radiant in a cream floor-length gown. Her voice shook slightly as she spoke her vows, but Alex held her hands and smiled his encouragement. From a few feet away, Réjeanne wiped discreetly at a few tears while David beamed with happiness. As he pronounced them man and wife, the justice of the peace thought that in his twenty three-years of performing marriages, he had never seen such a perfect couple.

* * * * *

On the same day, almost halfway across the globe, Anne Turner was lying exhausted in the delivery room. The doctor leaned over her and smiled. "You have a healthy baby boy."

She looked down at the shock of black hair on the baby's head and turned away. Just as she had expected, the little bastard looked exactly like his father.

"You're lucky," the doctor continued. "Most preemies are not as strong as he is. Your son will be fine."

Lucky, hah! How am I supposed to raise this kid all by myself, she thought, bitterly. *Just wait till I find that damned Alex Ivanov.*

The End

*Following is a preview
of the sequel to this book,*

*THE STING
OF THE SCORPIO*

PREVIEW
CHAPTER 1

I am safe, thought Brigitte as the plane began its descent into New York. It was only two weeks, since she had married Alexander in the small ceremony at the Paris, Hotel de Ville and already her life had been turned upside down. She was surprised at the swirl of emotions she felt, starring at the immense city below. It was a move she would never have made alone, but luckily Alexander was here, of course—she glanced lovingly at him in the seat next to hers—as were her son, David, and her friend and housekeeper, Réjeanne, so all was well at last.

She was landing in America, far from Paris and the threat of her stepfather. She still shuddered at the memory of Lucien, her step father, standing in the doorway, his eyes wandering over her body, as they had when she was just a child.

Réjeanne had taken one look at Brigitte's face and immediately realized something was terribly wrong. "Get out! Get out," she had shouted at the old man as she tried to push him out.

He had shoved her aside easily and walked toward Brigitte "What's the matter Brigitte? Don't you recognize your own *papa?*" he asked.

Brigitte stood paralyzed with shock. "You're not my father. Get out of here," she said, her voice trembling with emotion.

The old man chuckled. "Aw, Brigitte, you're breaking my heart. Where's your gratitude for everything I did for you? It looks to me like you've done well for yourself. You're living in this fancy place, and with a maid. Seems to me you could show some gratitude to your father and help him out a bit in their old age."

From the back bedroom, Brigitte heard David laughing, and she prayed to God Lucien would leave before her son walked in. "How dare you come here?" Her voice was like ice. "You are nothing but a filthy bastard. Get out of here and don't ever come back."

Her words had seemed to delight Lucien. "You're calling me a bastard? Me? I think you've got that wrong *ma fille*. It's your son who is the bastard, not me. And I have a feeling I might have a pretty good claim to that little boy. As a matter of fact I have a feeling I might have as much right to him as you do."

That was when Brigitte had collapsed and Réjeanne screamed. From down the hall, Alex and David had come running.

Alex took one look at the scene before him and grabbed Lucien by the collar. "What the hell did you do to her?" he shouted.

"Hey! Don't push me. I didn't do a thing. I was just leaving." Lucien walked out, and from the doorway, called out again. "But you can tell her that I'll be back. That's my boy she's got there and unless she and I can come to some agreement, she can expect a custody fight."

Brigitte shook her head, trying to rid herself of the memories. But she could not forget Réjeanne's and Alex's kindness when she admitted that Lucien was David's father.

Afterwards, David had taken her hand in his, and said, "He raped you, Brigitte. You shouldn't feel any shame." And rather than drive a wedge between them, her confession brought them closer.

The voice of the captain cut through her reverie. "We hope you enjoyed your flight and we thank you for using Pan Am."

The plane taxied down the runway and a few minutes later, Alexander held Brigitte's arm as they disembarked. She stepped down the portable stairs and turned to look at her husband, feeling an overwhelming rush of love for him. More than anything, she yearned to create the perfect family, the family she never had. I will make him happy, she vowed. I will be the best wife I know how.

But New York was alien. Everywhere she looked, she was surrounded by ugly grey buildings on city blocks the size of soccer fields. The streets were filthy. People looked angry, harassed, scared. They scowled at each other as they walked by. On the way from the airport, the cab stopped at a red light and a big black man with crazed eyes walked over to the car and stared openly at the occupants inside.

"Don't worry sweetheart, he's just another beggar." He rolled down the window and tossed a few coins to the man. A second later the man had already moved on to the car behind theirs. As Brigitte looked around at the unfamiliar city, she wondered if she could ever feel at home there.

Three days later, with Brigitte eager for a place to call home, Alex reluctantly signed a lease on an enormous loft in Greenwich Village. The building, an old warehouse, had been empty for over a year and the owner was desperately trying to rent it. "It isn't a residential building. I can't imagine how you can expect to live there," the man had exclaimed when Brigitte expressed her interest in renting it for residential purposes. However, the high ceilings, the large skylights, and the distinctly artistic community of the area appealed to Brigitte, while the low rent agreed to Alexander's sense of economy.

"How are we going to turn this into a home?" Alex asked, slightly skeptical, as he walked around the vast expanse of dusty space.

"Leave that up to me, *mon chéri*," replied his new bride.

With her boundless energy and her artist's flair, Brigitte quickly transformed it into a comfortable and imaginative home. The old hardwood floors were sanded and varnished. The brick walls were painted a flat white and the ceiling a starkly contrasting black. Walls were built to bedrooms and a bathroom, and the industrial-size windows and the skylights were cleaned until they gleamed.

"*Et maintenant*, all we need is some color," declared Brigitte.

"It looks great already," agreed Alex, putting more conviction in his voice than he really felt. It still looked like an empty warehouse to him. He wondered how his wife, who had left her luxurious apartment in Paris, could get excited over such a dump.

Brigitte set to work. Over the next few weeks she found a variety of old, but solidly built, second-hand furniture.

"You can't be serious," said Alex, getting close to the end of his confidence in the project. "I agreed to a loft because I know you need space and natural light for your studio. But I'll be damned if I agree to live like a pauper. This furniture is garbage. It's probably full of fleas."

"Don't be ridiculous. There is nothing wrong with this furniture. All it needs is new upholstery. You must trust me."

For days, samples of fabrics in dozens of colors hung from every available surface until Brigitte made the final selection. One morning a truck pulled up and all the old furnishings were carted away. Two weeks later they were brought back, looking like new.

The dusty old loft was unrecognizable. Huge screens in bright turquoise, sunny yellow, electric blue and bold pink, separated the living and the dining room from the kitchen area. One area was left totally bare, except for the professional size easel standing directly before the window. The space was to be Brigitte's studio.

From the ceiling, hung long rows of black spray-painted, upside down funnels fitted with light bulbs. The furniture looked like new, recovered in shiny, white vinyl. Tropical plants filled every corner, and every spare inch of wall space was covered with Brigitte's oils. The effect was electrifyingly modern.

Brigitte was triumphant. "*Voilà*," she said, jubilant. "Now what do you say?" she asked her husband.

"I say, you are a witch. A beautiful, talented, sexy witch." he took her in his arms.

From across the room, Réjeanne signaled to David and led him away. "Let's go for a walk," she whispered to him. "I think your *Maman* and Alex want to be alone right now."

Brigitte was consumed with passion for her husband. He was her friend, her lover, her savior.

THE STING OF THE SCORPIO

Sometimes she wondered what might have happened if she had not phoned Alex and prevented him from flying away that day. She shuddered at the thought.

For weeks, she had avoided Alex's attentions, until convinced she would never love him, he had booked a flight back to New York. If she hadn't picked up the phone and called him that day, God only knew what might have happened. One thing was sure. She would not be in New York any more than she would be his wife.

Since then her life had changed drastically. For the first time in a long time, she felt loved. Abandoning her career to follow Alex had been a miniscule price to pay for what she now enjoyed, a loving marriage, and the reassuring knowledge that at last Lucien was out of her life forever. Since the wedding a few weeks ago, there had been no more nightmares.

Alex carried Brigitte to their room and threw her on the bed. "Alex, what are you doing?"

He unbuttoned her blouse and buried his face between her breasts. Brigitte laughed throatily. At the beginning, she had been terrified of sex. But slowly, gently, and ever so patiently, Alex had helped her overcome her fears. Not only had he not seemed to mind Brigitte's inexperience, but it appeared to excite him. Now, he found one of her nipples and sucked greedily. She moaned. "Oh God, Alex, I want you so much."

"I've created a monster," he said, chuckling. He pulled up her skirt and slipped his hand inside her panties. "I love you," he whispered in her ear.

Brigitte's knees went weak as a surge of desire filled her. She felt so much love she thought her heart might burst. "And you'll never love anybody else?"

"And I'll never love anybody else," he repeated dutifully as he climbed on top of her. A moment later he was inside her, moving at a deliciously slow pace, until Brigitte could no longer tell where her body ended and his began.

* * * * *

By day, while Brigitte struggled to adapt to life in New York, Alex fought his own battles. Since his carefree days in Paris had come to an end, reality had set in full force.

Somehow, falling in love with Brigitte, and their quick decision to marry, had seemed logical in Paris. Now back in New York, it often felt more like insanity. *I'm only twenty-five years old. What am I doing with a wife and son*, he asked himself. It wasn't that he didn't love Brigitte. He was still completely captivated with her. And although he couldn't think of a single woman he would rather make love to, he missed the feeling of being free. Occasionally, he remembered the vows he had spoken on their wedding day, '...forsaking all others...' and he felt...trapped!

Also weighing heavily on Alex's mind, were his new financial responsibilities. It had been months since his last pay check, and he now had an extended family to support. Although Brigitte had insisted on helping financially, he was equally adamant about being the sole provider.

"Don't you understand?" he argued with her. "I don't want your money. I am your husband. What kind of a husband would I be if I allowed my wife to pay the bills?"

"But Alex, I really don't mind. We're married now. The least I can do is help until you find a job."

"Absolutely not. I won't have it."

Brigitte had grudgingly conceded. Over the next few months, Alex watched helplessly as his bank account, which he had so painstakingly grown to a considerable sum, dwindled daily. His sense of urgency rose.

Every day, rain or shine, while Brigitte busied herself with her new home, Alex continued his search for work. He searched the classifieds in the newspapers daily, applied with every employment agency and mailed countless resumes. He even swallowed his pride and went back to see William Brandon.

To his immense relief, he had not run into Anne Turner. At her desk was an efficient looking middle-aged secretary. She gazed at him with professional disinterest and ordered him to sit and wait.

"Mr. Brandon is busy. I'll see if he has a minute for you," she told him and left him in the reception area while she hurried down the hall to Brandon's office. Alex looked around. Nothing in the reception area had changed. The same expensive paintings hung on the walls, the same classical music played softly from the hi-fi. It was almost as though he had never left.

A voice suddenly broke through his reverie. "Alex, what the hell are you doing here, you old son of a gun?" It was Ben, one of the guys from the bull pen they had nicknamed purgatory. "I thought you had decided to stay in Europe indefinitely."

Alex chuckled. "Naw, life was too hard there. Who can take all that fine wine and *foie gras*. Give me a good old hamburger anytime. Is Andrew around?"

"Didn't you hear? Andrew left months ago."

Before Ben could say anymore, the secretary reappeared. "Mr. Brandon will see you now." Alex hurried down the hall to the executive office.

William Brandon sat back in his chair, puffing away at his eternal cigar and looking at Alex with thinly veiled distaste. "Well, if it isn't the wonder boy. You didn't do too well in Paris, did you? What makes you think you can just waltz back into your old job, now?"

Alex turned and walked out.

* * * * *

In the end, it was Brigitte who came up with the idea.

"Did you know that this building is for sale," she asked over dinner one night.

They were in the dining area, alone. Réjeanne had pleaded fatigue, put David to bed and retired. Now, Alex starred glumly at the *boeuf bourgignon* growing cold on his plate.

"Is it?" asked Alex, with disinterest. He picked up his fork and speared at his food. "What good does that do me? I don't have a job. And according to my last interview, I'm overqualified. The company can't afford to pay the kind of salary my experience demands."

Brigitte ignored his comment and said, "How much would you say this apartment would normally be worth?"

He put down his fork and looked at her blankly. "What are you talking about?"

She gestured to the room around them, and said, "Supposing we rented a place like this, one where we hadn't done all the renovations ourselves; how much could we expect to pay?"

"A hell of a lot more than we're paying now, that's for sure."

"How much more?"

He groaned with impatience. "How would I know? Double. Maybe triple. Why?"

"And how much did the renovations cost?"

"Very little actually," he answered. "I got all of the materials wholesale and I did most of the work myself."

Brigitte smiled victoriously. "I have an idea," she said and launched eagerly into her proposal.

Long into the night, Alex stayed up, going over the figures. He couldn't quite admit that Brigitte's idea was brilliant. But it was a good one, and he just might be able to pull it off. The down payment alone would take up nearly all of his savings. And every last dime of what was left would go toward the renovations, which would leave him with a real problem. He would have no more savings and no income. Without a job, how the hell would he get a bank to grant him a mortgage? By the time he climbed into bed, exhausted, the sun was already rising.

Brigitte stirred and opened one eye. "So, do you think we can do it?" she asked sleepily.

"I don't know. I'll have to think about it some more," he answered. He gave her a quick kiss, rolled over and fell asleep.

The next day he got on the telephone. After half a dozen calls, he finally located his friend Andrew McGregor.

"Why the hell didn't you call me sooner?" asked

Andrew when he heard Alex's voice. "How long have you been back in town?"

"Not long, and I've been pretty busy. I have a wife and a son," he told him. "And now I'm looking for work." Alex could imagine his friend's freckled face grinning happily.

"What! You have a wife? Well for Chrissake! When am I going to meet the lady?" then he realized what else his friend had said. "Wait a minute. How could you have a son? Last time I saw you was only about six or seven months ago."

Alex made up a story about David being Brigitte's son from a previous marriage. "Why don't you come over for dinner Friday night?" Alex asked afterwards. "That way you can meet both of them."

The following Friday, Andrew arrived punctually at seven, with a bottle of Dom Perignon.

"This certainly deserves a celebration."

He kissed Brigitte on the cheek and gave David a playful slap on the back. "I never saw anyone with hair redder than mine." He turned back to Alex. "I must admit that the color looks better on your wife than on me." He leaned forward, whispering, "She's gorgeous. No wonder you kept her all to yourself."

They sat and enjoyed a dinner of *coq au vin*, Réjeanne's specialty. They popped open the bottle of champagne, and during the meal, Alex brought Andrew up to date with his situation.

"You should have called me as soon as you came back," said Andrew. "You don't have to look any further. I have a job for you. You can start tomorrow if you like."

"What do you mean?" Alex didn't dare to hope.

"You can come and work for me. When I left Brandon & Associates, I started my own company." At the baffled look on Alex's face, Andrew explained. "My father agreed to back me financially." He chuckled. "Don't get the wrong idea. I'm not rolling in dough. The old man lent me the absolute minimum I needed to buy a tiny parcel of land just outside the city. That's where I plan to build a small residential project. And you, my friend, are exactly the person I need. Keep in mind I can't afford to pay much, but if you want it, the job is yours."

"Do I want it?" exclaimed Alex eagerly. "When do I start?"

* * * * *

A few days later it was official. With the confirmation of employment in his pocket, Alex put in an offer to purchase the building.

Brigitte was putting the final touches to a new painting when Alex burst in. He ran to her, picked her up in his arms, and twirled her around the room, almost knocking down her easel in the process. "Alex, *pour l'amour de Dieu*, put me down. What is going on?"

He pulled away from her. "You are looking at your new landlord," he said, beaming.

"Wh-what? Why didn't you tell me? When did this happen?"

"I signed the papers this morning. I wanted to surprise you."

"Well you did. You certainly did," said Brigitte. But she was not at all surprised. She knew that Alex had a brilliant mind and that someday he would be a very successful man. This was only his first, small step.

* * * * *

Alex settled back into working day and night with enthusiasm. This was the lifestyle he knew best and enjoyed most. He rose early every morning and worked all day by Andrew's side, drawing plans for inexpensive but well-constructed houses. This was a far cry from his old dream of developing luxury buildings, but at least he was earning a living. And he was grateful for the financial safety the job provided.

Evenings he came home to a quick dinner, and then spent hours renovating his building. Aghast at the way her husband was taxing himself, Brigitte tried to ease his load by helping as much as she could. During the day she ran his errands, ordered the long lists of building materials needed for the renovations. She supervised the electricians and plumbers, quickly learning the difference between good and shoddy work. Often, she surprised the workers by pulling on overalls and joining them in plastering and sanding. Being an artist, she enjoyed painting along with her husband, sometimes until she thought her arms would fall off. Even with her and Alex's combined efforts, it often seemed they would never see the end of the renovations. Most nights, they would crawl into bed so exhausted they had no energy left for talking, let alone lovemaking.

"Why don't we take the weekend off?" asked Brigitte one morning over breakfast. "We could relax for a change; maybe go out to dinner and a movie."

Alex was gulping down his coffee in his usual rush. "Sorry sweetheart. I wish I could, but I just don't have the time. I have some plans to finish for Andrew, and there's still so much work to do on the downstairs apartment."

Brigitte hesitated. "Alex, I hardly see you anymore. I miss you. David misses you. Couldn't you find some time, maybe just one evening a week, for us?"

Alex looked up at her, scowling. "Really Brigitte, don't you think you're exaggerating. I come home every single night. When I'm not home, I'm working. I have to finish that apartment and rent it fast. Do you think I'm made of money or something? I can't afford to keep paying the mortgage on this building without getting rent from at least one apartment soon. I would like your support, instead of this constant nagging."

Brigitte swallowed her disappointment and saw him off with her usual warm kiss. After Alex left, Brigitte sat and thought for a long time. Whatever she had expected of married life, this was not it. Sometimes she almost regretted having shared her 'brilliant idea' of buying this building with Alex. She knew that Alex was serious about building a successful career, and she appreciated his efforts, but she missed the quiet times they used to spend together, talking and cuddling. *I hardly see my husband anymore.*

* * * * *

Read about Alex and Brigitte's
life in New York in
*THE **S**TING OF THE **S**CORPIO*,
available soon!

Made in the USA
Charleston, SC
13 September 2011